THREE WHO VENTURED

⬩ CLUNY CLASSICS ⬩

Visit WWW.CLUNYMEDIA.COM *for other titles
from the Catholic literary tradition, including:*

ROBERT HUGH BENSON
Come Rack, Come Rope
Dawn of All
Lord of the World

GEORGES BERNANOS
Joy
Under the Sun of Satan

G. K. CHESTERTON
Wanderings over the World

MYLES CONNOLLY
The Bump on Brannigan's Head
Dan England and the Noonday Devil
Mr. Blue
The Reason for Anne & Other Stories
Three Who Ventured

ALICE CURTAYNE
House of Cards

GERTRUD VON LE FORT
The Veil of Veronica

MARIELLA GABLE, O.S.B. (EDITOR)
Many-Colored Fleece: Short Stories
Our Father's House: Short Stories

JOSÉ MARÍA GIRONELLA
The Cypresses Believe in God

RUMER GODDEN
Five for Sorrow, Ten for Joy
In This House of Brede

CAROLINE GORDON
The Malefactors

PAUL HORGAN
Things as They Are
Humble Powers

CARYLL HOUSELANDER
The Dry Wood

BRUCE MARSHALL
Father Malachy's Miracle
A Thread of Scarlet

FRANÇOIS MAURIAC
The Desert of Love
Thérèse: A Portrait in Four Parts
Vipers' Tangle

DOROTHY L. SAYERS
Whose Body?

IGNAZIO SILONE
Fontamara
Bread and Wine
The Seed Beneath the Snow

SIGRID UNDSET
The Burning Bush
The Wild Orchid
The Longest Years
The Faithful Wife

HELEN C. WHITE
A Watch in the Night

⬩ ⬩ ⬩

Three Who Ventured

A Novel

Myles Connolly

Introduction by Stephen Mirarchi, Ph.D.

CLUNY
Providence, Rhode Island

SECOND CLUNY EDITION, 2023

Three Who Ventured originally published
in 1958 by J. B. Lippincot Company.

This Cluny edition includes minor editorial revisions to the original text.

For information regarding this title
or any other Cluny Media publication,
please write to info@clunymedia.com, or to
Cluny Media, P.O. Box 1664, Providence, RI 02901

VISIT US ONLINE AT WWW.CLUNYMEDIA.COM

ISBN: 978-1685951948

Cover design by Clarke & Clarke
Cover image: Oscar Florianus Bluemner,
Old Canal Port, 1914, oil on canvas
Courtesy of Wikimedia Commons

CONTENTS

for Mary

INTRODUCTION

Published in 1958, *Three Who Ventured* was Myles Connolly's final major literary work, and it seems to have become his least well-known. Fewer than sixty copies[1] survive in libraries worldwide, as opposed to more than four hundred shelved copies of various editions of *Mr. Blue*, and more than one hundred copies each of his other two novels.

The format may have been a barrier for some. Unlike Connolly's previous books, *Three Who Ventured* was split into three sections—each a short novella describing the life of an extraordinary character. On the literal level, they are Fr. Dennis, a diocesan priest seeking perfect charity; Mann Timothy, the father of a large family seeking the miraculous; and John Martin, an ego-driven writer who decides to kill a prostitute and himself in order to consummate his ongoing existential dilemma. On the spiritual level, all three are seeking the divine: one moving towards the heroic, one hoping for the astonishing, and one approaching his childhood faith *via negativa*. All three are venturing in the Chestertonian sense,[2] and—as Connolly's original title of the book, *Many Mansions*,[3] attests—all three have places prepared for them,[4] if they but cooperate with grace.

As with Connolly's previous efforts, reviewers compared *Three Who Ventured* to the perennially popular Blue and found it wanting—not always for the best reasons. A quarrelsome article, for instance, in the Jesuit-run literary magazine *Best*

Sellers—which routinely reviewed dozens of books every two weeks, from Vladimir Nabokov to Fannie Hurst—admits that the novel "may very well convey something to the reader about the power of faith to strengthen and comfort those in adversity."[5] The reviewer finds Connolly's characters too unusual, however, such as the book's first hero, Fr. Dennis: "For one thing, his unsuitability for the secular priesthood would have become an issue long before he became a priest."[6] Even assuming that the writer means "diocesan" by "secular," the faith in seminary administration displayed by the reviewer has been rather tragically shattered in light of the abuse scandals. Given that psychological entrance exams for potential seminarians are still not absolutely required in all dioceses just in the United States, the reviewer's criticism functions in retrospect as ironic praise: Connolly was ahead of the curve in supposing that seminary formation would need reforming—an alarm bell he also tried to sound, albeit for somewhat different reasons, in his short story "Seminary Hill" (1953).[7]

---

1.   OCLC WorldCat, April 2020.

2.   See, for instance, chapter nine of *Orthodoxy*, titled "Authority and the Adventurer."

3.   Mary Connolly Breiner, email message to author, April 26, 2020.

4.   Connolly's original title is a reference to John 14:2, "In my Father's house there are many mansions. If not, I would have told you: because I go to prepare a place for you."

5.   James P. McDonough, review of *Three Who Ventured*, *Best Sellers: The Semi-Monthly Book Review* 18:13 (October 1, 1958), 248.

6.   Ibid., 247.

7.   That Connolly was a prophet of sorts in this and other matters is increasingly being recognized by scholars. See, for instance, Philip Gleason's argument that Connolly's mid-1920s defense of Catholic education at the college level anticipated the broader cultural move-

Such criticism of *Three Who Ventured* does not seem to acknowledge that one who writes about faith can be *both* profoundly involved in the workings and rituals of that faith *and*, as Marian Crowe has put it, deeply invested in offering "critiques [that] are more like lovers' quarrels or marital arguments. They are deeply felt and painful, yet still encased in love for the beloved."[8] Catholic authors of this time—or authors concerned with Catholicism, a crucial distinction in some cases—generally emphasized one of those poles to the detriment of the other.[9]

On the public side, Connolly may have suffered some loss of face because of his involvement in Leo McCarey's anti-Communist film *My Son John* (1952). Especially after the ruinous downfall of Joseph McCarthy, films like *My Son John* were seen as embarrassments: their ostensibly relentless dogma and maudlin messages were too sympathetic or apologetic for McCarthy and his witch hunts.[10] The success of works like Arthur Miller's *The Crucible* (1953) and

---

ment and even predated by several years Fulton Sheen's teaching on this point. Philip Gleason, *Contending with Modernity: Catholic Higher Education in the Twentieth Century* (Cary: Oxford University Press, 1995), 145, 148.

8. Marian Crowe, "The Catholic Novel is Alive and Well in England," *First Things* (November 6, 2007), https://www.firstthings.com/web-exclusives/2007/11/the-catholic-novel-is-alive-an.

9. For a recent academic treatment of this history in American literature, see Nick Ripatrazone, *Longing for an Absent God: Faith and Doubt in Great American Fiction* (Minneapolis: Fortress, 2020).

10. See, for instance, the analysis of the film in N. Megan Kelley's *Projections of Passing: Postwar Anxieties and Hollywood Films, 1947-1960* (Jackson: University Press of Mississippi, 2016), 101–108. For a more evenhanded yet sober analysis, see Bernard F. Dick, *The Screen Is Red: Hollywood, Communism, and the Cold War* (Jackson: University Press of Mississippi, 2016), chapter 9 ("Better Dead than Red").

E. L. Doctorow's much-later *The Book of Daniel* (1971) only
cemented such judgments in the minds of many.

Still, Connolly had once said that writing books was for
him not an economic activity but essentially about "entertaining people and telling them a fundamental truth at the
same time and telling them in a hearty, wholesome way—
through laughter."[11] Humor indeed plays a role in *Three Who
Ventured*, especially in scenes where piety clashes hilariously
with functionality, or when John, the self-consumed writer,
finds himself whisked away from his all too romanticized
dreamworld to destinations unknown by a larger-than-life,
rough and tumble producer (a character Connolly must have
laughed at himself, as many Hollywood denizens had that
very impression of him).

For all the humor in the novel, however, tragedy often
takes front stage, following as it ordinarily does on the heels of
deceit and treachery, a major theme of the book (which Connolly often calls "perfidy"). The golden-hearted priest Fr. Dennis is exiled from his diocese by a military-minded bishop;
Mann Timothy must confront the sudden, inexplicable death
of his ballet-loving child, Mary; and John Martin gains sure
knowledge that his actions have destined him to Hell. Each
of these calamities might be the rightful subject of its own
novel-length treatment, but Connolly kept them as novellas
and intertwined them with very short, intercalary paragraphs[12]
that bind them into a novel—somewhat like a voiceover that
might transport us to different scenes of the same film. To that

11. Walter V. Carty, "Myles Connolly Sings in His Books the 'Adventure
     of Catholicism,'" *The Pilot* (December 8, 1951): 9.

12. John Steinbeck had used to great effect a much more extensive ver-
     sion of this technique—entire intercalary chapters—in *The Grapes of
     Wrath* (1939).

end—understanding how these very different stories illumi-
nate each other—three particular moments are enlightening.

The first is a seemingly minor yet perceptively appro-
priate symbol. On the opening page of John Martin's story,
we see him noticing Rena—the prostitute he both lusts for
and wishes to kill—gazing into a "three-paneled mirror."[13]
Such mirrors were common in the time especially among artists and those in the beauty industry, to use the term widely.
Within the story itself, the three panels come to mean something more: John, Rena, and some idea of God, the latter rep-
resented by a cheap statue of the Virgin Mary, which will
come to play a most important role in John's redemption. As
to the wider scope of the novel, the three panels easily refer to
the three novellas, but given Connolly's theory of aesthetics
mentioned above, could they not refer to the novel, the reader, and the "fundamental truth"? We must be careful not to
overreach in our interpretations, but Connolly had a knack
for such literary devices, and we would do well to think on
the implications of what that three-paneled mirror reveals.

The mirror exposes one appetite or desire which Connolly expresses acutely in a conversation between Mann
Timothy and the story's narrator. Commenting on a murder
suspect he believes is innocent, Mann deems him not a devi-
ant but "a man hungry for mystery."[14] This apt description
fits just about every hero in every Myles Connolly work—
and its lack or void announces its conspicuous absence in
just about every Connolly villain. Far from making his characters homogenous, this commonality Connolly depicts

---

13. Myles Connolly, *Three Who Ventured*, introduction by Stephen Mir-
    archi (Providence, RI: Cluny, 2023), 166.
14. Ibid., 116.

distinctly—as uniquely as the individual panels of the same mirror do. And by *mystery*, Connolly means the rich complexity of that word in the Christian tradition: "Revealed truths that surpass the powers of natural reason…a supernatural truth, one that of its very nature lies above the finite intelligence."[15] The sacrament of penance plays a key role in at least two of the three parts of the novel, and what drives one to seek such a mystery in the first place if not a gnawing hunger for the strangely beautiful gift of mercy?

When offered such a grace, Connolly's narrators—who often remain unnamed—express old-world awe: a paradoxical interplay of wonder and fear. And here in Connolly's final work is an exemplary description of just that spiritual sensation as the narrator of Mann Timothy's story reflects on his friend's departure. This paragraph ranks among the most moving and inspiring in the novel and thus should be quoted in full:

> Nor did his new affection for me, born, I'm sure, of the new charity that had come out of his heartbreak and his conquest of despair, make it any easier for me. His last embrace and his last words had inspired me, for the moment certainly, with some of his greatness. I felt suddenly as if I were of heroic cast and had depths of courage and affection I had never dreamed of. I seemed, for that moment anyway, to have been lifted up to some towering height and there shared with him his vision of a world where, as he would have put it, the incomprehensible was clear and the impossible possible,

---

15. *CE*, "Mystery."

and audacity and affection inspired the hearts of
men, and where the haters, for all their enmity,
were in wonderment saying as they once had said,
"See how they love one another."[16]

As in Connolly's novel *The Bump on Brannigan's Head*,
"affection" here aligns with the classical *storge*, one of the
forms of love that describes a familial liking and intimacy
distinct from *philia* or friendship and discrete from sexual
attraction or *eros*. The whole drama of the crucifixion and
resurrection of Christ is recalled and invoked with the bold
phrase "his conquest of despair" and reminds readers of one
of Connolly's most important themes throughout his literary
career: the odd sensibility of redemptive suffering. We hear
echoes of Chesterton—as we do in almost all of Connolly's
works—in the narrator's sense of being illuminated by and
dilated with "greatness" simply by being in Mann Timothy's
presence. And in the startlingly counterintuitive final line,
Connolly asks us to imagine one of the most famous—and
possibly one of the most misunderstood—sayings about how
Christians act by reminding us of its likely context: it came
from the mouths of those who were enemies of the followers
of the Nazarene. These "haters" finally experience awe when
they glimpse Christians—their nemeses—actually and sub-
stantially willing the good of their foes.

Fantastically inspiring in *Three Who Ventured*, the above-
quoted paragraph could well be heard in the mouth of the
narrator of *Mr. Blue*, or from the narrator at the end of *Dan
England*, or as part of the voiceover at the finale of *The Bump*. Its
lofty spiritual themes and the summons to further conversion

---

16. Connolly, *Three Who Ventured*, 161.

effected by grace work beautifully—that is, both aesthetically and transcendentally—in those contexts. That Connolly wrote such an incisive, encompassing paragraph in his final book might prompt us, with wonder and awe ourselves, to ask: Did Connolly have further tales to tell? Alas, Connolly died about six years after the publication of *Three Who Ventured*, right in the backyard of these stories' settings at St. John's Hospital in Santa Monica.[17] One of the great bards of Hollywood who himself had been a lifelong adventurer in the truest Chestertonian sense of the word would, we hope, finally meet all his characters in the Tavern at the End of the World.[18]

Stephen Mirarchi
ATCHISON, KANSAS
MAY 8, 2020

STEPHEN MIRARCHI (Ph.D., Brandeis University) is Associate Professor of English at Benedictine College in Atchison, Kansas. His articles have appeared in journals like *The Edgar Allan Poe Review*, *Christianity & Literature*, *Religion & the Arts*, *Homiletic and Pastoral Review*, and *Dappled Things*; in a critical edition of Stephen Crane's *The Red Badge of Courage*; and in magazines and newspapers like *The Boston Globe*, *The National Catholic Register*, *Crisis*, and others.

---

17. "Obituary: Myles Connolly, A Film Writer, 66," *The New York Times* (July 17, 1964).

18. Chesterton's 1906 biography of Charles Dickens ends with this sentence: "And all roads point at last to an ultimate inn, where we shall meet Dickens and all his characters; and when we drink again it shall be from the great flagons in the tavern at the end of the world." *CW*, vol. 15, 209.

THREE WHO VENTURED

DENNIS

1.

It is many years ago now but I can still remember almost to the last detail that autumn evening, at Matt Easter's on the Pacific Coast Highway a few miles north of Santa Monica, when I first saw Dennis, tall, thin, bearded, slightly stooped, as he approached our booth to serve the wine.

He came to the table with a sort of humility, as if he were serving heroes and not Matt Easter and me, carrying the wine, a very ordinary California Burgundy, cradled in a basket, with such care and graciousness I was sure for a moment Matt had got his hands on some fine wine of precious vintage. He wore a black suit, very shiny and a little frayed, a white shirt and a white cotton wash tie, and this rather unusual apparel seemed completely proper to him, as if he had grown in it from his early youth. It was, in the few days I knew him, the only apparel I ever saw him wear.

He poured the wine ritualistically, giving Matt, my host, a little in his glass, then waiting for him to taste it.

"Fine," Matt said. "Okay."

"Thank you, sir." Dennis bowed appreciatively, a small smile lighting his face. His was a reflective, perceptive smile, not a smile of mere pleasantness, and it seemed almost always on his face.

He filled my glass, then added to Matt's glass until it was full, set the bottle down gently, bowed appreciatively again and withdrew.

I watched him walk away in his slightly stooped graciousness. Matt was studying my face, I knew, waiting for a reaction. "Collected another character, I see." I turned back to Matt. "Came in here in the rain one night about a week ago," Matt said. "He got off the Greyhound bus out in front on the highway. Said he liked the look of the ocean from here. So I gave him a job."

I sipped the wine. "He's a very interesting addition to your little private madhouse, Matt."

"He had never worked in a café," Matt went on, "but he had a simplicity about him that fascinated me so I created a job for him. Wine steward. How do you like that?"

"It was inevitable. Matt. Once you hired that French hitchhiker for a chef, the next step was a wine steward. How is the chef doing, by the way?"

"He's a little slow on learning to cook," Matt explained. "But he certainly knows his Voltaire."

"Tell me more about the wine steward. You will begin importing shiploads of fine wines now, I'm sure?"

Matt nodded. "Put in a big order yesterday. Champagne and everything. Carpenters are coming tomorrow to build an addition to the pantry with sloping shelves and special bins and the rest of it. My only regret is we have no cellar. Still I can call the pantry addition a wine cellar. The poetry of the event surely permits me some license with words."

"I don't suppose your wine steward knows anything about wine?"

"Not a damn thing. But I got him some books. He's learning. He has the greatest respect for wine. Yet, funny thing, he's a teetotaler."

I poured Matt and me more wine. "Strange place for him around here," I said.

Matt grinned. "I warned him. I told him the café was pretty much a rendezvous for tipplers. I told him I was an alcoholic myself." He leaned over, lowered his voice. "He's the sort of fellow you tell the truth to. He wasn't shocked. His smile went for a moment, that's all. And do you know what he said? He said, 'The alcoholic is given his purgatory here. What anguish after folly. What despair. What a cross he has chosen for himself on earth.' That's what he said."

I looked over to where Dennis was humbly and graciously serving wine at another booth.

"That's extraordinary talk even for this place, Matt," I said. "He sounds religious."

"Every morning around daybreak he gets up and goes out. I see him sometimes when I am going to bed. He's a strange duck." Matt joined me in watching Dennis. "He gives me the impression he walks with the daybreak around him all day."

"At night too," I added.

"He's a puzzler all right. I don't know whether Dennis is his first name or his last name or whether it is his name at all. He gives no hints about his past or background. He's evidently well educated."

"Looks and acts like an Oxford don."

"Don't let that narrow, brown beard of his fool you. In most ways he's as American as a Down-East country store. Why do you suppose he ever took a job like this? It can't be money. He refuses all tips. He seemed embarrassed when I gave him his first pay."

"My first guess would be alcohol," I said. "My second, dope."

Matt shook his head. "He doesn't even smoke."

"Maybe he's mad."

"I've thought of that. But that smile, that throws me. There's no lunacy behind that."

I studied Dennis again. "Yes, he's sane. I'm sure," I said.

"When I think I have him pegged," Matt went on, "he will come out and say the damnedest things, fantastic things. Early this evening I discovered him in the kitchen deeply concerned about some wine that had been spilled from a bottle. I told him not to worry about it, not to be so reverential about it. It was just ordinary wine. Do you know what he said? He turned gravely to me and said, 'Mr. Easter, there is no such thing as ordinary wine, not since God chose wine to be His blood.'" Matt drained his glass of wine. "What do you think of that?"

"Maybe he is mad after all," I said.

2.

Perhaps a word or two about Matt Easter and his place might not be amiss before going on with Dennis.

Matt had in his youth been a copywriter for an advertising agency in mid-Manhattan. He was good at it and had done well. One of his accounts was a group of orange growers in Southern California. After a while, oranges became a pleasurable fixation with him. He lived oranges, so to speak. He, who had never seen an orange tree, save perhaps a dwarf plant in a Madison Avenue florist's window, now beheld the deep green growing on the trees, smelled the fragrant blossoms, watched the colorful fruit appear, followed it through to the golden harvest. His words, colorful as the illustrations that went with them, came to life on the glossy pages of a hundred magazines.

Matt looked down on the magazine pages, read his words over and over, and a feeling grew in him that he had somehow had a part in the creation of, if not the orange tree, at least the orange industry. It became therefore a common pastime for him (aided by the magazine illustrations) to picture himself sitting in a colorful sport shirt on the veranda of a red-tiled stucco ranch house looking down over a great orange grove, gold and dark green in the sun.

One bright May morning, as was inevitable, he being Matt Easter, he resigned his job, took his not inconsiderable savings and boarded an airplane for California. In a month he was proprietor of an orange grove in the Los Angeles area. He had a red-tiled, stucco ranch house and he sat in his sport shirt on the veranda and looked down on his orange grove, gold and dark green in the sun.

Matt was not, however, as successful growing oranges as he had been growing words about them. Every bug and blight in the book were soon drawn to his trees. His crops grew poorer. His trees grew more and more barren. His investment dwindled. But, as often happens in Southern California, while the value of his orange grove was growing less, the value of his land was growing greater.

A new highway was built along his property. Two real estate developers fought to acquire Matt's land. The bids rose and finally Matt, in an equitable mood, sold half the grove to one developer and half to the other, and happily retired. He had tripled his investment.

Matt was a tall, huge man, a good six feet two inches in height, with a deep fondness for food and drink. His palate was above ordinary although he was no epicure. He grew tired of dining out. Being a bachelor he could not endure dining home. But being, further, a man of great faith in his imagination, he hit on what he considered an easy solution to his problem. He would buy a restaurant, be always his own guest, be a host when it pleased him, and thus enjoy both the pleasure of dining home and dining out.

His fancy was caught by a little place, a small café with rooms above it, built on stilts out over the surf on the Pacific Coast Highway. It had a "seagoing look," he said. He bought it for twice what it was worth, painted it red, brown and yellow inside and out, hung some white-washed life preservers here and there, and, as a last touch, put up a gold-lettered sign describing the place rather incongruously as: *Chez Easter*. Nobody, however, ever called it *Chez Easter*. It was known simply as Matt's place.

But if anyone thought for a moment because it had a sign, *Chez Easter*, out in front it was wide open for business, he was headed for disillusionment. There were some six booths and eight tables in the restaurant. On each table in the booths and on the floor there stood a small gold-and-black sign with the word *Reserved*. And reserved is exactly what Matt meant.

The first booth was exclusively Matt's booth and he invariably occupied it by himself or with guests. He was always the host at this table (and sometimes at other tables as well) and when he was host he considered it unbecoming for the check even to be mentioned. "You wouldn't ask to pay if you were dining at my house, would you?" he would always say.

From this booth, Matt had command of the entrance door. Charlie, the waiter, would hold up any possible customer until a signal from Matt—a glass raised to admit—was given. Matt had mysterious standards for admittance, most of them being unknown to anyone but himself and, sometimes, it seemed, unknown to himself as well. Poetic intuition is what he depended on, he maintained. He would be more likely to admit a derelict in rags than a man of affairs in white tie and tails. He had an intense and constant dread of practical people.

I must say that the customers he selected were, more often than not, interesting and even entertaining. Quite a few of them were parasites, of course, but Matt did not mind that if they amused or diverted him. He also had a great weakness for ladies of the evening, romanticizing them beyond ordinary discretion, seeing all of them as soft of heart, victims of the callousness of mankind.

It can easily be discerned then that Matt's place was more of a private club than a restaurant. He kept no books, knew nothing about such things as unemployment insurance or social security, and his only knowledge of income tax was that he took a loss each year. This loss he considered a sort of triumph and gloated over it.

There is no mystery as to how the restaurant was run at a loss. Seldom were more than three or four tables permitted to be occupied. I have sat in the main booth with Matt night after night for a week without seeing the *Reserved* sign taken from a table once. No glass was lifted in approval. No customer at the entrance had satisfied the demands of Matt's poetic intuition.

I was the chief of Matt's guests, which made me therefore the chief of his parasites though that did not occur to me at the time. Matt was about forty, some fifteen years older than I, and seemed to me very old and very wise. He would say things like, "The Good Book tells us to love our enemies but I say let us begin by trying to love our friends," or with a drink he would give a toast such as, "Let us be worthy of our sins!" and such sayings of his would appear to me to be profound and original.

"I like poets," Matt would say. "Only poets know the infinite value of the immediate and fleeting moment. That's why I like you, son. You are a poet."

If Matt meant I liked to sit hours on end talking and drinking with no regard for the morrow, then Matt was right about my dedication to the immediate moment. I think the truth is Matt was always lonely after nightfall and needed a good listener and I was, I suppose, a good listener.

Matt's hospitality was very welcome to me in those days. I was two years out of college and working on a Santa Monica newspaper. I was no adventurous reporter with a thousand tales to tell. I was merely an odd-jobs man around the office, a combination rewrite man and office boy.

But I did have what might be called a poetic side and being young I had, of course, my dream of greatness. I lived in a shack in the Malibu Hills a few miles from Matt's place. It was very primitive, this shack, with an outhouse and with such running water as would run supplied from a roof tank which had to be filled by a water service company from time to time. But the shack, with the dappled-black, cinnamon-brown higher hills rising steeply into the sky behind it and with the gray-blue-green Pacific spreading vastly before it, had a startling and inspiring view. It was this view that prompted me to rent the shack. Here my dreams of greatness were to come true.

I had, at the time, the idea that I should write the epic story of California in dithyrambic blank verse. The primitive shack in the hills was the very place for me to work on the heroic poem in my spare time. Thanks to Matt, and, in smaller measure, to my own indolence, I never wrote a line.

It could be that publishers' readers everywhere have reason to be grateful.

I'm afraid, looking back, that my only distinction then was that Matt considered me another of his characters.

3.

The next night when I joined Matt in the first booth, Matt was talking to Roland, the itinerant Frenchman he had plucked from the highway and, in his imagination, had turned into a chef. Roland cut a striking figure, standing before Matt, a lofty, thin six feet, in a long loose apron, with a chef's hat like a great rumpled white muffin adding another eight or ten inches to his height. His long, narrow, sallow face, like a drawn single piece of copper, gave him a slightly malevolent air.

Matt was patiently explaining to his chef how he wanted a little mashed banana added to the potatoes, just so much and no more. The chef listened distantly from his great height.

Matt realized he was not making much progress. "Roland," he said, "for two weeks now there has always been too much banana or too little in the potatoes. What is the solution?"

"Cut out the banana," Roland replied with a crisp accent.

Matt laughed. "That is your trouble, Roland. Always too much or too little. I don't know why I keep you. Do you?"

"I am your conscience," Roland replied crisply again. Then, tilting his head back in severe importance, he turned sharply and went back to the kitchen.

Matt was entertained. "The Gallic mind at its best. I am very grateful for him."

I sat down opposite Matt. "He seems rude to me. What does he mean—he is your conscience? I don't get that."

"He is right," Matt replied. "He is my conscience. That's why I cannot let him go."

Dennis approached, carrying a cradled bottle of wine with his customary graciousness.

Matt continued, "Roland is a man of cold intellect. He is an agnostic and yet an ascetic. I am a Catholic and yet I am a libertine and a drunkard. Roland is here to keep me from forgetting my weaknesses, to remind me of my sins." He turned up to Dennis who now, his little smile on his face, waited to pour the wine. "Dennis, my life is dedicated to self-indulgence. I have no virtues. I am damned."

"You are generous, Mr. Easter." Dennis bowed ever so slightly. "Generosity is next to godliness."

"But I'm generous because I like to be generous. It is another form of self-indulgence, Dennis."

"A higher form, Mr. Easter. Holiness too is a higher form of self-indulgence, a transcendentally high form of self-indulgence." Matt laughed. "You are very consoling, Dennis. You must never leave me."

Dennis bowed. "Thank you, sir. It is a privilege to be here." He poured the wine ritualistically as he had the night before and went back to the kitchen. I was completely fascinated by him.

Matt held up his glass of wine. "He's a character all right."

"Your best, Matt," I said.

Charlie, the waiter, came to the booth. Charlie was a gray elfin sort of man with that air of constant optimism that usually adorns horse players. Charlie had a system for betting on the horses. He used astrology, carefully casting the horoscopes of all the horses and jockeys in a given race.

His system kept Charlie busy, much busier than did the café with its reserved tables. It also provided him with a limitless source of hope. His horses rarely won.

Charlie had come to the booth to announce that Gloria, one of Matt's ladies, was outside. Gloria was always admitted, always treated royally, but because of her profession she was inclined to be diffident and always waited on Matt's invitation.

I had met Gloria on several occasions. She was in her late twenties, a husky brunette who featured a black lace headdress, like a small mantilla, black dresses and much deep red costume jewelry to match her deep red lipstick. I suppose she saw herself (or had at one time) as a sort of femme fatale. Her lips quivered until she had had a few drinks. Her dark brown eyes were cloudy and blue-circled, her face soft and slightly puffy.

Matt considered her quite pretty. "The older I get," he said, "the more convinced I am there is no beauty without pathos. It is the ruined village that sleeps most beautifully in the moonlight. It is its melancholy that makes autumn the most beautiful of seasons. It is the sorrowful madonnas who are the loveliest. It is pathos in a woman's eyes that gives her the most profound, the most appealing beauty."

Whether Matt actually believed this about Gloria or not, I do not know. Matt so liked ideas—conceits is perhaps a better word—so liked the feel of them, so liked to play with them that you could never be too sure how deep was his realization of what he said. Not that he was insincere. His devotion to his conceits was vigorous. It was his devotion to his conceit about oranges that originally brought him to California and to the ownership of an orange grove. It was his conceit about being a host or a guest as he chose that brought him to the ownership of a café. He was a happy host to Gloria because he liked to associate pathos and sadness with her.

Matt ordered Gloria a double bourbon over ice, her usual drink. Dennis served it. He served it graciously but not as ritualistically as he served wine.

I noticed Gloria as she discovered Dennis, saw the excitement that began to glow in her cloudy eyes. She did not take her gaze off him. She watched him while he served the bourbon, while he bowed and left. She watched him until he had disappeared into the shadows near the kitchen door.

The moment Dennis was out of view, she straightway drank down her entire drink.

"Who is that?" she asked making no effort to conceal her excitement. "Who is he?"

Matt explained how Dennis had appeared at the door in the rain one night a little more than a week before.

"That's for me," she said, her voice trembling. "He's beautiful. Let me have another drink."

Matt and I exchanged glances. We both had the same reaction. We were a little startled—startled and disconcerted is probably a better way of putting it—at this woman's sudden desire for Dennis. It was not merely astonishment that Gloria should consider the male animal anything but a client, as was her cool custom; it was a feeling this was impropriety on her part, indecency even. If she had shown any similar sudden infatuation for Matt or me, say, we would have considered her simply out of character, or, more likely, out of her mind. But for her to have an infatuation for Dennis, that was somehow wrong.

"Lay off him, honey," Matt said quietly.

"Why? I won't hurt him."

"It isn't that. He's…" Matt paused for the right words. "He doesn't seem that kind."

"All men are that kind," she replied intensely. "Only some are more so. I know."

"But he's poor, honey," Matt declared. "He can't afford you."

"I don't care. Maybe I can afford him. How about that drink, Matty?"

Matt ordered the drink from Charlie, a double bourbon again, and Dennis served it. He served graciously as he had served before. Again Gloria did not take her eyes off him.

After she had watched him go, she turned back to Matt and me. She was more excited than before. "My God," she whispered hoarsely, "imagine anything like this happening to me!"

She sipped her drink in tense silence for a minute, then drained the glass. Abruptly she got up and left the booth.

Matt and I, ill at ease, watched her go into the kitchen.

"Why don't you stop her?" I asked Matt.

He shook his head. "I'm sure Dennis will take care of himself. He is of the greatest innocence."

I was not so sure of Dennis. "She has a sort of evil charm to her," I said, "the sort of charm that is especially appealing to innocence."

Presently Dennis appeared serving wine at a nearby booth.

"You see," Matt said triumphantly.

But later when Matt called for new drinks, it was Charlie who brought them.

"Where's Dennis?" Matt asked.

"He went out with that hooker," Charlie said. "They went out to look at the ocean," he added with a wink.

Our chagrin must have showed on our faces. Charlie, misinterpreting Matt's reaction, said, "It's okay, Boss. There's no business." Then, leaning over, he whispered confidentially, "I got a nag, a sure one in the fifth at Bay Meadows tomorrow. A Scorpio."

Matt and I, who usually joked with Charlie about his horses, could only sit and stare at each other, unable even to manage a smile.

4.

Matt and I sat alone in the café and drank and talked. We avoided with care any reference to Dennis or Gloria, a care prompted by our disillusionment with Dennis. We hardly knew him and yet strangely, vaguely, we felt as if he had that night failed us. Somehow he was for us a hero fallen. A flag on a distant and, I must admit, hazy rampart had been struck.

Matt was in a quiet mood. He talked about death. I am sure Dennis was responsible, however obscurely, for this change in him.

"I am going to get myself a skull," he said after a long silence and considerable wine, "a human skull, a fine, highly polished human skull and keep it here on this table before me."

"*Memento mori*," I said.

"No. *Memento vivere* or however the Latin should go. Remember we must live. You've heard those stories about people who go to physicians and are told they have only six months or a year to live and how they then begin to discover the startling loveliness and surprise in the ordinary things around them: a human face, a breaking wave, a dragonfly, the morning star, a friend's voice, a shadow pattern in the late afternoon sunlight, all the myriad things they had not really seen or heard before. It is the man given a few months before the adventure of death who realizes best the adventure of life."

I could not help being a little amused at his unaccustomed solemnity.

"I want the skull before me," Matt went on, "I want death on the table here before me to increase my capacity for living. With every glass of wine I shall remember death, and every glass of wine will be that much sweeter to me. The food will be more succulent. The coming of dusk will be more moving and beautiful. With the skull before me, I shall see life as it is, startling, inexplicable except in terms of death. With the skull before me each immediate moment will be more surprising and more precious. I shall be more mystified and therefore more diverted, more humble and therefore more grateful. Right now, with merely the thought of the skull, the polished skull, on the table before me, I feel a sudden inspiration of gratitude for your presence and friendship."

I thanked him but he hardly heard.

He mused a moment. "What would you think if I had here the skull of a once beautiful woman, a woman of disciplined passion, a disturbing, life-giving woman? She would not only dramatize the present moment, she would give it the melancholy, the pathos of womanly beauty forever gone, the melancholy and pathos without which there is no supreme beauty."

This was an old theme of his and he sensed my awareness of the fact.

"You aren't finding this morbid or depressing, are you?" he asked.

I shook my head. "No, I too am looking for the kingdom of the absolute," I said.

This pleased him as I had an idea it would.

"Good," he said. "Very good. Beauty is a mystery. It must always be strange. And if it is true beauty, its strangeness, its eternally baffling, eternally impenetrable strangeness will always be a source of pleasant melancholy. Man and supreme beauty is a love affair that can never end in marriage. It is a union that can never be consummated."

"Maybe it's better that way," I ventured to comment. "Man in love with beauty will thus never be surfeited."

He smiled, pleased. "You grow in wisdom," he said.

Roland, now without his chef's hat and apron but still tall and important, approached from the kitchen.

"The kitchen is closed," he announced.

"Fine," Matt said. "Thank you. I'm sorry you hadn't come out sooner, Roland. We've been talking about the skull of a beautiful woman and the pathos of beauty."

There was an air of superiority about Roland as he said, "You live by your emotions, Mr. Easter. You shall die by them."

Roland left the café. Matt watched him let himself out.

"I live by my emotions. I shall die by them. That is good, very good," Matt said. "He is truly my conscience."

"I wouldn't care for a conscience like that," I said.

Matt gave no heed to my remark. He talked on, elaborating further his strangely solemn conceit of the skull on the table. The idea of the skull of a once beautiful woman especially enchanted him.

"It is one of my very best ideas," he said. "I shall find such a skull tomorrow. I know a place in town."

While he was talking, Gloria and Dennis appeared at the entrance. Dennis, gracious as usual, stood back and bowed her in.

Gloria turned and came directly to the booth. Dennis went on through the shadows into the kitchen. Gloria, frowning, sat down next to Matt. She sat there in sharp silence and stared into space, the frown hardening her soft face.

After a moment Matt said, "Like a drink, honey?"

"No. I don't want a drink." Her voice was angry. Presently, as an afterthought, she added, "A drink wouldn't do me any good."

Matt was pleased. "Looks like I was right."

"He's crazy," she whispered harshly, "crazy as a bedbug."

"Don't take it so hard, honey." Matt winked at me. "You're beautiful, Gloria, but you're not completely irresistible."

"Have you talked much with him?" She toned to Matt.

"Not as much as I'd like to."

"Well, talk to him some time. He looks like he's making sense, he acts like he's making sense, but half the time he isn't. He's tough to follow."

"He does talk strangely sometimes," Matt said.

"Strangely?" Gloria obviously considered that something of an understatement. "Why, when I sashayed up to him in the kitchen here to give him the business, I remarked, kind of polite-like, I hoped he didn't mind the intrusion. Do you know what he said? He said with that little bow he gives, he said, 'I'm very grateful for your speaking to me. I'm always grateful when anyone speaks to me. I don't deserve it.' What do you think of that?"

"It sounds like him," Matt said.

"Well, that threw me off balance right off," Gloria went on. "'I'm always grateful when anyone speaks to me.' That was too much for me. Later when we were out on the beach, he got talking even more fancy. I must say he was handsome out there in the moonlight. It seemed sometimes like the moonlight was inside of him. But the way he talked! He talked about someone he called his lady and he said the stars were his lady's jewels, and he talked like he believed it. The competition was too tough. I all but fell in his arms but he didn't make a pass at me. He'd have no part of me."

Matt nodded. "She's tough competition all right."

Gloria turned to him in surprise. "You know what he was talking about?"

"Distantly. Too distantly. Catholics call her the Virgin Mary, the Mother of God."

Gloria was clearly bewildered. "You think God has a Mother?"

"Mary was the mother of Jesus Christ who is God."

Gloria was more bewildered. "But Christ, he's the fellow they killed. You think some people killed God?"

"That's right, honey." Matt was gentle. "Some people killed God. It's hard to understand. It's hard for anyone to understand."

"Brother! I think you're nuts too. Matt, I'll take that drink!"

Matt went to the bar and came back with drinks for the three of us. Gloria drank her bourbon almost at once.

After the drink, she softened. "He's crazy the way I said," she said quietly. "Crazy as can be, but he's real beautiful. No one ever talked to me the way he did. Not even when I was a kid. He made me feel good and kind of important." Suddenly she began to sob. "I'm sorry, boys. I got to bawling out on the beach too. I told him I was no good. Do you know what he said? He said he wished he was as good as I was. I told him he didn't know the half of it. I told him what my business was. And he said—" she sobbed again—"he said I had a beautiful soul. You should have heard the way he said it. I felt new and young again."

She began to cry openly. "I love him! I guess I'm crazy too. But I love him!"

Abruptly she jumped up, left the booth and ran out of the café.

Matt and I sat in silence.

At that moment, as if on cue, Dennis came quietly out of the kitchen into the dark café.

It was an extraordinary appearance he made. In the dark, his body seemed faintly luminous, especially his face, as if he were carrying a hidden candle. It was startling. Matt and I stared wide-eyed at him.

Dennis bowed to us, said a courteous good night and went up the stairs that led to the rooms above. Spellbound, we watched him until the upstairs door closed behind him.

Matt turned to me. "Did you see what I saw?" he asked in a hushed voice.

"Fantastic," I said. "Looked like phosphorescence."

There was complete silence.

"There was a time when they'd probably call that the glow of sanctity," Matt finally spoke. "Could be it is." He got slowly to his feet. "Let's go over to the bar and get a drink."

5.

The next night I was back at Matt's, in the first booth with him as usual. There were no customers, Matt's poetic intuition presumably having found none worthy of his favor this night. Also, I suspect, his mind, after the experience of the night before, was especially occupied with Dennis, as was mine, and he wanted no distractions.

Matt had the skull he had talked of already on the table. It was small, of a pale ivory color and highly polished and while the effect of it on the table before me was dramatic, the skull was not repulsive as I had thought it might be.

Matt looked pensively down on the skull.

"Woman?" I asked.

"So they told me. A young woman," Matt answered. "But I cannot find out if she was beautiful. We'll assume she was beautiful." He tapped the skull softly with his glass. "You were very beautiful, dear lady, beautiful with the great beauty that breeds heroes and destroys kingdoms. I am deeply in love with you." He raised his glass to his lips. "Now I begin to live!"

Dennis came and went with his customary graciousness. We made no comment on the phenomenon of the night before and if he saw any special curiosity on our faces, he gave no sign of it. He appeared to like the idea of the skull on the table as Matt explained it to him.

"It's too bad," Dennis said with his little smile, "we cannot have our own skulls on the table before us."

"A wonderful idea," Matt nodded.

We watched Dennis as he walked away from the booth. "Could it ever be your Dennis is what you call a saint?" I suggested. "You have some such idea in the back of your head, don't you?"

Matt hesitated. "Saint is a precious word and should be applied only with the greatest of caution. Still, that phenomenon last night, I can't get it out of my mind."

"Could it ever also be," I suggested further, this time with a smile, "that Matt Easter is going religious?"

"I suppose," Matt nodded after a moment, "you could say since Dennis arrived I've become somewhat religious, though, I must say, only in a conversational way. He makes me feel important, as he did Gloria.

"Ordinarily the thought of the hundreds of millions of people crawling this planet appalls me. How in such a multitude of multitudes can one soul matter, I ask myself? But talking with Dennis, the millions somehow cease to be masses. They become individuals. As he is. And I am one. I take on size. I no longer am appalled."

"Dennis does all that for you?" I asked in some surprise. I was well used to Matt's extravagant way of talking but at the moment he seemed to be beyond himself.

"That and more. When a man says, 'I'm grateful when anyone speaks to me,' as Dennis said to Gloria, you run head on into the extraordinary phenomenon of supernatural humility. You are shaken up. It might well be you will never be the same again. The universe begins to grow cozy and comfortable. The individual begins to grow large and radiant.

"And when I saw him as I did last night in the dark with the light of his unique individuality about him, I saw him, an almost nameless nobody, as someone superhumanly important. I felt warmth at being a member of the human race."

About this time, Gloria appeared at the entrance and was waved in by Matt. Her eyes intently searched the café for Dennis. He was not in sight.

"A double?" Matt asked her as she sat down beside him in the booth.

Gloria discovered the skull. She drew back in horror. "Is this real?" she whispered.

"Real as can be," Matt said easily. "Once belonged to a girl as beautiful as you, Gloria. About your age, too."

"Take it away, will you?"

"You'll get used to it," Matt smiled. "It's a very common object. We all have one, honey."

"Well, keep it away from me, will you, Matt?" There was pleading in her voice.

"We'll move it over here near the lamp."

Matt moved the skull over under the lamp near the wall. It was more highlighted, more striking there than before, but out of the way. "What you need is a drink, Gloria," he said. "How about that double?"

"No thanks."

"Single?"

She shook her head. "Nothing," she said tensely, obviously on edge. "I'm going to try and cut down on the stuff."

"Dennis?" Matt's eyes twinkled.

She turned on him angrily. "What are you always snooping into people's business for! You squat there half-crocked and squint down at the rest of us like we were all a lot of fleas in a flea circus! Who do you think you are anyway? You're for the zoo yourself, you ought to know that by now! Let me alone, will you?"

"I'm sorry, Gloria," Matt apologized. "I'm terribly sorry. I was impertinent."

At that instant, from the highway, came the sudden screech of automobile brakes jammed on, followed by the high, single, hysterical scream of a woman, then instantly by the abrupt, shocking crash of two cars colliding, crumpling, then silence.

We rushed to the door, Matt leading, I after him. Gloria followed fearfully. Roland came quickly, excitedly, out of the kitchen. Then Dennis appeared with his usual composure.

On the highway, two dark, heavy cars had apparently smashed into each other head on, and had been spun around so they were almost off of the highway. All lights on the cars were out and the two wrecks looked like huge crumpled black boxes in the dimly lit dark.

On the black pavement a few feet from the car nearer the café, the white figure of a woman lay on her side. She was moaning.

Matt ran back into the café to telephone the police. I moved on to the highway, followed by Roland. Gloria hung back and could be seen framed in the soft light of the doorway to the café.

A ranch wagon, approaching from the direction of Malibu, stopped on the highway. Its headlights illumined the ugly scene. More cars stopped from moment to moment and soon the highway was played on by many headlights.

I went to the woman on the pavement. She was quite young and wore a white evening dress. The white dress looked startling against the black of the pavement. I leaned over her and said as quietly as I could, "Take it as easy as you can, miss. The ambulance will be here in a few minutes."

She was trying to say something in her moaning but I could not make the words out.

Matt came back out from the café, joined us.

"She's trying to say something," I said to Matt. "I can't make it out."

Matt leaned over her.

"She wants a Catholic priest," he said tensely. "Go and ring the Catholic Church at Malibu, will you? Put the call through as an emergency. Hurry!"

Roland looked down at the woman on the pavement and shrugged. "It will be too late."

As I hurried back to the café, I met Dennis hurrying out. He was fixing a purple stole around his neck.

He went to the woman and knelt down beside her, his black suit very black against the white of her dress. He made the sign of the cross over her and leaned close to her.

I could see he was hearing her confession.

Later we stood at the bar. Matt, Gloria and I.

Dennis had gone on to the hospital in the ambulance.

Gloria, putting her glass down, said, "I'm sorry. Matt, I bawled you out tonight."

"Forget it, honey," Matt said quietly.

"I've got to be going," Gloria said.

"You aren't going to wait till Dennis gets back?" Matt was surprised.

"I've made enough of a fool of myself as it is," Gloria answered.

She said good night and left.

"It's the damnedest thing, isn't it," Matt said. "Dennis a priest. I can't wait till he gets back. I can't wait till I hear his story."

6.

I was back at Matt's place the next night and was surprised to be met with a sign on the door reading, *Closed for Alterations*.

The door was open, however, and I pushed on in. The café was dark but there was a table light on in Matt's booth. He was sitting alone there reading a large black-bound book with red-edged pages. The book was propped up against the skull on the table.

"I left the door open for you," Matt said.

"What alterations are you planning?" I asked with an effort at lightness as I sat down. "Going to add more reserved tables so you will have more empty chairs?"

"The alterations are to be in me. I hope." He solemnly closed the book. "I've had quite a time of it, quite a night, quite a day."

"Dennis ever show up?"

He paused, then added quietly. "No, Dennis never did come. Nor will he."

"Perhaps he stayed on at the hospital," I suggested, though at heart I shared the finality of Matt's judgment.

"I telephoned. He's gone. I have a very definite idea he's again on a Greyhound bus again bound for nowhere."

"He may be hitch-hiking from Santa Monica." I tried to be helpful.

He shook his head sadly. "He could have walked from Santa Monica by this time. No. If he had any intention of returning I would have heard from him." He coughed to clear the emotion from his voice. "I can tell you, son, it's been quite a day. The place has been empty, empty. I miss him."

I looked around the dark café. "I miss him too. He was a character."

"He was more than a character," Matt said with intensity. "He changed the quality of my feeling, of my thinking. Without his presence the café has become an enormous vacuum. I feel small and unimportant. I feel crowded again, stooped. I feel complicated. I do not know what Dennis' life story is but I do know he somehow achieved timeless living and he could share his achievement with others.

"This afternoon I went to his room in the wild hope he had slipped in without my seeing him. The room was bare except for this book. The bed was neatly made. In the dresser I found a white cotton shirt, a pair of nylon shorts, a pair of cotton socks, a razor, a toothbrush, a tube of shaving cream, a tube of toothpaste, a cheap brush and comb, two clean handkerchiefs and nothing else. All his possessions could have been carried in a paper bag, as they were when first I saw him.

"Earlier this evening I went back up to his room to see if I could find any trace of an address or any indication of his identity on his clothes. I found none, nothing."

"You have the memory of him," I said, trying, lamely, I'll admit, to console him.

"What a poor bromide that is," Matt said quietly. "The memory of his presence is a hurt to me." He paused, then continued. "I would give a great deal to find him again. I would travel a long distance to see him again. I know not merely that I miss him but now he is gone I know I need him." He tapped the skull. "Tonight my lady reminds me, not of the brief sweetness of life, not of the sudden excitement of the immediate moment but of the long dull emptiness of death."

Again Matt was beyond me so I said nothing. There was a profound silence, especially profound in the dark café with Matt mistily staring at the polished skull in the light of the single table lamp.

After a while, Matt held up the book he had been reading. "This was his breviary," he said.

"Maybe he'll come back for that," I said. "It looks like quite a book."

"It was his only possession, really," Matt went on. "Note how worn the pages are. His life was a strange life for a priest but you can see he did not fail to recite the Divine Office. He must have loved this book but I am sure he will not return for it. No. His secret is revealed, or, rather I should say, a part of it is revealed and his simplicity would never permit him the embarrassment of facing our questions. No. He is gone."

Matt thumbed the pages of the breviary. A small card, such as is used for a place marker, fell out of the pages. He picked up the card and read a quotation on it.

"This is good," he said. "Listen. 'Great is the power and courage of love, for God is its prisoner. St. John of the Cross.'" He looked over at me. "All right, isn't it? 'Great is the power and courage of love, for God is its prisoner.' Somehow I can imagine Dennis going around with God as his prisoner."

As Matt spoke, I noticed printing on the back of the card. I called Matt's attention to it. He turned the card.

His face immediately showed excitement. "I think we have something. I know we have something." He hastily passed the card over to me. "Read that. It's a memento card. It gives the story. Read it."

I read, "Dennis Browne, First Solemn High Mass, St. Aidan's Church, Ipswich, New York."

"There's the story!" Matt exclaimed.

"It's only the beginning of the story," I said. "Look there at the small print. It's dated ten years ago."

"Yes, it is only the beginning of the story but it's enough," Matt agreed, his excitement growing. "It's the starting point of the quest."

That night Matt's idea of a quest I considered an inspiration of the mood of the evening that would pass as the evening passed. But I underestimated his devotion to Dennis.

The next night when I returned to Matt's place I found the *Closed for Alterations* sign on the door of the café as before. But this time the café was completely dark and the door was locked. Matt was not there.

He had already, it turned out, gone on his quest, as he in his rather literary fashion had put it.

7.

Weeks, months went by. Thanksgiving, Christmas, New Year's Day highlighted the passing of time. And I heard not a word from Matt.

Then late one early February evening, a Saturday, he telephoned the office. Would I come out to his place that night? There was excitement in his voice but he gave no hint of what he had in his mind.

I drove out the Coast Highway in a heavy rain. The *Closed for Alterations* sign was still on the door. The café was dark. But the door was open and I went on in.

The café was dusty and needed airing but otherwise it was as I had last seen it months before.

Matt sat in his usual booth under the single table lamp with the skull before him, looking exactly as I had seen him last. There was only one change, a major change it eventually turned out to be. Beside Matt, near the window, sat a young woman I had not seen before.

So striking was the woman I could not keep from staring at her. Her hair, flaxen and bountiful, fell to her shoulders, defining a strangely pale, high-cheekboned face, set with dark, lazy violet eyes and a large, sensuous mouth. Her cheeks looked as if she were ever so slightly sucking them in and gave her face the appearance of unusual sensitivity. Her body was slender and yet voluptuous. She was an engaging, slightly disturbing combination of commonness and distinction.

Matt enjoyed the impression he could see she made on me.

"Meet Miss Wren," he said, introducing us.

I joined them, sitting across from them in the booth.

"I am going to tell you the story of my quest," he announced grandly, "the story of our friend Dennis. I have been to many towns and cities. I've talked to many people. I do not have the whole story as yet but I have much of it. The end I hope we will soon find out."

So Matt began.

8.

No one enjoyed Matt's manner of talking—his extravagance with words, his fondness for his sometimes hazily mystical conceits, his grandiloquent apostrophes and the rest of it— more than I, but I'm afraid if I put down Dennis' story exactly as Matt told it, it might come out a little too discursive, too vagrant with irrelevancies and, in a word, too protracted for any one-volume work. I shall therefore play my part as a rewrite man and tell Dennis' story as directly and succinctly as I can. Matt's comments will be interpolated here and there when they appear particularly pertinent. If I should appear to improvise on occasions, that is Matt's doing, not mine.

Dennis was born Dennis Browne in a small city in upstate New York, a city which, for the purposes of this narrative, I have called Ipswich. He was an only son. His father owned and operated a hardware store in the heart of town and was reasonably prosperous. Mr. Browne had dreamed of a large family but his wife had other ideas. Her one experience with childbearing was all she wanted. Mr. Browne, tolerant, patient, abided by her wishes.

Dennis' father was a serene, simple man, a Catholic and a devout one. His mother was also a Catholic but could hardly be described as devout. She fancied herself a woman of great allure (there was no question she did have considerable physical charm), much too bewitching for her husband and his small city. The shops, the dressmaker, the beauty parlor and the theater, motion picture and legitimate, were the chief claimants on her time.

Dennis deeply loved his father and mother and when he grew into his teens and discovered his mother's inclinations and his father's unhappiness over them, he too became unhappy, as unhappy as a sensitive, reflective boy can be. He humored his mother in all her flippancies and small indulgences and strove to show her constant affection and tried, as subtly as he could, to suggest to her how deeply she was hurting his father. But the boy was unable to influence her.

Secretly she had, as it turned out, a highly romantic notion about her destiny and it did not include the small city of Ipswich and the devout and plain father and son.

When Dennis was in his last year in high school, his mother had an affair with the leading man in a musical comedy road show playing in the city and went off with him. It was, naturally, a shock and a scandal, especially with the help of the local newspapers. Dennis and his father walked the darkness of heartbreak and helplessness. Presently, the mother instituted divorce proceedings on the grounds of cruelty and incompatibility. She declared no special interest in Dennis. Dennis' father did not contest the divorce.

These months brought the father and son more closely together. By an unspoken pact, no mention of the mother was made again. The father never did recover from his wife's perfidy and two years later, when Dennis was a sophomore at

Georgetown in Washington, he died in his sleep. Everybody who knew him believed he died of heartbreak.

Dennis tried to reach his mother in New York City, where her husband was a star in a new musical, to tell her of his father's death. He reached the actor but not his mother. She had already divorced him and married a Chilean millionaire playboy. It was a lonely youth who saw his father laid to rest.

Dennis had never considered he had any special calling to the priesthood. But in those days after his father's death he suffered particularly from a sense of the brevity and futility of life in general and of the guilt of his mother in particular. He began to meditate the becoming a priest as an act or, perhaps, as a life of reparation for her.

So the idea of a vocation began. It grew in intensity. Then, a year after his father's death, his pastor and confessor recommended he enter the diocesan seminary. If the young Dennis had any doubts as to the validity of his vocation, which he did have, they soon vanished after his enrollment at the seminary.

He was well remembered at the seminary. He showed some talent for letters but he was best remembered for his extraordinary humility. It is told of him, for example, how the prefect of discipline once hearing the crash of fallen crockery in the kitchen hurried in to find Dennis picking up the pieces of a broken platter and murmuring contritely, over and over again, "Forgive me, Lord Jesus, I broke Your dish. Forgive me, Lord Jesus, I broke Your dish." He was completely unaware of the prefect's entrance. It was a picture of childlike humility as the prefect described it.

In the seminary library under a reproduction of Rembrandt's etching, *The Crucifixion*, was a framed typewritten poem Dennis had written. It is given here not so much as a revelation of his talent for letters as another evidence of his humility.

GOOD FRIDAY

Christ is nailed to the two-branched tree.
His blood runs fast, His blood runs free.
Where have all fled?
Where are the sick His love made well?
Where are the lost He kept from Hell?
Where are the living He raised from the dead?
Lazarus, His friend, where is he?
Where is the son of the widow of Nain?
Where is she?
Where are the blind He made to see?
What of His lepers, His sick, His lame,
His deaf, His dumb, His sore-distressed,
His poor, His lambs, His devil-possessed?
Where are all He kept from Hell?
Where are all His love made well?
Where are all on this lonely day?
Where are they?
Christ is nailed to the two-branched tree,
His blood runs fast, His blood runs free.
Where am I?
What of me?

After his ordination, Dennis was assigned to a parish in a large city. His pastor, a monsignor, a stern extrovert of the old school, looked on Dennis with a critical eye. He did not feel in any way honored by the appointment of Dennis. He considered him much too naive and, generally, ineffectual.

Dennis was, for example, hardly what could be called a forceful preacher. He was shy in the pulpit. He talked rather than preached. His themes were often (too often, the pastor thought) from St. John of the Cross, the Spanish Carmelite, to whom he had a great devotion. We have already seen one quotation from the great mystic, the one on the memento of his first Solemn High Mass, "Great is the power and courage of love, for God is its prisoner." That this was one of his guiding thoughts in the pulpit can be surmised from the honor he gave it.

Another favorite theme of his talks, also from St. John of the Cross, was in the quotation, "An instant of pure love is more precious in the eyes of God and the soul, and more profitable to the Church, than all good works together though it may seem as if nothing were done."

It is a beautiful thought, and true, I'm sure, but it can be understood how a busy, unmystical pastor of a city church striving for lay cooperation and contributions would look on this declaration that pure love is more precious and profitable than all good works put together.

There were some understanding souls among the parishioners who liked Dennis, strange and other-worldly though he must have seemed to them, but generally the rough, tough parishioners agreed with their pastor and considered him high-flown and ineffectual. There were also the few, as there always are, who were concerned for him because he was handsome and could therefore come to no good end.

His stay in the parish would at best have not been long but it happened it was considerably shortened by the events that are about to be related, events that proved to be determining factors in Dennis' future.

9.

It was a warm, placid July late afternoon. Father Dennis was in his room reading his favorite saint's meditation on his poem *The Living Flame of Love*, and was deep in the spiritual romance of the Bride and her Beloved. Mrs. Guinness, the housekeeper, knocked on the room door. The first knock Father Dennis did not hear. Nor the second. But the third was a thumping that brought him abruptly out of his mystical adventure.

Mrs. Guinness eyed the curate coolly. She had little use for curates but for this curate she had hardly use at all.

"Sorry to wake you up, Father," she said, nodding her head sharply as she spoke, a habit of hers when she wished to give significance to words that had no apparent significance otherwise.

"I was reading," Father Dennis meekly explained.

"If you don't mind my saying so, Father, I think you ought to get out and around more. Get to know the parish and the parishioners," she advised with advice that turned out to be anything but wise. "Mrs. Dutton is downstairs in the parlor with Mrs. Galvin. Mrs. Galvin is the wife of Mr. Galvin, the roofer, who plays golf with Monsignor. They came to see Monsignor but he is out and I thought it might be a good thing for you if you discussed their problem with them."

"Thank you, Mrs. Guinness," Father Dennis said. "I guess I haven't been as concerned with parish life as I should be."

"They're in a high dudgeon about some rascality." There was a trace of satisfaction in her voice. "They're a pair of dragoons, I might as well tell you."

"Good," Father Dennis said with his little smile. "I'm sometimes afraid the fine virtue of indignation has been lost."

Just what Mrs. Guinness meant by Mrs. Galvin and Mrs. Dutton being dragoons is not clearly known unless somehow she was thinking of dragons, but a pair of amazons they certainly were, huge, red-necked and excitable almost to being apoplectic.

They were truly in a high dudgeon. It seems some ladies of the evening had taken a house in Mrs. Galvin's and Mrs. Dutton's neighborhood, a slightly shabby but still proud neighborhood of ancient red brick and brownstone fronts.

The ladies had a stream of callers from early evening until late at night.

"But aren't they the crafty ones!" Mrs. Galvin exclaimed. "They're as quiet as mice. We can't get no complaint against them for disturbing the peace!"

"At noon they walk around the streets bareheaded in the sunshine takin' their exercise as free and easy as if they were honest women," Mrs. Dutton complained.

"They're brazen, that's what they are!" Mrs. Galvin's face as well as her neck was red. "Those floozies!"

Mrs. Galvin and Mrs. Dutton had complained to the police. "And the sergeant at the desk was a Catholic too," Mrs. Galvin declared indignantly, "Sergeant Matthews, a married man with a family and a member of the Holy Name! And he never lifted as much as a little finger. I'll bet somebody's payin' him off. He said he knew about the girls but they didn't do no soliciting so his hands were tied. It was a job for the vice squad. He reported it, he said."

"The vice squad indeed!" Mrs. Dutton snorted. "The Jezebels are too slick for those young weasels in their Sunday suits. They laugh at them!"

Father Dennis listened without comment to the two parishioners. It was a problem indeed.

"It's a disgrace to the parish and to all decent women," Mrs. Galvin orated. "Why, do you know yesterday noon the floozies out walking stopped in front of my house and talked to my little girl who was playing on the steps. 'Hi, honey,' they said," Mrs. Galvin gave an imitation of the voices making them what she considered musical and therefore presumably sinful. "'How you, sweetie?' Where did you get those golden curls?' 'You're a cutie, do you know that?' The gall of them, talking to my sweet little baby! I let them have it from the window. I'm a lady but I called them 'hores, that's what I called them! And that's all right, isn't it. Father? That's what they are! And did they run? They did not! They stood there and laughed at me and then sauntered off as easy as you please. What do you think of that, Father?"

"Let us pray for them," Father Dennis said.

That suggestion really raised the hair on the good women's heads. They hadn't come there asking for prayers, they had come because they wanted action, they announced. They wanted Father Dennis to call up the chief of police that very minute and give him a piece of his mind. They wanted immediate action. They wanted results.

Father Dennis was in difficulty. He had no inclination whatsoever for calling up the chief of police and giving him a piece of his mind. He was incapable of giving anyone a piece of his mind. Further, much as he was in favor of what he had called "the fine virtue of indignation," he had the feeling the two good women had gone more than a little beyond bounds on that noble emotion.

"Maybe if someone talked to the poor girls," he suggested mildly, "maybe they might give up their life. Maybe Monsignor might find jobs for them."

Mrs. Galvin and Mrs. Dutton stared at each other in disbelief. They had not expected much from the curate in the first place. But this was sheer insanity. Talk to the poor girls! Indeed!

"Father," Mrs. Galvin said with a restraint that nearly burst her wide open, "you do not understand. You are too young. These are wicked women who should be put in jail."

"And kept there!" Mrs. Dutton added.

"They are a threat to morality and the sanctity of marriage," Mrs. Galvin continued as if speaking from memory.

"And to the Christian home," Mrs. Dutton appended.

"What time does Monsignor get back?" Mrs. Galvin asked abruptly.

"About six."

"We'll be back," Mrs. Galvin declared. "We'll be back at six." Father Dennis sat weakly down on a black horsehair sofa in the parlor. He felt he should do something. Mrs. Galvin and Mrs. Dutton had, for all their emotion, one point in their favor. The conduct of the girls was sinful and not to be condoned. But what to do?

What would St. John of the Cross have done?

He must do something, Father Dennis kept telling himself. Mrs. Guinness was right. He should get out into the parish. He should get to know the parishioners and their problems.

Suddenly he had an inspiration. The day before, July 22, had been the feast day of Mary Magdalene and now he vividly remembered the Gospel of the day. He remembered Christ talking to the sinful Magdalene. He remembered and a resolution began to take form. He remembered and slowly he got to his feet. He knew now what he should do.

10.

Father Dennis pulled the doorbell at the door of the ancient brownstone front.

After a moment, the door was opened the few inches a restraining chain would permit. Ada, an older girl who was a madam of sorts, peered out. She was in a pink robe and her hair was in curlers.

She gasped in astonishment as she saw the tall, bare-headed young priest standing outside.

"Just a minute, please," she managed to mumble and closed the door.

At that moment, it so happened, Mr. Sheridan, an undertaker and an usher, was approaching his house across the street. Mr. Sheridan, as a leading parishioner, was more than a little on the rigorist side. Naturally he was astounded to see the young curate standing humbly waiting for admittance to the house of pleasure which, of course, Mr. Sheridan knew it to be.

It must be said of Mr. Sheridan, if he viewed this scene with suspicion, he had what he considered good reason for doing so. Father Dennis was generally suspect with him. Once he had given a talk from the pulpit urging the use in funerals of a plain wooden box such as is the custom of the Carmelites rather than the plush and expensive caskets in vogue, and that idea, it is understandable, could hardly have stirred enthusiasm in an undertaker. Similarly the young curate was suspect with all the florists in the parish. On several occasions he had spoken of what he considered the folly and futility of spending money on flowers for a corpse.

Mr. Sheridan hurried up his stairs and into his house and called loudly for his wife. She came quickly. They both rushed to the front parlor window to watch the curate as he still stood in the late afternoon sunlight outside the disreputable door.

Mrs. Sheridan, quite understandably, shared her husband's unfavorable opinion of the young priest. She also was one of the parishioners who was sure the curate was too alluring to the young women of the parish ever to come to any good end.

Meanwhile, Ada and the four other girls in the house held a quick, nervous conference. Two of the girls were Catholics and they urged admittance of the young priest. He didn't know what the house was and had probably come to sell them tickets to a raffle or a picnic. It would be bad luck sure if they turned him away.

Ada returned to the door. Again she opened the door only the few inches the chain would allow.

"Well take some tickets, Father," she said, "whatever it's for."

"There are no tickets," Father Dermis said. "I just wanted to come in for a visit if you don't mind."

Ada was stunned but she remembered what the two Catholic girls had said about bad luck.

Mr. and Mrs. Sheridan, in the parlor window across the street, watched stony-eyed as Ada, in her curlers and pink robe, opened the door wide and admitted the curate.

Ada led the way into the parlor off the hall just inside of the entrance door. It was a large, drear room with heavy maroon draperies blacking out the afternoon light. Ada drew the draperies ever so slightly but enough to reveal a scuffed dirty carpet, an ancient, stained, marble mantelpiece with artificial daisies in a vase on it, and a set of over-stuffed, frayed, faded green furniture.

Father Dennis looked around the room, saw it was empty.

"There are other girls, aren't there, Miss?"

Ada was alarmed. Evidently he knew the truth. She did not know what to say and so said nothing.

Father Dennis looked at her with eyes that hardly saw her, with eyes that certainly did not notice her large coarse, world-worn face, her red-dyed hair and her worn, frilly-laced pink robe. "I just wanted to have a little talk with everybody," he said.

Now Ada could see his young innocence and sense his harmlessness. She indicated a chair. "It'll be a minute or so, Father."

Ada hurried out into the hall and up the stairs that led to the upper floor. Father Dennis sat in the indicated chair and fixed his gaze on the artificial daisies. He had a feeling of satisfaction. The first, vast step had been taken. He was at last truly about His Father's business.

Matt Easter, telling the story in his booth in the café that night, made a point here. "I sometimes think," he said, "that God is more fond of His sinners than His saints, and the same in a certain fashion could be said of Dennis."

It was some time and the shadows were long outside before the girls made their appearance. The five came slowly down the staircase and filed into the parlor. Now they were all in their evening best—their display clothes, so to speak—satin gowns of different colors and in very high heels. Out of deference to the priest they wore very little make-up. All were nervous and one girl, Cara, the only young and attractive girl in the five, was frightened.

Father Dennis got to his feet as they entered. Ada was slightly over medium size and the others were under and the young priest in his tallness seemed tall indeed. He bowed to the girls and asked them to be seated.

Then, his head slightly back, his little smile on his face and his eyes on infinity, as Matt put it, he began to talk.

"Do you know what he talked about?" Matt asked.

"So far as I was able to gather, he spoke to those uneasy and puzzled women of Christ and His love of them. He spoke of Him, in one phrase that was remembered, as a rich but hungry beggar knocking at their hearts.

"It was pretty strange and heavy stuff for them and, you may be sure, they, like Gloria, did not understand much of what he said. But they did sense they were beholding an extraordinary phenomenon. They may not have been persuaded that some god loved them but they knew this man before them loved them.

"They sat humble and in tears. The doorbell and the telephone rang quite often as evening came on but nobody was interested in answering. Dusk filled the room and still he talked. And one girl, Cara, she who was young and pretty, declares there was a strange light in his eyes as he talked, a light that grew as the darkness deepened.

"I must say Cara was not necessarily a good witness. Transported, she had fallen in love with the young priest. Like Gloria, she had fallen in love with his innocence."

It was dark and the street lights were on when Father Dennis left the house.

11.

Mr. and Mrs. Sheridan were already at the rectory when Mrs. Galvin and Mrs. Dutton arrived.

Mrs. Sheridan lost no time in telling the two parish stalwarts of the shocking sight they had seen.

Mrs. Galvin was the first to comment. "He slipped in to have a little chat with them and perhaps a spot of tea," she said with sarcasm that chilled the little parlor. "He mentioned some insanity of the kind when we talked with him here today."

"Maybe he and the little dears said their beads together." Mrs. Dutton was equally bitter.

"It's a scandal," Mr. Sheridan said ominously. "It'll do our parish no good I'm telling you, no good at all."

"It's no place for a priest to visit, a house like that," Mrs. Sheridan said sadly. "We'll look like fools to our Protestant neighbors."

"We'll have to hang our heads in shame," Mrs. Dutton said.

Mrs. Galvin summed it up. "The curate, he's more of a problem than the 'hores."

The monsignor entered.

He listened to his indignant parishioners tell their tale out, and tell it out they did with many an embellishment.

When the parishioners had finished, he said curtly, "Father Dennis probably went to the house to make a sick call."

"That he didn't, if you don't mind my saying so, Monsignor," Mrs. Sheridan spoke up. "They must have kept him waiting outside for ten minutes. They wouldn't have done that if they had sent for him, would they?"

The monsignor resented this criticism of a priest, even his curate, by parishioners.

"Suppose, my dear people," he said with the severity permitted a pastor and a monsignor, "suppose you leave Father Dennis and the problems of the rectory to me. Such parish problems as the house of prostitution are not uncommon in a city parish and there is a way of handling them, I promise you. Those women have illegally and under false pretenses rented an honorable house and they will shortly be evicted."

The housekeeper, Mrs. Guinness, appeared at the parlor door to announce dinner and that closed the meeting. The parishioners filed humbly out, more impressed than ever by the authority of their pastor, the monsignor.

Once the housekeeper and the pastor were alone together he said, "Ask Father Dennis to come here, will you?"

"There's been no sign of him, Monsignor, since he went out this afternoon," Mrs. Guinness answered.

"He's not home yet?" The monsignor lost his austere calm. "Have you heard from him?"

"No sign of him at all, Monsignor." Mrs. Guinness imagined the agitation of the monsignor was due to the curate's being late for dinner. It was an iron rule with him: a curate was never to be late for dinner. The monsignor had got rid of curates who had broken the rule.

The monsignor's face colored slowly with wrath. "This is a fine kettle of fish," he said half aloud, "a fine kettle of fish." Then he sharply recovered. "Serve dinner, Mrs. Guinness. If Father Dennis comes, you will serve him only after I have left the table."

"Yes, Monsignor." Mrs. Guinness, sensing that something more than appeared was afoot, turned quickly and hurried toward the kitchen.

The monsignor was sipping his coffee when Father Dennis came in.

"Good evening, Monsignor," he lightly greeted the pastor.

The monsignor eyed him coldly, did not return the greeting.

Father Dennis said grace and sat down at the end of the table. His face was slightly flushed, his eyes bright.

"You seem exhilarated over something, Father," the monsignor said coldly.

"I am, Monsignor. I am very happy," Father Dennis said ebulliently. "I feel I've done a good afternoon's work."

"You visited that house of ill fame on Vernon Street, or so the neighbors inform me." The monsignor's voice was metallic. "Is that the good work?"

The curate in his high spirits did not notice his pastor's antipathy. He nodded enthusiastically. "I thought it was about time I got out and around the parish."

The monsignor studied him, seeking to assay the value of this declaration. "Did you ask those—those women to get out of there?"

"I didn't. Monsignor. I never thought of asking them to leave their home."

"Why on earth did you go there then?"

"I thought perhaps if I gave them a little talk, a little conference, sort of, it might help them."

"You were there quite a while for a little talk. You are late for dinner, I suppose you know that."

"I'm sorry, Monsignor. I'm afraid I don't have much sense of time."

"Lack of sense is never acceptable to me as an excuse." The monsignor paused for a moment to put his emotions in order. Then he said as quietly as he could, "You're aware,

I'm sure, you could give great scandal, a young priest like you going into a house like that? I hope you have made up your mind not to do so again. I might as well tell you some parishioners have already been here to protest your behavior."

Father Dennis' exhilaration left him. "It never occurred to me I might give scandal. No, Monsignor. I looked on those girls as so many children, so many Magdalenes to be cherished. It has often seemed to me I have a special devotion to the Magdalenes."

The monsignor paused again. "What did you talk about, may I ask?"

Father Dennis' exhilaration began to return. "I talked on the extravagance, the prodigality, the abandon of God's love. It is a talk I gave the nuns in the convent two weeks ago."

The monsignor's incredulity finally broke the fine discipline of his face. "A talk you gave the nuns?"

"Yes, Monsignor." The curate's enthusiasm was completely renewed. "It's from a beautiful thought of St. John of the Cross. It goes like this—"

But Father Dennis did not get to the quotation. The monsignor got abruptly to his feet, interrupting him. He said grace as if he were saying a prayer over a corpse, turned sharply and left the dining room.

Father Dennis, finally disconcerted by the monsignor's pointedly abrupt departure, got slowly to his feet.

Mrs. Guinness entered with a cup of soup.

Father Dermis shook his head. "Thank you, Mrs. Guinness, but I don't think I'll have any dinner if you don't mind."

"No dinner at all?"

"No thank you. I'm not hungry."

Mrs. Guinness, for all her disdain for curates, and for this curate especially, was still a woman who believed young men should eat. "We have roast lamb tonight, Father. It is very good."

"No, nothing, thank you." Then, meditatively he said, "Monsignor seems to be angry at me about something. I think he thinks I gave scandal this afternoon. I could have. I could very well have. I'm afraid I do not have good judgment."

Mrs. Guinness for the first time since she had known the curate was sympathetic. "You were late for dinner, Father," she said. "But I'm sure you couldn't help it."

"It's more than that, I'm afraid, Mrs. Guinness," the curate said quietly.

Mrs. Guinness nodded. "Yes, it could be, though there are few greater sins for Monsignor than being late for dinner. He did, just now as he was going through the house, ask me to pray for you."

Father Dennis turned quickly, earnestly to the housekeeper. "Oh, please pray for me, Mrs. Guinness! Please pray deeply for me! I try hard but I'm such a poor priest, such a poor priest!"

Mrs. Guinness was startled by the curate's sudden emotion. She backed toward the pantry door.

"I'll get you a glass of milk anyway," she said, desperately in need of an excuse to go.

She turned and hurried from the room.

12.

The monsignor's next few days were troubled days. He had to make a decision. The monsignor had his own rigid standards, perhaps too rigid, but he lived by them himself and he sought to be just.

The curate problem with Father Dennis was unlike any

curate problem he had had heretofore. Father Dennis was deeply religious, there was no question about that. He did not smoke or take a cocktail or even go in for pastimes as innocent as handball. Such spare time as he did not spend in his room in meditation, he spent in the confessional or before the altar.

What the monsignor had to decide was whether his curate was merely young and immature and thus capable of being brought to reason by careful supervision and the passing of time or whether he was irremediably unbalanced and irresponsible.

Father Dennis presently helped the pastor to come to a decision.

It was a drowsy afternoon three days after Father Dennis' visit to the girls' house. The pastor was out at the barber shop. Father Dennis, now determined to be of practical use, was in the office working, not too successfully, at bringing the parish records up to date.

The telephone rang. Father Dennis, at the desk, answered it. It was a young woman's voice. She wanted to talk to the young priest.

When Father Dennis answered that he was the young priest, the young woman's voice grew vibrant. She was Cara, she said, a girl at the house he visited the other day. Would he come to visit her?

Father Dennis was embarrassed. He could not visit her, he said. He must have given her a wrong impression when he was at the house.

The girl's voice was suddenly intense. She had to see him. She wanted to become a Catholic.

Father Dennis was immediately relieved. He was also grateful. His visit had not been a blunder.

He was very pleased, he told the girl. She had made a decision that would bring great happiness to her life. But it would be best that she come to the rectory. They could talk more leisurely there.

The girl said she could not come to the rectory. She would be embarrassed.

Father Dennis said he could not go to the house. His visit the other day had had unhappy consequences.

The girl, her voice growing in emotion, pleaded with the young priest. He had to come to see her. She would never go to the rectory. She would be ashamed.

Now it was Father Dennis who pleaded. Shame, he said, was a small price to pay for her soul. If she came in the evening nobody would see her.

But the girl refused. It was impossible. Finally, reluctantly she ended the conversation.

Father Dennis was profoundly disturbed. He felt a deep obligation toward this girl. His visit to the house, his talk, had borne fruit and with all his heart he wanted it harvested.

He went across the cement walk to the church. Inside he knelt before the altar of the Virgin and pleaded for guidance.

Matt paused in his narration. He had made coffee and he poured fresh cups for himself and me.

The first pale gray fight of daybreak was misting the dark gloom of the café and troubling the placid black ocean beyond the window. The table lamp was making a sickly protest against the coming of day. The skull on the table shone whitely as if with some subtle life of its own.

The girl was slumped back in the corner of the booth peacefully asleep, her flaxen hair looking silver in the gray shadows.

"Father Dennis, on his knees before Our Lady's altar," Matt went on, the coffee cup in his hand, "was facing the crisis of his life. This girl's soul and its salvation were now, he felt, I'm sure, his sole responsibility. The blame for her damnation, if she were damned, would be laid directly to him.

"On the other hand, his going to the house again would be against the pastor's wishes if not his orders. He might give scandal. He had before…"

13.

Cara, in a pale green cotton dress, opened the door. Her deep violet eyes grew bright with surprise and delight as she discovered the young priest standing there. She quickly loosened the door chain and let him in.

She looked quite pretty in an earthy way, with her flaxen hair falling to her shoulders framing her pale, high-cheekboned, full-lipped face. But if she thought Father Dennis saw her in her attractiveness, as she most probably did, she was wrong.

As Matt put it, "Father Dennis rarely saw anyone—that is, as others see people. As a metaphysician might put it, he saw only their essence. It might be said he saw their souls."

Cara led Father Dennis into the shabby parlor. She noticed he glanced up the staircase as he went through the hall.

"I'm alone in the house," she said. "The other girls have moved away."

"It is good the girls have moved away," Father Dennis said.

"I don't know how good it is," Cara commented. "They simply wanted to get out of the parish. They didn't want to hurt your feelings."

"They are daily in my prayers. I have great hope for them," Father Dennis said. "They are really good girls. Are you moving away?"

"I stayed to be near you, Father."

He noticed the emotion in her voice. He was disturbed.

"I think you should get a room for yourself in some good home," he said. "Maybe I can help you get a job."

"Could you come to see me if I had a room in some good home?"

"That all depends on the circumstances," he said gently. "I shouldn't be alone in this house with you now, my child."

"I wanted to see you again," she said, and now her lips quivered slightly with her emotion.

Father Dennis grew more disturbed. He took a paper-bound catechism out of the side pocket of his coat.

"This is a catechism," he said, "a little book that gives the truths of our Holy Faith. Suppose we sit down and I'll go over the first chapter." They sat down, the girl on the sofa, the young priest on a nearby chair. "I want you to study this and learn the answers. You can come to the rectory once a week and we'll talk over each lesson. I should tell you there is a great deal more to Mother Church than is in the catechism."

Her dark eyes were fixed on his face. "Can we be alone if I go to the rectory?"

"I'll answer the door and nobody will see you, if that's what you mean." He opened the paper-bound book. "Suppose we run over a question or two just to get the idea." He read from the book, "'Who made you?' That is the first question and the answer is, 'God made me and lives in me.' Suppose I ask you then, 'Who made you?' and you answer, 'God made me and lives in me.' Now, 'Who made you?'"

Her voice was low, vibrant. "'God made me and lives in me.'"

"Very good."

"Father?"

"Yes, my child."

"Do priests ever marry?"

"Not in the Latin Rite. Why do you ask, my child?"

"I was just thinking."

"Suppose we go on to the second question, 'Who is God?' The answer is, 'God is our Father in Heaven.' See if you can repeat that then. 'Who is God?'"

"'God is our Father in Heaven.'"

"Very good. Very good."

She moved along the sofa to be nearer to him. "Isn't it unnatural for a man not to have a woman, Father?"

He looked at her in surprise. "You're not interested in this lesson are you, my child?"

"No, I'm not, Father." She moved slightly closer.

He closed the book. "I must warn you—what is your name?"

"Cara."

"I must warn you, Cara, that it is not easy to become a Catholic." He got slowly to his feet. "You must want to with all your heart and all your soul. You must pray, pray."

Suddenly she slipped from the sofa to her knees on the floor and flung her arms around his knees, her flaxen hair tumbling over his feet. "I just wanted to see you again." Now she was sobbing. "I never met anyone like you. I never knew there was anyone like you in the world. I just had to see you again."

Father Dennis pulled back and broke her embrace. "My child, my poor child, you are starved for the love of God."

She, still on her knees, lifted her face to him. Tears shone in her dark eyes. "I love you, Father."

"Hush. Hush, Cara. I was not born for a woman's love." There was a great kindness on his face as he talked. "You love genuinely, Cara. You love deeply. Many sins are forgiven you because you have loved so much. I shall give you my blessing."

He made the sign of the cross over her while she sobbed on her knees, and gave her his blessing.

He then leaned down and taking her arm raised her to her feet. "I must go now, my dear."

He put the catechism down on the table and turned to leave. "Pray, pray hard, my child," he said. "Mother Church is your home, the home for all who love much and have lost their way." He went out into the hall and to the front door. She opened the door, her eyes still filmed with tears.

"I shall remember you each morning at Mass," he said as he went down the stairs. "Goodbye, my child. God loves you dearly."

She stood in the open door and sadly watched him go.

Across the street, Mrs. Sheridan had come into her parlor to wash the windows, waiting, as was her custom, till the afternoon when the sun was gone from them and shone on the other side of the street. She looked out and saw the curate going down the stairs and the flaxen-haired harlot standing in the open doorway with tears down her face.

It is understandable that Mrs. Sheridan dropped her wash bucket to the floor.

Matt sipped his coffee. The dawn beyond the window was widening across the sky and splashing the ocean with flame.

"You wonder perhaps how I know so well what went

on in that house that day?" He turned to the sleeping, flaxen-haired girl beside him. "This is Cara. I shall tell you her
story later."

His announcement was no great surprise to me. I had
already had a good idea our flaxen-haired companion was
Cara.

14.

Father Dennis sat in the reception hall of the bishop's residence, a dark, musty room slightly overdone with religious
pictures. On a carved wood table was a stack of religious
magazines.

Father Dennis went through the motions of looking
through the magazines.

A young, husky, blond monsignor, the bishop's secretary,
came into the hall from the living room. He seemed austere
and, to the troubled Father Dennis, a little terrifying.

"His Excellency is free now," he said. "Please."

From his look Father Dennis knew the secretary considered him of more than ordinary interest. Father Dennis
followed him into the drawing room.

The secretary withdrew, closing the door behind him.

The drawing room was ornate, heavy with a dark red
oval rug and massive, dark red upholstered furniture. The
bishop, in a black cassock with narrow purplish-red piping,
sat at a mahogany table in a tall, thronelike chair. On the wall
a short distance behind him hung a Raphael-school madonna in a wide gold frame.

The bishop was of medium size, perhaps five feet ten or
so, but in the tall chair he looked quite small. His hair was
white, his face thin, ascetical.

Father Dennis went to him, knelt on one knee and kissed his ring.

There was silence. The bishop tapped the table softly with long pale fingers.

"You know why you are here, Father?" the bishop finally broke the silence.

Father Dennis bowed his head humbly. "Yes, Your Excellency."

"Sit down, won't you? Do you feel you have been maligned? Is there anything you would like to say in your defense? Or in explanation perhaps?"

"No, Your Excellency," Father Dennis replied quietly as he sat in a chair by the table. "It is all true. I have made a fool of myself."

The bishop's lips tightened for an instant. "I'm afraid you have done more than that, Father." He paused, then went on. "I am going to be very brief with you and very much to the point.

"There is a virtue called prudence which is a great virtue and an especially great virtue in a priest. It is the first of the cardinal virtues, as you know. It is circumspect and it is wise. It directs the other virtues. Indeed it might be said the other virtues depend on it. You are aware of this, of course?"

"Yes, Your Excellency."

"I know you can say the virtue of prudence has seemingly been often disregarded by the saints. The history of almost any saint will reveal extravagance in action, extremity in self-mortification, for example. It was certainly foolhardy for little St. Francis to make his hazardous trip through a land of hostile infidels to see the sultan. The ecstasy of the Little Flower when she saw the coughed-up blood that meant her early death can hardly be interpreted in terms of the golden mean as we know it. But they did not give scandal. And they were saints. Most of us, alas, are not saints."

There was sadness in Father Dennis' voice as he said, "I know that too well, Your Excellency."

"But to get back to your case, Father," the bishop resumed, apparently unaware of any emotion on Father Dennis' part. "I'm afraid in your recent actions you have sinned seriously against prudence, how seriously you alone can know.

"Charity toward those fallen women could, prudently practiced, have been the greatest of virtues. Imprudently practiced as it was, it may have been a source of scandal and serious sin, and was, I'm afraid, foolhardiness itself. Your being alone in that house with that woman was particularly foolhardy."

"Yes, Your Excellency," Father Dennis said in great humility. "I am sorry. I am sorry from the bottom of my heart."

The bishop nodded slowly. "Well and good. But I must point out to you that your contrition is not the complete answer. I don't know that there is any complete answer. But I do know that the priesthood is a corps with a proud record of prudent conduct through many, many centuries. Their prudence has often demanded the virtues of the field of battle: bravery and loyalty and sacrifice.

"Right reason applied to practice is not always easily come by. The record of the priesthood is a golden record of brave discretion, of dauntless prudence. There is no other corps, military or otherwise, can boast of so glorious an achievement through so many centuries."

The bishop paused, hesitated as if he did not want to say what he was going to say. "I have a special point to make, Father. Your actions may have been ignorance on your part. They may have been plain stupidity. I am sure they were not intentional. But nonetheless, you, I have to say, have failed the corps.

"In a small way, in this parish in this diocese, you have besmirched its golden record. I say this in all charity, Father, but it is necessary I say it."

Father Dennis' head was bowed and his voice almost inaudible as he said, "I'm sorry, Your Excellency. I shall be sorry for the rest of my life."

"Well and good." The bishop nodded. "I have said about what I wanted to say. Do you have a home you can go to?"

"No, Your Excellency." Father Dennis' head remained bowed.

"It is a pity. You see, Father, you are quite a serious problem." He glanced at a typescript on the table before him. "There is considerable question as to your fitness for parish work of any sort. This has not directly to do with the particular foolhardiness we were just discussing. Your approach to even the most ordinary problem seems unrealistic. You have been described as irresponsible and from the record it appears as if the description is just.

"It will take me some time to decide just what disposition is to be made of you. Do you have any money?"

"I don't know, Your Excellency." Father Dennis felt lamely in his pockets. "Yes, I have some."

"Good. Suppose then you go away for a few days and I'll see what can be done. Think things over. Think especially of the virtue of prudence. And pray. Pray, Father. Pray for guidance. Perhaps if you could go to the Trappist monastery in Kentucky and spend the time there you might find the proper illumination. I shall pray too. Have you any questions?"

Father Dennis got to his feet. "May I have your blessing, please?"

Father Dennis knelt by the bishop's chair. The bishop rose and gave the young priest his blessing.

"Thank you, Your Excellency," Father Dennis said as he got to his feet. His voice was almost a whisper as he added, "I know now I have loved God too little. I shall try to love Him more."

Father Dennis turned and went slowly out of the room. The bishop, a trace of puzzlement ruffling his disciplined face, watched him go.

15.

Late that night, in the deserted warehouse district in the downtown area of the city, two policemen in a cruising car saw a bareheaded young man with a handkerchief around his neck wandering aimlessly along the empty sidewalks.

They were suspicious and drew the car up alongside the curb.

"Looking for somebody, bud?" one of the policemen asked from the car.

The young man came over to the car. His face was deeply troubled. "I am looking for illumination from the Holy Spirit," he said.

The two policemen were going to laugh but they saw his simplicity, his earnestness. They put him down as a mildly deranged, harmless religious crank.

"Don't look for it in any warehouse," the officer said as the car drove off.

Such is the way Matt told it.

"Those were not fanciful words that Father Dennis spoke, and it is understandable why he spoke them," Matt declared. "He, like his Master, was calling in anguish, 'Not my will but Thine be done.' He, too, heartstricken, was crying out for illumination.

"He had not gone back to the rectory after leaving the bishop's house. Indeed he was never to see the rectory or his pastor again. Nor was he to see the bishop again except once under rather extraordinary circumstances, an event I will tell of presently.

"He wandered the downtown streets the whole night long. Dawn, creeping down the empty, dark ravines of the city, found him still plodding the brick and asphalt floors, bareheaded, tortured, looking for the light he could not find.

"He came to an ancient, once elegant now dilapidated church. He saw a few people, mostly old, going into five-thirty Mass, a special Mass for those who finished work late or went to work early. The people entered quickly in the shadows, singly and with that curious quality of secrecy that attends people moving in city streets in the early dawn.

"Father Dennis entered the church just as Mass was begun. The altar and chancel were aglow with light. The rest of the church was a deep shadowy dark.

"Father Dennis knelt in the almost black obscurity of the last row of pews. He bowed his head and prayed. He prayed to God the Father, God the Son, and God the Holy Spirit. He prayed to God's beautiful Mother. He remembered it was the feast of Ignatius, a saint to whom he had a special devotion since his days with the Jesuits at Georgetown. He prayed to Ignatius.

"Then, suddenly, the illumination came.

"The celebrant had reached the moment of the Consecration of the Host. Christ was about to come down to Earth again. Father Dennis knelt rigidly upright, his head back. He said the words of the Consecration of the Host along with the priest on the altar...*Hoc Est Enim Corpus Meum* ...for This is My Body....

"Then, in that instant, he received the illumination of the Holy Spirit. Then, in that instant, he knew the tremendous and, in some ways, tragic decision he must make."

Two days later the bishop received a letter, without any return address, signed by Father Dennis.

The letter told of his deep sorrow at his failure as a priest. It told of the tortures of his search for illumination. It told of the moment when at Mass in the ancient church the light finally came to him and, with the light, the knowledge of his decision.

"I saw the truth," Father Dennis wrote, "the almost intolerable truth. I saw why I was irresponsible, and incapable of prudence, and why I failed the priesthood.

"It was because my vocation was not a true vocation. The idea of becoming a priest had come first to me with the idea of offering reparation for my mother's sins. It did not come first out of a desire to save my soul and a love of the service of God.

"The fundamental fact is, Your Excellency, I am not good enough to be a priest. Others, I am sure, are good enough to stand at the altar and command Christ's immolation again. I am not. Others can lift Him up again on His Cross. I cannot. I am not worthy to hold God in my hands.

"Forgive me. I shall see to it I trouble you no more. I realize once a priest, always a priest, and I shall try to act accordingly. Please in your charity remember me in your prayers."

16.

Father Dennis' life and wanderings were unknown for the next few months. It was assumed that he got himself odd jobs here and there downtown and became lost in the multitudes of the city.

It is not certain whether his pastor made any effort to find him. It can be imagined neither the pastor nor the parish greatly bemoaned his loss. The bishop, who had been somewhat disturbed at the end of his interview with Father Dennis and by the intense sincerity of his letter, could not get him out of his mind for several days. But soon, in the press of his own many and grave responsibilities, his concern gave way to the idea that the young curate, being deeply religious, would return, and his problem was vaguely filed away for the future.

Sometime in the late autumn, Father Dennis turned up working in a large downtown bookstore. The store had a sizable religious books department. It was here Father Dennis was stationed. He was remembered as a self-effacing man who was good in the department.

He was not to stay at the bookstore long however. A woman member of his former parish dropped in to the religious books department. She was an ardent reader of Catholic verse and was in to see if anything new had appeared.

She recognized Father Dennis. This was not difficult at this time because he had not yet become stooped and thin from his austerities nor had he grown his beard. She was scandalized.

Straightway she went to the manager. She told the manager his clerk was an "ex-priest" who had had an affair with a woman and had been kicked out of the clergy. The store wouldn't sell many religious books to Catholics, she warned, once the truth about the clerk got around.

"And she warned further," Matt added, "she would see to it the truth got around."

Father Dennis next turned up working at a religious goods store. It was some weeks before Christmas. What happened at the bookstore happened again here. Except this time it was a man doing his Christmas shopping early.

"He was a fine Christian, I'm sure," Matt commented sarcastically, "and a dutiful parishioner. Was he not doing his Christmas shopping, and already abounding in the Christmas spirit?"

Again, apparently, Father Dennis took to wandering the streets. But this time his feet—"his angel," was the way Matt put it—led him to a haven where he was to enjoy some years of happiness and peace.

On Christmas Eve, in the middle of the afternoon. Father Dennis went to visit the chapel of the discalced Carmelite sisters. He had worked out a sort of rule for himself and he wanted to spend his appointed hours of meditation in a church or chapel not overrun with the hurried and the worldly, no matter how devout they might be. He went to the Carmelite convent, to the quiet chapel of contemplatives so he might be at peace.

He knelt in the deeper shadow in the rear of the chapel. The afternoon wore on. Now and then a neighbor dropped in for a visit, knelt a minute or two and departed. The unseen sisters came to their choir and chanted the Divine Office and after that there would be silence. The chant, reverent to begin with, seemed more reverent sifting from the invisible choristers through the walls into the hushed quiet of the chapel.

Father Dennis felt a great peace, a peace he had not known for a long time. It seemed to him he was at last somehow at home. He was living in a sort of dream, he was sure,

and its ending would come with the end of day but while
it lasted he drew in deeply every moment of its sublime
content.

His beloved St. John of the Cross was much in his mind,
as might be expected—St. John, the Carmelite, being the
spiritual father of the dedicated contemplatives within the
walls.

Dusk crept with its usual delicacy into the chapel. He
was alone. Words from St. John of the Cross came to his
mind like a whisper. "O sweetest love of God, too little
known! He who has found Thee is at rest."

The whisper in his mind sought for utterance aloud.
Involuntarily he whispered to the tabernacle, "O sweetest
love of God, too little known! He who has found Thee is at
rest."

Immediately after he had spoken, he was embarrassed to
discover a woman standing just inside the side door of the
chapel, looking sharply at him. She was a large buxom woman in her early fifties. One sturdy hand supported an electric
floor polishing machine by her side.

"I hope I'm not bothering you," the woman said, "but I
have to polish the floors."

Her voice was rather loud and matter-of-fact—too
much matter-of-fact, Father Dennis thought, for a chapel
with its Divine Mystery.

Straightway the woman plugged in the electric cord in a
wall outlet and began to work on the tiled floor. The machine
made a din that destroyed the peace of the chapel.

Father Dennis, ill at ease, watched the woman as she
pushed the polisher along the front of the church. She
worked with a vigor and an efficiency that seemed to him to
be irreverent. The front finished, she lifted the heavy machine

and pushed on through the altar rail gate into the sanctuary, genuflecting with some difficulty because of her bulk as she came directly before the tabernacle.

There was a moment of quiet as she transferred the electric cord to a wall outlet near the altar. Then the din began again.

Father Dennis grew more ill at ease, partly because he felt he should offer his help to this woman, partly and more strongly because he was unhappy at the profane way she barged around the sanctuary.

He was a shy man and slow to decision but finally he made up his mind. He left his pew and went reverently into the sanctuary, genuflecting humbly and long before the tabernacle.

"Madam," he said in a reverent whisper, "may I help you? May I do the polishing?"

His decision, unimportant though it seemed at the moment, was to change his life.

17.

The robust Mrs. Welsh—she with the floor polisher—was very much in need of help. The convent had no outside sister and Mrs. Welsh, who lived across the street, was its only auxiliary. That evening she had yet to dust the pews. She had yet to arrange the new flowers on the altar for Christmas morning. She had yet to set up the breakfast table in the refectory for the celebrant of the Masses in the morning.

She promptly and gladly turned over the floor polisher to Father Dennis. It was a small chapel and he was soon finished with the floor. He joined Mrs. Welsh at dusting the pews and again he was welcomed. After that he helped her arrange the new flowers. He showed such aptness for the job and such reverence at the altar that she commented on it.

"You're an old hand, I see," she said in the loud, matter-of-fact voice that discomforted Father Dennis. "You've been around an altar before, I can see that."

It was dark when Mrs. Welsh got to setting up the breakfast table.

"Now," she announced, "I must get me an altar boy or a pair of them for the morning. It's no easy task any more getting boys who will get up in the dark. In the old days Christmas Eve was a quiet time and everybody went to bed early so they could be up at the crack of day. Now they stay up and celebrate in the evening—some go to Midnight Mass—and sleep the beautiful Christmas Morning away."

"I'll serve the Masses, ma'am," Father Dennis said.

Mrs. Welsh studied him, saw him wasted and shy. "You sure you can now?"

"I'm sure I can."

"Well, that's a load off an old lady's shoulders!" Mrs. Welsh exclaimed loudly. "I'll be depending on you. There's to be no Midnight Mass this year—too many roisterers used to crash the services—so the first Mass will be at five. Don't be here a moment later than four-thirty."

"Yes, ma'am."

"Are you going home for your supper?"

"No, ma'am."

She studied him again. "You look like a good meal wouldn't do you a bit of harm. I've got an oyster stew on the stove and some homemade rolls warming in the oven. I live just across the way. I might even cut the fruitcake in your honor."

Father Dennis was a little ill at ease. "I don't think I'd better, ma'am."

"Come on, come on," Mrs. Welsh insisted. "You can leave right after supper. I suppose you, like the rest of the world, have Christmas shopping still to do."

"No. I have no Christmas shopping."

"Well, come along then. I won't eat you." She started through the refectory toward the reception hall of the convent. "You'd be doing a person a kindness. It gets kind of lonely being alone on Christmas Eve."

So one thing led to another, as Matt put it, and Father Dennis had supper with Mrs. Welsh.

Mrs. Welsh, a widow of many years, owned a two-story, timeworn, elaborate frame house across from the ancient red-brick convent. When the convent was built, the neighborhood was comfortably suburban, but the city had reached out and the well-to-do had moved on before the advance of the poor. Most houses took in roomers, as did Mrs. Welsh's.

It was part of Father Dennis' new rule that he eat very little, a rule in his poverty he had found easy of observance. That evening at Mrs. Welsh's he ate so little, she became worried about him.

As he was about to leave the house and had opened the front door, snow began to fall. Mrs. Welsh looked out at the wintry night and then at her guest. She saw him in all his wretchedness: thin, in the cheap white shirt and white cotton wash tie he had now begun to wear, hatless, without an overcoat, and the concern she had for him at the supper table grew.

"I better call a taxi," she said. "You'll be soaking to the bone before you've gone a block."

He was alarmed. He had no money to pay for a taxi and no place for the taxi to go. "No, thank you," he said quickly. "I like to walk. I like to walk in the snow especially."

She surmised immediately the reason for his alarm. "Young man, I'll bet you don't have a dime in your pocket!"

He looked at her gravely and said, "I've never had much acquaintance with money, Mrs. Welsh."

"I knew it! I knew it." She was her loud, commanding self again. "You look like death eating crackers! Come. I have a warm room for you and a comfortable bed."

He was disturbed. He had not known kindness for a long time. He tried to protest.

But Mrs. Welsh would have none of his protestation. She was a woman who, once she saw her way, went dead straight ahead. "You have to get up at four o'clock in the morning, young man!" she declared.

So it began.

Father Dennis stayed at Mrs. Welsh's house that night. In the morning he served the Christmas Masses. After breakfast the celebrant told the sister at the turn—the turn being the revolving, half-barrel in the reception room wall through which ordinary communication is maintained with the unseen sisters—that never before had a Mass of his been served so reverently and beautifully.

Later, the sister at the turn talked to Father Dennis. Even the sisters, hidden in the choir, she told him, had been aware of the humility and reverence in his responses at Mass. How they all wished he could serve Mass every morning!

He would try, he said. He would try.

He was happy someone wanted him.

So again one thing led to another. Father Dennis stayed at Mrs. Welsh's Christmas night and served the Mass on St.

Stephen's day, the next morning. And the next morning after that. And the morning after that...

In a short time Father Dennis was an institution at Carmel. He was acolyte, sacristan, messenger, outside gardener—a beloved factotum.

But to him, taking the name of his favorite saint, he was simply Brother John, janitor. And as Brother John, janitor, he was to find a purpose and peace.

For a time.

18.

The janitor job seemed providential and Father Dennis felt that as Brother John he had finally found his station for the rest of his life. The sisters fed him the little he ate, usually only milk or coffee and Carmelite bread, and Mrs. Welsh gave him a room. Both the Carmelites and Mrs. Welsh grew very fond of the janitor and they affected him more than he knew.

The usual Carmelite good humor brought out a latent humor in him and his little quips soon became a source of amusement to the sisters behind the walls. And their affection for him made his heart often sing with joy.

Mrs. Welsh's loud practicality at first frightened him but, after a while, he began to like it and benefit from it.

Once, Mrs. Welsh, smelling smoke in the middle of the night, got out of bed and made an inspection of the house. She found no fire but she did find Father Dennis out of his room and his bed not slept in. She was much disturbed.

She made coffee and sat up the night in the parlor. At the beginning of daybreak, she heard a door being closed in the monastery across the street. It was Father Dennis coming out of the chapel.

Mrs. Welsh sat Brother Janitor down in the parlor.

"What in glory's name are you doing out moping around at this hour?" she demanded.

"I was just making a visit," he answered meekly.

"Making a visit! Your bed wasn't slept in. This is regular procedure, is it?"

He said nothing.

"Is it?" she asked, "or isn't it?"

"I do go over to the chapel quite often," he admitted.

"Why? Why on earth would you do a thing like that?"

He hesitated and then did not speak.

"Why? Why do you give up your night's sleep? Why?"

He hesitated again but this time he spoke. "I just figured Our Lord might be lonely over there during the long night."

"Glory be! You're going to take care of the Lord, are you?" She was indignant. "The Lord, I promise you, can take care of Himself! And that's more than you can do. Why, you poor creature, you don't eat, you don't go anywhere, and now you don't sleep. You're dying on your feet. You're already getting to be stooped like an old man and you're so thin I wouldn't know you had a face if it wasn't for that stubby beard you're growing.

"Well, I'll tell you one thing, young man. If I'm going to give you a bed, you're going to sleep in it! I'm not going to have you die here on your feet. You hear?"

"Yes, Mrs. Welsh." He smiled, deeply grateful for her solicitude.

But she did not understand his being grateful. "Wipe that smile off your face! I have eyes in my head, haven't I? Your dying is no laughing matter."

"I appreciate your worrying about me, Mrs. Welsh," he said quietly.

"Well, start worrying about yourself a little bit, will you? Don't leave it to me to carry all of the burden." Then she added, looking him straight in the eyes, "What do you want to be? A good janitor or a bad corpse!"

He was silent a moment. Her last remarks had made an impression on him. "You have a point, Mrs. Welsh."

"Indeed I have. The Lord has given you a job to do. Do it."

"Yes, Mrs. Welsh."

"I noticed yesterday the pews weren't dusted," she said coldly.

He was chagrined. "The pews were dusty?"

"Dusty. Yes. There in the middle where people don't usually sit. Now, I know you're doing this job for nothing. But you're eating and you have a roof over your head and you seem happy, and all that's a lot more than you were before you came here if I know the score.

"Let the Lord take care of Himself, if you want my advice, and you take care of you. I tell you right now you'll be in a wheel chair in a couple of weeks at the rate you're going. Then you won't be doing any job, for free or otherwise."

He nodded slowly. "It would break my heart, Mrs. Welsh, if I lost my janitor job."

"Well, get to bed and give up the nonsense. Get on with you. Good morning!"

Father Dennis went obediently to bed. And, so far as Mrs. Welsh knew, in any event, he gave up his middle-of-the-night visits to the chapel.

19.

Father Dennis was a little more than three years at Carmel before word of his saintliness got around. The nuns had had an idea from the beginning he was not ordinary, and Mrs. Welsh was sure of it, but no one else. He worked unobtrusively at his many odd jobs and spent such spare hours as he did not spend in the chapel in a small patch of infertile ground which was euphemistically known as the outside garden.

It was the garden that first revealed his uniqueness. There he grew flowers for the chapel altar and it soon was evident his flowers were more beautiful even than those grown in the carefully cultivated gardens in the cloister. He especially grew red roses.

They were roses of the deepest red, large and long-stemmed and graceful. Once, in May, after he had been at Carmel for three years, he brought an armful of the roses to the nun at the turn for the Virgin's statue within the walls.

The little nun, Sister Imelda, exclaimed in rapture as she took the flowers off the turn, "Never, never have I seen roses so red and so beautiful!"

"Those are special roses. Sister," he said. "Saint Thérèse grew them for me."

Truly, the roses Brother John grew were red, deep red. They lasted long and kept the deepness of their color even when wilted. They made blood-red clusters on the altar and before the shrines much to the wonder of the sisters and the faithful. Everyone agreed that never had there been roses so red.

When asked how he grew roses so beautifully red, always he would give the answer he gave Sister Imelda. Saint Thérèse grew the roses for him. Once when Sister Imelda asked him how he was so sure Saint Thérèse grew the roses for him, he said, "I ask her to," as if that were all there was to it. Then he added—and this was the only time he made this comment—"Blood red was a color very dear to Saint Therese."

The sisters realized then what they had long before surmised: that their Brother John was someone of importance. They began to turn hopeless petitions and lost causes over to him, saying to the petitioners, "Go and see Brother John. He has more influence than we have."

The number who sought him out grew with the passing of the years. Finally he had to keep a list of the names of the petitioners, and the list became so long that the paper with the list reached to the ground. Always when before the altar, he kept the paper before him and methodically, carefully interceded, one by one, for all.

It was inevitable his accomplishments, sometimes being remarkable ones, were finally called "miracles." The idea he performed miracles profoundly distressed him. Any good thing that happened he attributed to the intercession of his dedicated friends within the walls, the Carmelites. It was also inevitable that he be called a saint. And this, when it happened, embarrassed him so much and hurt his humility so deeply he would keep himself aloof for days.

"In his humility, he felt that this reputation he was achieving was fraudulent," Matt said, "and after eight perfect years at Carmel, he began to be ill at ease. He saw himself simply as a man not good enough to be a priest, and his sole purpose in life was to do penance for what he considered his great sins of imprudence. He loved God with all his heart, and hoped he could save his soul. The idea of his being saintly was incomprehensible and painful to him.

"One spring night, Mrs. Welsh, watching Brother John as he came through the front door with the dark behind him, thought she saw a sort of luminosity about him. It

seemed especially to be around his head and in his face as we
observed it that night last autumn here in the café.

"Mrs. Welsh was startled, naturally. She said nothing
and kept her excitement to herself. The first thing the next
morning she was over in the monastery asking Sister Imelda
at the turn if she should believe her eyes.

"'Of course, my dear,' Sister Imelda whispered as if the
report were too marvelous for a normal voice. 'This sort of
luminosity is a well-known phenomenon of mysticism. It is
not necessarily supernatural but in Brother John's case it may
well be. We're all sure he's a saint, if we can call anyone a saint
who has not been canonized.'

"'He's a saint sure enough, canonized or no canonized,'
Mrs. Welsh said. 'He changes the world he walks through.
After you know him, you're never the same again.'

"Of course," Matt went on, "word of what Mrs. Welsh
had seen got around and the more it got around the more
it was distorted. People thronged the chapel, especially on
weekends, looking for 'the man with the halo.'

"Now for the first time, Father Dennis began to meditate the possibility of leaving Carmel. He had the idea Satan
was somehow working for his destruction."

One little incident that happened at this time Matt nar-
rated with more than ordinary emotion. It seems the bishop,
visiting the local parish church to administer Confirmation,
was told of the holy janitor at Carmel nearby. He decided he
would go and see Brother John.

The bishop, with the monsignori and priests in his retinue, six in all, found Father Dennis working in his little
garden.

Father Dennis was frightened. He wanted to flee. He
was sure he would be recognized.

But the bishop did not recognize his priest, now abnormally thin, stooped and bearded.

Father Dennis, trembling, kissed the episcopal ring and kneeling, asked for the bishop's blessing. The blessing given, the bishop told him he had heard of his piety and asked for prayers.

"I sit in a high place, weak and alone. Brother John," the bishop said humbly. "I need your prayers."

Father Dennis, still trembling, took his roll of paper with its long list of petitioners from his inside pocket. He unrolled it and it reached as usual to the ground. He then fumbled in his outside front pocket until he found a stub of a pencil. At the bottom of the roll, near the edge of the paper, he wrote, "The bishop."

One of the monsignori frowned. "His Excellency's name should be put at the top, Brother."

Brother Janitor hesitated a moment, then he said, "There are many poor people before the bishop on the list, Monsignor, people who are sick and in need and dying. I could not put the bishop first."

The bishop smiled. "As you wish, as you wish."

The bishop and his retinue left.

Father Dennis, watching them go, felt suddenly sorry for the bishop. He took out his roll of paper, scratched the bishop's name from the bottom and wrote it at the top.

The bishop, as his car pulled away, looked back at the stooped, bearded, thin man in the garden. In a voice that trembled slightly, as much from emotion as old age, he, said to his retinue, "Would that your bishop or one of his priests were a man like this man here."

20.

"It was probably inevitable, Cara or no Cara, with the ever-growing crowds making pilgrimages to see him, some in the quest of miracles, some only out of curiosity, that Brother John would eventually leave Carmel," Matt went on. "But it was Cara who hastened the day.

"Cara came back into his life in the aftermath of one of his miracles or wonders, as I prefer to call them. This was a particularly dramatic one. A girl of the streets—Mary Price was the name she went by—had been stricken with paralysis. It was not polio but a sudden stroke that brought on the paralysis and no doctor—certainly no doctor such as she could afford to see—was certain of its cause or of any course of treatment for a cure.

"On a June afternoon, a sister in the profession, one who had visited Brother Janitor looking for consolation in her frailties, brought Mary to see him, wheeling her there in a wheel chair. The poor creature, to use Mrs. Welsh's expression, was a pathetic sight, no beauty to begin with, she now was ugly in her infirmity.

"Father Dennis laid both hands on her shoulders and prayed over her. At the touch of his hands, she began to tremble from head to foot. A few moments after he had lifted his hands she got out of the wheel chair. She tried to walk. She fell down. Father Dennis and her friend helped her to her feet. She swayed back and forth for a minute. Then she walked."

Matt looked out the window at the growing splendor of the day breaking over the ocean. "Of course, the girl's paralysis was probably psychosomatic. At least that's the way it sounds to me. And the cure may well have come from the tremendous surge of hope and faith the saintly priest inspired.

The ailment was psychic and the cure was psychic, I'm sure. Even so, it was still wonderful indeed. But the newspapers heard of it and to them it had to be a miracle. I can't say for sure they weren't right but they certainly were jumping to conclusions.

"That was the beginning of a real problem for Brother John, janitor."

Crowds of men and women, old and young, healthy and ill, overran the chapel and the outside grounds. Many of the ailing came on crutches and in wheel chairs. Father Dennis tried to hide in Mrs. Welsh's house but the pilgrims were at the doors and windows and it was a troubled sanctuary he found there. All who saw him insisted on touching him so his virtue and power would go out to them. Some insisted on embracing him. They plucked buttons off his coat and snipped pieces of cloth from his clothing until he was in tatters.

His peace, his happiness, were ebbing from him. He prayed and he begged the Carmelites to pray that the crowds would diminish and soon desist so he might return to the simplicity of his old life. But the prayers were in vain.

He told the newspaper reporters that if anything unusual had happened, it was the Carmelites' doing, not his, and they should talk to them. He gave them no opinions on his saintliness because in his humility he had none. But they manufactured opinions.

They quoted him at length in words he did not speak. They took pictures of him when he was unaware they were doing so and published them with their stories.

The "Janitor Saint" they named him.

"The Carmelites were perturbed," Matt said. "The bishop was concerned. He issued a statement giving the Church's stand that no phenomenon is miraculous and no man a saint until declared so by the Church. He warned the faithful on hysteria. Father Dennis was distraught, wretched.

"Only Mrs. Welsh was happy. If this was a flagrant display of superstition as a sociologist in a nearby college described it, it wasn't to Mrs. Welsh. To Mrs. Welsh it was faith at work, faith triumphant.

"Father Dennis, despite Mrs. Welsh's enthusiasm, grew more and more miserable. Here were all he loved, here was his home of many rich and happy years, yet he felt in his heart the day might be near when he would have to give all up and go away."

After a moment, Matt, his voice lowered, spoke again. "It was Cara here, as I have said, who hastened the day of Father Dennis' going."

Cara, unregenerate, still plied her trade but now on a more elegant and prosperous level. She and another girl shared an attractive apartment. They dressed well, lived well and could have been, to all appearances, two sophisticated young ladies living off a moderate inheritance.

Cara's attention was caught by a picture of the Janitor Saint in a newspaper. She read the account of the man's simplicity and saintliness. She returned to the picture. She studied it. Suddenly it occurred to her whose likeness this was.

"She alone recognized in the eyes, in the bearded, drawn face the sanctity she had once known, if only briefly," Matt went on. "It could be she alone remembered his sanctity because, during his short time as a curate, she was the only one who had recognized it.

"She had the gift of her profession of not remembering but she remembered the innocent young priest. She remembered vividly his two visits with her. She remembered them not as any religious experience, for she had had no interest in religion. She remembered them with a physical rapture. She remembered them as times when she was overwhelmingly in love with—and desired—his purity and innocence.

"She had known many men, more men than she could recall, since she had had her meetings with the young priest but he was the only man she really remembered.

"She was sure, looking at the picture, that this was he. The old excitement returned to her. She would go and see him."

21.

On a warm, june evening, a little before dusk, Cara, her flaxen hair falling richly to her shoulders, her light blue frock and her very high-heeled slippers presenting her physical attractiveness at its fullest, climbed the stairs to Mrs. Welsh's house. She had looked vainly for Brother Janitor at the monastery and had been directed to the house across the street.

Mrs. Welsh answered the doorbell. She was a little startled at the obvious charms of the girl she discovered standing at the door. Cara, she could see, was not one of the distressed, the poor or the ill, not to the ordinary eye certainly.

Brother Janitor, Mrs. Welsh explained, had retired to his room. He was not seeing anybody.

But Cara was not so easily put off. She was more sure of herself now than when years ago she had asked the young curate to come to see her. She was an old friend, she said, of many years' standing. Brother Janitor would want to see her if he knew she was here.

Mrs. Welsh's curiosity was stirred. She ushered Cara into the shadowy parlor and went to call Brother John.

When first Father Dennis entered the parlor, he did not recognize Cara.

"Yes, my dear," he said coming forward.

She smiled in anticipation of his surprise. "I am Cara, Father—the girl in that house you came to visit years ago."

Father Dennis remembered immediately. About all he clearly remembered in the blur of his past were the occasions of his imprudence.

"You recognize me?" He was disturbed.

"Easily, there is only one of you on Earth, Father." Cara looked into his eyes, saw they shone more brightly and more passionately with his sanctity than before. "I would recognize you anytime anywhere," she said with a voice that trembled slightly. "I'm beginning to think I was the only one who really knew you in the old days. I knew you were not like other men."

"You won't tell anyone, will you, my dear?" There was a touch of pleading in his voice. "You won't betray me? I thought you were a friend of more recent years or I wouldn't be here."

"It'll be our secret," she said softly, and she liked the feeling of what she said. Now, she felt, they had a bond between them.

He grew more ill at ease. There was silence as she rested her avid eyes on the thin face that glowed slightly in the shadowy room. By so much as he had mortified himself through the years, by so much as he had sanctified himself, by so much more did she desire him now.

It took resolution on his part to say, "Won't you sit down, my dear?"

She sat down. He sat down across from her. He found he was trembling.

She noticed he was trembling. "You are trembling, Father. So am I. It's the excitement of us seeing each other again after all these years."

"I am unhappy you found me out," he said in a voice a little more than a whisper.

She smiled now. In her command of the situation she could afford to be whimsical. "Don't you want me to become a Catholic?"

"Of course, my dear. Of course," he said with quick intensity. "Haven't you done anything about it?"

"I learned the catechism you left in the house that day. I mean I learned the first three questions. That's one more than you asked me."

"You did? These questions have important answers."

Still smiling, she got to her feet and crossed the room to a chair near him. Her body moved vibrantly with the physical pleasure of the moment.

"I remember them still. So you'll believe me. I'll say them for you. 'Who made me?' 'God made me and lives in me,'" she recited in a low throaty voice, a voice hardly tuned to the catechism. "Who is God?' 'God is Our Father in Heaven.' 'Why did God make me?' 'God made me to know Him, to love Him, and to serve Him in this world so that I may be happy through Him in this life, and with Him forever in Heaven.'" She sat back, pleased. "Was I not a good pupil, Father?"

"Excellent, my dear." His uneasiness left him. "My visit to you long ago was not in vain."

She moved closer to him. Her eyes shone. "I have never forgotten you." Her red sensuous mouth quivered ever so slightly. "I can't."

He was uneasy again. "You should go to see a priest for instructions, my dear. Go to the pastor of your local church."

"I went to see you, Father, after your visit. That's why I learned the three questions. At the church, they told me you were being transferred." Her voice grew in emotion. "I hunted everywhere for you. I must have telephoned twenty churches. I even went to the bishop's office. I couldn't find you. I loved you so much I thought I would die without you."

Father Dennis got to his feet. "Hush, my dear. Hush," he said.

She slowly got to her feet, faced him. "What's wrong with love?" Her passion was in her voice. "I've always wanted love. I took to the life I'm living now because I wanted love. I have never found love. What is wrong if I believe I can find it now? In you?"

"You have God's love, my dear." He was gently understanding now.

"God won't take me in His arms, will He?" She grew more emotional. "He won't kiss me, will He? He won't make love to me, will He? Will He?"

"That kind of love fades and dies, my dear. God's love never dies."

"Couldn't you love me?" She was suddenly direct, realistic.

"I do love you," he said gently.

"You do?" Her eyes widened with her surprise.

"I have not forgotten you since first I saw you," he said quietly. "Your soul is one of the souls I love most in the world. Daily I have prayed for you. Next to my mother's and father's and my own soul, I have prayed to God for your soul. I have always thought of you as an instrument of His Providence." He drew himself up to his full height. His sanctity was a flame in his eyes, his innocence a smile on his lips. "But much as I love you, God loves you more, far more than

I ever could. If I had the strength of a million men and lived a million years, I could never take His place. Goodbye, my dear. Pray. Pray."

He turned and left the room. She, speechless for the moment before his startling sincerity and innocence, watched him go. When she was recovered, Mrs. Welsh was coming into the parlor.

The next evening Cara was back at Mrs. Welsh's house. But the only one there was Mrs. Welsh, forlorn and wretched and red-eyed from weeping. Brother Janitor had gone away during the night.

22.

Now the day had broken fully across ocean and sky. The café was aglitter with light, the first time I had ever seen it so.

"Well, that's about the end of the story of my quest," Matt said. "Mrs. Welsh and Cara, sharing their grief over Brother John's going, became friends.

"Cara, moved by Mrs. Welsh's devotion to the priest, revealed his identity to her. Subsequently, Mrs. Welsh wrote a letter to the bishop and thus it was the bishop learned the truth about Brother John. He kept it very much to himself, however, and it was only in the hope the truth might help me find Father Dennis that he told it to me.

"Cara left her name and address with Mrs. Welsh in the event he should return or write to her. Thus it was I got in touch with Cara and learned her part in the story."

He looked affectionately down at the sleeping girl. "She has the pathos of true beauty, don't you think?"

"She certainly has her charms," I said.

"She came west with me because I persuaded her a change of scene would be good for her," Matt said. "In her heart, though, it's more likely she came in the hope of seeing Father Dennis again."

"Is there such a hope?" I asked. "He seems capable of pretty thorough disappearances."

"Well, Cara found him at Carmel, didn't she?" Matt went on. "We have one hope, a thin hope I'll admit, but a hope. After he left Carmel some two years ago he sent post cards of his wanderings back to the nuns and to Mrs. Welsh. He never gave any address. But the post card would identify the town and city and he would indicate what he was doing. From here he sent a post card of Santa Monica Bay and quipped about his job as a wine steward.

"On his travels, he would visit Carmelite monasteries but in each case, it appeared, the monastery had outside sisters and after a short stay he would move on. In between times, he would work, usually in restaurant kitchens. He wanted, I suppose, a few dollars to enable him to continue his wanderings. That is the reason, I'm sure, he stopped here.

"His real purpose, I think now, is to get as far away from his past as he can. I have an idea we'll find him. Mrs. Welsh is to let me know if she or the nuns get any communication from him. That will give me his town or city. If there is a Carmelite monastery in the neighborhood, we'll know where to go.

"We've got to find him. I have to see him. I need his help.

"I have some real news for him too. His mother has been back looking for him. She is in widow's weeds and pious now. Whether it is merely the piety of a woman growing old

I do not know. If it's genuine, it's a miracle by Father Dennis, a miracle of grace. She is rich, but generous to the poor. She gave Father Dennis' monsignor, his former pastor, a large donation for a summer camp for the children of the parish.

"The pastor was quite surprised his irresponsible curate should have so worthy a mother."

Matt got to his feet, stretched vigorously. Cara opened her eyes sleepily, blinked in concern till she saw Matt, then yawned deeply behind her hand.

"You did all right, honey." Matt beamed down at her with evident affection.

She smiled a small smile. "Next time you start talking, darling, I'm going to bed."

Matt grinned. "You'll be in bed all the time."

Matt looked out the window at the radiant morning. An early sailboat made a small white triangle on the rim of the gleaming ocean.

Matt glanced down at his wrist watch. "I think I'll go to Mass in Santa Monica," he said abruptly.

"You?" Cara laughed softly. "You haven't been to church since I've known you."

"Another miracle?" I was amused.

"No," he said. "I just feel I've got to do something about this morning. It's so beautiful."

I could see he was trying to talk away the transformation that had taken place in him.

"And you, Cara," he went on, "you're so beautiful, I've got to do something about you. Say," he said to her as if with a sudden idea, "how about you coming to Mass with me?"

"Me? Not me, darling." She was decisive. "You kiddin'?"

"Just out of curiosity," he urged.

"Nope. Thanks. Not me." She slipped out of the booth. She was taller, I could see now, and even more physically attractive than I had thought. "I'm still sleepy." She yawned again behind her hand and managed to look good doing it. "I'm going up to that room and go to bed."

So Matt went to Mass. Cara went to bed. And I went up to my shack in the mountains. And thus ended the long evening.

23.

Matt came to the end of his quest sooner than he dreamed.

On a bleak, chill morning, four months less a few days, after he had told Dennis' story in the booth in the café, we, Matt, Cara and I, stood by a simple grave in the potter's field of a northern California city.

A plain metal plate with the single name "Dennis" marked the head of the grave.

It had been raining for several days and the earth of the grassless grave, one of a row of comparatively new paupers' graves, was muddy. The cemetery itself was a desolate wide field bordered by scrubby, brown hills and cheap building developments. None of the beauty that, it seemed to me, should have attended the burial place of such a man was visible so far as the eye could see.

We could not speak for a long minute after we had come upon the grave. Cara was sobbing, her body shaking.

Finally I, seeking for an epitaph, said, "Friendless he died, and alone. The end of a saint."

"No, not friendless, not alone," Matt said, and so deeply moved was he, he could hardly speak. "He died happily in the presence of his greatest friend."

The circumstances of Father Dennis' death had been strange and it was not hard to understand how Matt saw the event as the curtain of a divine drama.

Matt, in the months after his return to his café, had received two post cards from Mrs. Welsh. The first placed Father Dennis in a central California town where Matt found on inquiry there was no Carmelite monastery.

The second, several months later, placed Father Dennis in a northern California city. Matt telephoned long distance to the diocesan chancery. He found there was a Carmelite monastery in the city. A half hour after the call, Matt, Cara and I were racing north on the Pacific Coast Highway in Matt's powerful automobile.

The monastery was a beautiful place, far different from the monastery where Father Dennis had served as Brother John, janitor. Two beautiful, wrought-iron gates opened on the driveway. A pink stucco wall covered with ivy guarded the privacy of the monastery. Acacia, olive and camphor trees and low-hanging pepper trees adorned the grounds.

The sister at the turn, sounding exactly like the sister in the eastern Carmel, was very kind. There had been a man named Dennis there for a few days. He had come and asked if he might work around the grounds. He was employed as a night dishwasher in the kitchen of a café in the city and he would like now and then to enjoy the sunshine and beauty of Carmel, he said.

Permission was granted him. The monastery had a part-time gardener already and there were two outside sisters and so there was little for the new gardener to do.

The outside sisters, on the few occasions they met with him, found him kind and pleasant. They worried about him. He seemed to be ill as if of some wasting disease.

He was most devout and spent, they observed, most of his time in the chapel.

He had been visiting Carmel for only two weeks when he stopped. For ten days or so nobody saw him.

Then, one early morning, the outside sister who was sacristan, coming into the sanctuary to prepare the altar for morning Mass, found him stretched out on the dark red carpet at the foot of the altar. He was lying prostrate, his head toward the tabernacle, his arms outstretched.

His body was in the form of a cross.

It was an extraordinary sight to her but she was a simple woman and, looking from the sacristy door, she reached a simple explanation.

Mr. Dennis, she decided, had been in the dark of the chapel the night before, unaware of her when she locked the doors. Now, in the morning, he had prostrated himself in extraordinary devotion before the altar, much as a young priest at ordination prostrates himself before the altar.

But when the outside sister went to him and, in her simplicity, called to him, "Mr. Dennis. Mr. Dennis, you must get up," he did not respond or move.

She saw then he was dead.

At the grave, Matt, head bowed, grief-stricken, said again, "No, not friendless and alone. He died happily in the presence of his greatest friend."

Suddenly, Cara, still sobbing, fell to her knees in the mud, careless of her fine dress and fine stockings.

Matt and I, startled, watched her.

After a moment, she began to pray. "'God made me and lives in me,'" she sobbed. "'God is Our Father in Heaven. God made me to know Him, to love Him and to serve Him in this world, so that I may be happy through Him in this life and with Him forever in Heaven.'"

She was reciting the three answers from the catechism. It was for her a prayer, the only sort of prayer she knew.

As she sobbed her prayer. Matt looked down on her with great compassion. When she had finished, he raised her gently to her feet.

"*Come*, honey," he said softly, "Father Dennis is not here."

MANN TIMOTHY

If you found Dennis in his adventures wanting in good common sense, then you may well find Mann Timothy in his adventures even more so. I'm afraid there isn't much the rest of us can do about such people. Once they start out, once they are headed for the Absolute, so to speak, there is no stopping them.

1.

I had been living in Seaview only a few weeks and I was sitting in Mr. Bosdick's barber shop waiting my turn—there were two ahead of me—when I heard Mann Timothy's name mentioned.

Mr. Bosdick and his customers were at the moment deep in the discussion of a recent theft in the town, he presiding, as he always did, in his precise and authoritative way. Mr. Bosdick, an erstwhile English actor, was no common man. He was tall and lordly, having played, I am sure, many an English butler in his stage days or, perhaps more likely, many an English prime minister. His face was long, thin, and severely drawn, his hair thick, grayish and always in need of trimming.

The theft Mr. Bosdick and his customers were discussing was the theft of the Archer house. Art Archer is a very wealthy man and is the largest property owner in Seaview. He acquires his wealth in petty loan and mortgage companies, which is legitimate enough but he makes enemies abundantly and is generally disliked in the community. His answer to the dislike is a sustained attitude of sullen contempt. He lives alone or, rather, he lived alone in a redwood cottage set beautifully in the heart of five flat acres in the hills. He had gone down to a clinic in La Jolla for a physical check-up and when he returned he found his house had been stolen.

The flagstone walk and the boxwood hedge lining it were there, the patio and the hibiscus bushes were there, but the house and its furnishings were completely gone. The foundation gaped cleanly up at the open sky. The removal of the house was a remarkable operation, especially so in view of the fact that the house was quite far up in the hills and the five acres were enclosed by a high wire fence, which was said to be electrified.

The police were thoroughly baffled. There were no wheel or tire tracks on the grounds or on the road leading up to the house.

"Tracks or no tracks, it's got to be a professional house mover's job," Joe Barry, the young editor of the *Courier*, said from the barber chair. "Don't you think so, Mr. Bosdick?"

Mr. Bosdick—he was always Mr. Bosdick, and never Boz, and never called by his first name, for no one would ever think of addressing him with such familiarity—Mr. Bosdick stood back from the chair, his scissors poised carefully in one hand, his comb in the other, and after a solemnly meditative look into the sunlight beyond the open door, announced to the room, "The theft must be considered in the realm of the mysterious. It is a problem, gentlemen, that only The Mann Timothy can solve. No one else."

He said this with a gesture of the scissors to indicate this was the last word on the subject and turned back to Joe Barry's head of hair. There was a murmur of approval from the customers.

Mann Timothy. The name started my memory groping back through the mists of twenty-five years. It was the name of a man I had known when I was in my early years of law practice in Los Angeles.

He had been known first as McMann Timothy, McMann being, as I remembered it, his mother's name, but soon the Mc was dropped and he became known as Mann Timothy though no one then called him The Mann Timothy, as he was called in Seaview.

The Mann Timothy I had known was a brilliant young lawyer, much too old for his years, given over to making heavy and humorless speeches at every possible opportunity, at lunch, at dinner, on sidewalks and street corners, in corridors—anywhere, indeed, he might come upon you. He believed fanatically in progress, or Progress, as it is perhaps better written, described by him as the inevitable perfection of man on earth through what he called the Divinity Within. (A faith not uncommon in those days.) He sounded as a combination of Emerson and Thoreau might have sounded, with, now and then, a flavoring of John Burroughs and Whitman added. He was what, I suppose, at one time would have been called a transcendentalist, believing in some misty sort of God-in-Nature, rather than in a personal God but, whatever his God, his religion was Progress. I could see he was a strong personality, in a severe sort of way, and had been well educated, but I was never impressed much by his speeches. He was much too abstract and rhetorical for me. He had a following, however.

Now, sitting there in Mr. Bosdick's barber shop, remembering this Mann Timothy and mellowed by the beneficence of time, I began to think that perhaps my opinion of him in those old days had been a little unkind. He had been passionately dedicated to an ideal, there was no question about that, blurred though the ideal may have been, and he was handsome, handsome in a poetic way, as solemn and prematurely old young men seem so often to be. And he was a brilliant lawyer, with a gift for going directly to the heart of a case. It had to be the same man. He had probably retired and moved to Seaview as I had.

Talk in the barber shop continued about him and I gathered he had acquired quite a reputation in the community as an amateur detective. The role of a detective, amateur or professional, hardly fitted the picture of the dark visionary I had in memory but still I could understand how, with his gift of going to the heart of a case, he might be good at it.

"You are next, sir." Mr. Bosdick bowed slightly in my direction and I took my place in the chair.

"A light trim, please," I ventured humbly, very humbly, for Mr. Bosdick had given me the impression he was accepting me with considerable condescension—an impression he gave all who came into his shop.

As Mr. Bosdick bowed and began with his scissors, I said, "This Mann Timothy I heard you talking about—this extraordinary detective—he's a lawyer, isn't he?"

"No, sir. I'm sorry, sir." Mr. Bosdick continued with the scissors as he spoke. "He's a worker in wood, a sort of cabinetmaker, sir."

I thought a moment. "You mean, Mr. Bosdick, this is a hobby he has? He's retired, is that it?"

"No, sir. Not at all, sir." Mr. Bosdick did not hesitate a moment with the scissors. "He's a working man, though very much on the artistic side. He put in those shelves for me there, sir."

Mr. Bosdick pointed his scissors at the corner where the

shelves had been installed. It was a neat, trim job with the shelves slightly scalloped and darkly stained.

I studied the shelves. "That's one on me," I said. "I never expected to find two men named Mann Timothy in Southern California. Or anywhere for that matter. The man I knew was a lawyer." Then a thought struck me. "Perhaps this is his son. Boys do sometimes go off in strange directions. How old would you say he was?"

Mr. Bosdick stopped in his work and meditated a moment. "I'm sorry, but it is very hard to say, sir. He must be very well on in years and yet, most curiously, he gives you the impression of being young, of being very young indeed. It is quite curious."

I was sure then that he was not my Mann Timothy. Despite the names being the same, I was completely sure of it. Mann Timothy, in a wild venture of the imagination, might have become a woodworker, and a somewhat artistic one, and even a detective of sorts, but the ancient youth I remembered could never, I was certain, have become what Mr. Bosdick described as "very young indeed." That struck me as impossible.

2.

Daybreak and the time immediately following, even if it is raining or foggy, is my favorite time of day. This early hour is for me alive with promise and anticipation, and I have the feeling then that some great new work has somewhere been begun, some new creation, some shining enterprise that never has been begun before, and I am somehow about to be part of it. I know, and tell myself, that at dusk it will have been just another day for me, a day different, if at all, only in minor variations from the days for some years before, but still I nurture the illusion and never fail to find excitement in it.

This pleasure of being up and about at the beginning of day is, I must explain, an easy pleasure for me. I am an insomniac. No pity for me, though. I am an insomniac by choice. Once, when I was young and there was a death in the family and I did not go near bed for three days, I discovered what so many discover, that a short nap can often bring more refreshment than a full night's sleep.

I was ambitious in those days, and the thought of having more time for use than my fellows sustained me in my resolution. Thus I have rarely slept in a bed in thirty-odd years, and on those occasions I was ill. I doze off as it pleases me in a chair or on a sofa or on a cushion out under the sun and awake completely refreshed. I feel I have almost doubled my lifetime with the waking hours I have added to my days.

I know my design for sleeping does not always fit in with the routine of other lives and it is disconcerting to people if I doze off when I am with them, especially as I sometimes snore. But my friends are usually tolerant, and about the others I do not concern myself too much.

Another pleasure my sleeping pattern allows me is the pleasure of being awake and up and about in the dead of night. The dark, secretive silent hours are rich hours for me. They bring no qualms or fears, make no demand on me for three-o'clock courage. Rather, they give me a delicious feeling of aloneness—a feeling I as a chronic bachelor cherish—and they afford me an ideal time for tranquil reading and what I could, I suppose, call rumination.

One morning a few days after my visit to the barber shop—the third morning, I think it was—I took my usual daybreak walk along the beach before my house. It was

early May and the morning fog we so often have during that
month was heavy over the water. My sweat shirt was damp
from the fog as if from a light drizzle. The only visible thing
in the bay was the blurred white breaking of the surf and its
froth on the sand a few feet away.

I heard a foghorn, such a horn as the lighters that ply the
bay usually employ. It sounded quite near. Although I knew
this was probably a trick played by the fog, and the horn might
well be a mile or more away, I turned to search beyond the
breakers for possible sign of the lighter. The lighter with its
horn was hidden in the fog but, as I stood there searching, a
small skiff came into view a short distance out. It drifted ghostily into view, taking on the vaguest of outlines and the even
vaguer outline of a person in it. At times, the fog would close
so thick about the skiff it would become invisible, and then the
fog would thin out and I would see the vague outlines again.

The skiff came slowly nearer and nearer, and after a
while I could hear the small grating sound of the oars in the
oarlocks. Then, a moment later, I made out the shadowy figure of a man at the oars. He rowed indolently, almost sleepily, barely dipping the oars into the water. As I watched, the
oarsman stopped rowing, and presently the eerie little skiff
glided to a stop.

It was some early morning fisherman braving the fog, I
was sure, and meditating a catch of perch or, perhaps, bass.
But, as I watched, the oarsman put down his oars and got to
his feet. The fog lifted a little and I discovered he was fully
dressed in regular street clothes—what we in Seaview call
"city clothes"—even to a gray felt hat. Now, that was quite
extraordinary, for fishermen in our waters favor the most
informal and practical and, more often than not, the most
slovenly of clothes.

He moved carefully out to the bow of the skiff and stood there quietly, a ghostly figure looking out into the fog.

A minute or so passed. The fog closed in on him again and blurred his silhouette, and wisps of the fog seemed to hang from him and he became more and more ghostly a figure. Finally, when it seemed he would be lost to my view, he stepped up on to the bow seat. Delicately he balanced himself there for a moment and then, hat and all, he stepped deliberately over the rail of the boat into the water.

He stepped over the rail of the boat into the water in the easiest sort of way, as you might step from the last step of your stairway to the hall floor or from a bus to the sidewalk. The moment he stepped over the rail, the fog closed in more thickly and immediately he and the skiff were lost to my view. I heard a splash. Then there was complete silence.

I waited tensely to hear if he would cry out for help. There was no cry or sound of any sort. I felt I should try to do something. If the man was attempting suicide, it was still an obligation—perhaps even more of an obligation—for me to try to save him.

I keep a little flat-bottomed rowboat up on the sand against the bulkhead before my house. It is light of weight and is ideal for me when I go fishing, for I can carry it easily and launch it single-handedly when sea and surf are running not too high. I ran to the rowboat, kicked off my loafers, rolled up my trousers and lifted the boat to my back and shoulders, carrying it, as I do, upside down so that its bow inside is like a hood over my head.

It was probably only a few minutes but it seemed forever before I had the boat launched and was rowing out into the fog where last I had seen the man and the skiff.

After a while, the skiff began to stand grayly out in view.

I could not see the man at first but I could hear him splashing about in the water and when I came alongside I could
make out a single hand holding on to the opposite rail of the
skiff. I rowed around the skiff and there he was, holding on
with one hand while with the other he was diligently trying
to retrieve something in the water. I came closer and saw it
was his felt hat which was floating on its brim a few yards
from him.

It seemed rather ridiculous, the ado he, who had stepped
deliberately into the water, was making about saving the hat,
especially to me who had rushed out there to save his life. It
struck me he should at least have anticipated the losing of his
hat. Straightway, my concern for him vanished.

I rowed to the hat, picked it up and, without a word,
tossed it into the skiff.

"Thank you," the man said. "Thank you very much. I was
afraid it might drift off into the fog before I got back into the
boat. It is my Sunday hat."

He grabbed the rail with both hands and hoisted himself up into the skiff. He dropped with a splash into the
middle seat by the oars and looked out at me through the
soaking hair that fell flatly over his face. He was still fully
dressed and, in his sopping wet clothes, black and shiny, he
resembled a black cat caught out in the open in a downpour.

He pushed the hair back from his face. Then, he called
out, "Why, Tom! Holy mackerel! It's you! Isn't this the sort
of crazy thing you would expect to happen—meeting you
out here?"

Now I could see the smiling face. It was thinner, imm-
ensely younger, but it was the face of Mann Timothy. If I had
not heard about him in the barber shop, I would probably not
have recognized him, but having heard, I knew it was he.

"Hello," I said. Panting, and considering myself more than a little foolish, I did not share his enthusiasm at the moment. And meeting him out there, under those circumstances especially, was certainly not, as he suggested, the crazy thing I would expect to happen. It was the last thing in the world I would have expected to happen.

"You recognize me, don't you?" he asked, shaking his head vigorously to shake some of the water out of his hair. "Don't you?"

"You're Mann Timothy. Yes." I was hardly what could be called cordial.

He seemed entertained. "It's really a coincidence, isn't it, Tom? I heard you had moved into town and I was going to give you a call. I was going to give you a call this very day. Now we meet out here. Like this. On the sea in the fog. As if someone had arranged it."

I was unable to join in his good spirits. I kept my patience and said evenly, "Mann, suppose you follow me into shore. We'll beach the skiff and go up to my house. You can dry out there and we'll have some coffee."

I turned and started to row for shore. I had taken only a couple of strokes when I became aware he had not moved. He was leaning a little on his oars and staring out into the fog. I stopped.

"Anything the matter?" I called to him. "Lose something?"

He turned to me slowly. "No. Everything's all right. Thank you, Tom."

His smile had gone. His voice was very quiet, almost solemn, especially so in contrast to its happy excitement of a few moments before.

He began slowly to pull on the oars. I waited until he had come abreast of me. The whole proceeding, his stepping out into the water, his light mood afterwards, and now his change to this sudden and strange gravity, had me, as it would have had anybody, completely mystified.

I rested the oars and looked over at him. "Mann, tell me, will you?" I asked. "What on earth were you trying to do out here anyway?"

He looked back over his shoulder into the fog again and on his face was a sort of wistfulness as if he were wishing for something that might have been.

"I was trying to walk on the water," he said.

I stared at him. He had lost his mind through the years.

He watched me with vaguely wondering eyes. He was, I reasoned afterwards, surprised at the concern which must have been very obvious on my face.

"You were trying to walk on the water?" I tried to put the words as gently as I could.

"Haven't you ever tried to walk on the water?" he asked me with a voice that had the mildly wondering expression his eyes had.

It was as if he felt his question was most reasonable, a natural though slightly unusual question, as if he had asked me if I had ever tried to judge a person's character from his hands or had ever tried to make someone turn around by staring at the back of his head.

There was no doubt but that he thought there was something wrong with *me*.

The fog grew heavy again.

"Let's go in and get the coffee," I said in order to say something.

3.

It turned out that all my meetings with Mann Timothy were to be extraordinary in one way or another but that first meeting over coffee in my house seemed the most extraordinary of all, probably because it was the first after twenty-five years.

The change in Mann through those twenty-five years was almost incredible. The solemn, prematurely old Mann Timothy had at thirty looked about fifty. Now, at more than fifty, he looked thirty or even under. He was older in years than I, and yet there was no sign of gray in his hair while mine was well on its way to being completely so. He not merely looked young for his age, he *was* young.

A smile, something he had not possessed when I had known him before, was almost constantly on his lips, and changed as constantly as his thought—bemused, tolerant, wistful, demurring, meditative, understanding—the modulated smile of a philosopher. But it was his eyes that held me. I remembered his eyes as dark and solemn. They were still dark but now they shone—shone is the only word for it—with a bright expectancy, like the eyes of a small boy entering the Big Tent for his first circus or coming slowly down the stairs in the dark of early Christmas morning toward the glitter of the Christmas tree.

He was definitely leaner and looked taller, but on that first meeting it was hard for me to see him clearly for his eyes.

He sat in the living room. He had had a shower and we had put his clothes out in the kitchen to dry. He wore a robe of mine which in his leanness was much too large for him.

"Tell me," I said when the coffee was before us, "what is all this walking on the water business about?"

"One day, some twenty years ago, I read the New Testament," he said, as if that answered my question, and sipped his coffee.

That, naturally enough, did not make much sense to me. "Thousands of people, hundreds of thousands, millions, perhaps, read the New Testament," I said, "but they don't go around trying to walk on water."

"How do you know?"

I studied his face. He was serious. "I've never heard of anyone trying it," I said. "I've never seen anyone trying it except you."

"Maybe they try it at night," he said. "Or maybe when the fog is thicker."

Had I not, a few minutes before, seen him deliberately step out of the skiff into the water, I would have thought he was joking.

"Would you mind disclosing to me, Mann," I asked, "why under heaven would anyone want to try to walk on water?"

"It's a great test of faith," he said.

"Faith in what?"

"Faith in the impossible."

I began to see the light. "I remember. Like Peter in your New Testament."

"Like Peter," he said.

"But Peter also got dunked, if my memory of a sermon I heard in my youth is correct. Even with his Lord right there on the sea with him to encourage him."

"And his Lord said to him as he began to sink, 'Why did you hesitate, man of little faith?'" he quoted softly. "I'll bet St. Peter was back out on the water the next night and I'm sure on his second try he didn't hesitate. He made it."

I was certain then my surmise outside in the fog that he was mad was right. "You're going to try again, I suppose?" I asked, though I knew what the answer would be.

"Oh sure. Until I make it."

It was unkind, I know, but I could not keep from laughing.

"Mann," I said, "do you mind if I suggest the next time you try it, you wear swimming trunks?"

"No, Tom, I could never do that," he spoke gravely. "If I dressed in trunks, I would be admitting before I tried to walk on the water that I did not fully believe I could do it. That's why I wore a hat. The next time I think I'll carry a book under my arm.

"You have to believe fully first," he went on. "To him who believes, everything is possible. So the Lord—the Lord of the Impossible—declared time and again. But we cannot be hesitant, we were warned, or have any reservations." He waved out in the direction of the ocean. "I had a flash of uncertainty out there at the moment when I stepped out of the boat and my feet touched the water. I lacked faith. That's what sank me."

"You sank all right," I said. Then I added, "You really believe this completely?"

"Of course. His words are too uninventible not to be true."

"Too what?"

"Too uninventible. Too impossible for anyone ever to think up." He looked at me but I was sure he did not see me, and when he spoke again it was a little sadly. "I'm pretty much of a failure in believing. I failed again this morning. My early years are against me. I just don't have the simplicity."

"You don't have to worry about that," I assured him.

"You are like a child. You must be two or three hundred years younger than when I saw you last."

"It could be I've made a little progress. I have believed a few things into coming true." He was meditative for a moment. "But this walking on water is a hard one. I've got a long way to go."

I pondered what he meant when he said he had believed a few things into coming true.

"Holy smoke," he exclaimed. "Here we are meeting again for the first time in twenty-five years and all we talk about is me!"

"It's a little difficult," I returned, "not to talk about a man who believes he can walk on water."

"I've been in the pulpit, too. I'm afraid," he went on in a manner most humbly apologetic. "I'm sorry, Tom."

I sipped my coffee, studied him. It was still hard for me to realize that this quietly smiling young man was the old, solemn Mann Timothy of a quarter of a century before.

"Mann," I said, "it's none of my business but it seems curious to me why, when you decided to change your life, you didn't go off to a monastery or some place like that."

He slowly shook his head. "Too much security in a monastery. Too much for me, in any event. I've been deathly afraid of security, that is, of economic security."

He looked around the living room where we were having the coffee. My home is, I must say, a rather elegant home, especially for the beach, and I saw him note my fine books, my original Rembrandt sketch, and my small and exquisite girl's head in the purest of marble by Rodin.

"You have a problem too," he said.

"Burglars?"

"No, though burglars go with it. Possessions."

This comment was not what I had expected and was, as one may imagine, a considerable disappointment to me. But, as a host, I let the comment pass.

After a moment, still looking the room over, he asked, "You're married and have a family?"

"Just a born bachelor," I gave my usual answer, "dedicated to the principle that he travels fastest who travels alone."

He smiled a small, demurring smile. "You really have a security psychosis, haven't you?"

He must have read annoyance on my face for suddenly he was contrite. "I'm sorry, Tom. Now and then I have an ache in my old arrogance. I lack charity. It is the worst of faults. Pray for me."

His contriteness was very genuine but it did not inspire me to forgive him.

"I am retired," I said coldly. "I have ease and serenity. And you are some sort of carpenter doing odd jobs for barbers and the like."

"I shudder at the very idea of retirement," he said quietly. "It is the anteroom of death." After a moment, he went on, "There came a time, Tom, when it was impossible for me to continue on as an attorney. It's entirely personal but I felt something like a parasite on life. I decided it was important I should become an artisan of some sort and, if possible, an artist. As a boy I used to dabble at woodcarving and had a liking for it so I took up working in wood. I make very little but I am much happier at it than I ever was at law.

"Now I feel like I'm a part of Creation. I have my hand in, so to speak."

He stood up. I finished my coffee and joined him.

He was mad all right, thoroughly sincere and thoroughly mad.

He was, however, happy beyond question, and, more persuasive than that, he, while I and our contemporaries were old and growing older, was young, and, I could believe, growing younger. That, at least, was an intangible but invincible argument in his favor. How I hated growing old!

His clothes were now dry enough. He seemed amused at something as he dressed, but he said nothing. After he was finished dressing, he studied himself in the mirror.

"I think I have a wonderful idea, Tom," he said. "The next time I try walking on water, I won't carry a book. A book under my arm, as I stepped on to the water, might suddenly strike me as an affectation and cause me to waver. I think I'll carry a walking stick."

"A walking stick?"

"Yes, a walking stick. As an indication of faith in my walking on the water. It's my best idea yet."

He was mad, no question about that, and yet at the moment I envied him.

"I wish, Mann, you would share your secret of youth with me," I said, hoping the lightness in my voice would disguise my interest. "This childlike simplicity, the kind you say you're striving for, do you feel that has something to do with it?"

He nodded slowly. "It might, that and the right amount of material insecurity."

He moved to the door.

"Tom, I'll give you a little suggestion—a tip, I might call it," he said. "Read those books of the New Testament sometime. Some sort of biochemical change might well come over you. You'll come, for example, across a little passage where the Lord says, 'Behold, I make all things new.'"

I opened the door. The fog had lifted and the morning sunlight deluged sky and sea. He went through the door. I followed him. He threw his arms back and looked up into the shining sky.

"'Behold,'" he quoted again, softly. "'I make all things new.'"

His words, I could see, were not so much a comment on the coming of the sunlight as they were a sort of invitation for me to join him in the secret of his youth.

4.

We went out over the bulkhead to the sand where we had beached his skiff.

"Mann," I asked as we walked, "so long as we're putting pieces together, I wonder if you'd tell me something? What's all this detective business about? It mystifies me just as much as your being a woodworker and," I added, "almost as much as your being young and mad and wanting to walk on the water."

"Detective?" he looked at me blankly.

"At the barber shop the other day, I heard the townspeople talking about you. It struck me they looked upon you as a Master Sleuth. 'Mann Timothy: Woodworker, Prophet and Private Eye. By Appointment Only.'"

"A method, that's all I have. Sometimes it works." Now, as he talked, he began to scan the sea and the surf breaking on the shore as if in search for something. "My approach is that every crime is like a story built about a plot. I merely try to find out what the plot is. And to find the plot I make a point of sketching out the *dramatis personae*. It's Edgar Allan Poe's idea really."

We walked on toward the cove. He seemed interested now in the sand along the beach.

"This Archer business, have you any guesses as to that?" I asked. "At the barber shop they seemed to think the house was stolen. That's a dreadfully fantastic idea."

"The house was there and it is not there now. It was stolen all right."

I looked at his face. His eyes were now searching the reeds and weeds in the sand. Close to the surface of the water, a long single file of great pelicans glided gracefully, following the air draft in the curve of a breaking wave. A swarm of fat sea gulls screamed and complained overhead like so many badly spoiled young children.

"What puzzles me," I said, "—what puzzles me far more than the motive, is how the house was stolen. Do you have any guess as to that?"

"I have no guess on that." He smiled. "I know, I'm sure, exactly how it was done. The house was stolen from the air."

"By someone in an airplane, you mean?"

He nodded. "In a helicopter or, more likely, helicopters. A man, possibly two, was landed from the helicopters. Then the helicopters, hovering above the house, lowered light grappling irons such as are sometimes used in salvage of sunken boats, and the comrade or comrades on the ground attached the irons."

"The helicopters would certainly have been heard by people in town," I objected.

"The sound of helicopters is no novelty around here," he said. "The important point is that up at Archer's place in the hills, nobody would be seen. The house, you must remember, was a small redwood cottage and weighed little. It was probably lifted away in two or three sections. A very neat and imaginative operation, I'd say."

"Why should anyone want to steal a house? Have you

any reasoning on that?" I asked. "Especially, why should he go to all that trouble to do it?"

"It wasn't much trouble, not as much trouble as a professional house mover would have had in bringing that house down from the hills." Then he said, "I know Mr. Archer and I think I know the characterization needed for the construction of the plot. His philosophy is the philosophy of the jungle. Victory is to the ruthless, that is his philosophy." He pointed to the south. "You know the Marines have an air base a few miles below here. Even in your short time in town you must have heard their helicopters whirring around at all hours, day and night. Well, I can see a young Marine, probably recently married, getting in debt to Archer over his new home, or his parents' new home or what, and Archer moving ruthlessly in on him.

"One night when the helicopters are going up for night flight training, I can see that Marine, knowing Archer is out of town, saying to his buddies, 'Whadaya say, fellers?' and in the morning, the Archer house is gone. If Archer were smart, he would have been aware of the philosophy of a Marine in combat. My guess is Mr. Archer, for once, made a very expensive mistake."

"It sounds fantastic," I said. "Still it has a reasonable quality about it."

"Usually, in the case of the fantastic only the fantastic can be reasonable."

A dark, Marine helicopter whirred by overhead, flying north.

"Tell me," I said, watching the helicopter, "does your surmise go as far as a guess as to what they did with the house?"

He turned around to the reeds and seaweed up in the dry sand. "You see that accumulation of little pieces of wood up there?" He waved to them. "I had an idea about now I'd find something like that washed up in the cove. Driftwood usually ends up here in the cove. That's why I came to look."

"They're shingles," I said.

"Yes, shaker shingles. Archer's house was the only house in town that had shaker shingles."

"They dumped his house into the sea?"

"A most audacious conclusion, Tom," he said, laughing softly and at me, I am sure.

5.

Seaview being Seaview, there were many rumors about Mann. One was that he in his youth had been a Franciscan friar. Another was that he was an addict of a secret Yaqui Indian drug that inspired a man to see visions, especially religious visions, and gave him a sustained euphoria. This rumor was, I am sure, a sort of folk-legend explanation of his youthfulness and his extraordinary love of living and his many declarations that life was an incomprehensible experience and in faith alone was there any real understanding and enjoyment of it.

Mann was, as must be apparent, outrageously religious.

I remember on one of my first visits to him in his home, I was asking him about Seaview and he said, "It is a tolerant place. Here, I am sure—and this is the ultimate test of a community—here the idiosyncrasies and excesses of sanctity would be accepted for what they are, the normal expressions of great love. Here, in Seaview, Simon Stylites could plant his pillar on the street corner outside the Murphy Drug Store and sit there on top of the pillar for all his days and no one would bother about him very much. Here, little Francis could run naked through the town as he did once through his native Assisi and nobody, I feel certain, would send for the police. Yes," he mused, "Seaview would be a very comfortable place for a saint. I remember when I first came here I used to expect, at every corner I turned, to run into a saint. Perhaps if I stay here long enough and turn enough corners I will."

I was amused at the time at the peculiar—the unrealistic, I might call it—quality of his enthusiasm. "It is evidently a very comfortable place for a man who is determined to walk on water," I said.

"Yes, it is," he, unaware of my amusement, said seriously. "It is a very comfortable place for anyone like that."

It must not be imagined from what I've said of Mann Timothy thus far that he lived in some sort of smiling dream world and was incapable of deep hurt or heartbreak or indignation, and I have done him an injustice if I have given that impression. There were many times when he was anything but other-worldly. There was one occasion, in particular, when he stood tall and fiery-eyed in wrath. That was when a friend of his was accused of murder. The friend was dead and unable to defend himself, and all the evidence was against him, so much so that he was pronounced without reservation guilty of the crime, but Mann Timothy stood by the memory of his friend, stood angrily and valiantly alone by that memory.

This little narrative would hardly be complete without telling of Mann Timothy on this occasion and I shall come to it presently. The philosopher in him had never been more alert and inventive, and his indignation had never, to my knowledge, been more inflamed.

However, more about this presently, as I have said. Now,

it seems to me, might be a good time to give a little picture
of our town.

Seaview is, to all appearances, another Southern California coastal town bisected by the Pacific Coast Highway,
with the hills rising inland from the Highway and the land
on the other side edging or sloping down to the shore and
the ocean.

The Highway is our main street, as it is for so many of
the coastal towns, and the motorist, speeding north to Los
Angeles or south to San Diego sees little more of the town
than the little roadside row of buildings that house some of
our main institutions: Mr. Bosdick's barber shop, the beauty
shop, the country store, the café, the post office, the *Courier* office, and such minor institutions as the laundry, the
liquor store, the tailor and the like. This row of buildings of
various sizes and shapes, of brick and wood and stucco, of
many colors, suggests the picturesque mixed Spanish and
American-Western character of the town, and is known as
the Arcade, though except for a few stucco arches it is not an
arcade in any sense at all.

I find myself often beguiled by the town's quietly idyllic
appearance, especially at the shore.

You look out over the bulkhead. The sky is a radiant blue
white, the sea is a shimmering blue black, the surf foams
and curls and endlessly laces the beach; the houses, strung
as far as one can see along the shore that curves widely and
gracefully out to the Point, are like bright, colorful gift boxes—green, gray, rose, yellow, blue, white, mostly white—set
delicately down on the glistening sand. The house next to
mine to the north, the Ellerton house, in its blue and white,
seems especially chaste and idyllic.

Here resides, you are confident, the beautiful medium

life the ancients extolled, the serenely ordered life free from
madness and perversity. Here, you find yourself saying to
yourself, is the dwelling place of the rarely lived normal life.

Now, I don't mean to intimate that our town is deeply
and drastically in contradiction to its rather idyllic appearance and is, if you explore it, a place of evil and infamy. We
have evil and infamy, of course. We also have goodness and
laughter. But our goodness and laughter are not completely
conventional, nor are our evil and infamy. Our virtues and
vices are both, I think, of slightly unusual dimensions.

Take those two adjoining stucco houses, down the beach
about a hundred yards beyond the Ellerton house. They are
identical houses, white with a narrow red trim. One is newer
than the other but still they appear very much related, as if a
father, who lived in the older house, had built the other for
a recently married daughter. They are related, it so happens,
but hardly in so amicable a way.

One of the houses belongs to Major Von Manheim. The
other belongs to his wife. They live completely separate lives.
He does not go near her. She rarely visits him. When first
they came to Seaview, I am told, they lived, though hardly
normally, in one house. After several years they had the second house built. The major moved into it and thus apart they
have lived ever since.

The major, according to the talk of the town, was a major
in the German infantry in the First World War and it is
said he was gassed. He is a tall, solemn, gray man who is an
alcoholic. He has a man servant, a stocky, taciturn Bavarian,
a wartime private in his command.

The major keeps the window shades drawn on all the
windows of his house day and night. He lives glass in hand,
in this twilight through the day, no matter whether the day

be warm or cold, sunlit or rainy. He has never been seen to leave the house during daylight. The major is always slightly drunk but never staggers and never raises his voice.

Only after dark is he ever seen about and then infrequently as when, glass in hand as always, he goes out to the bulkhead to survey sky and sea. On such occasions as he does this, he does so methodically, gravely, very much in the manner of a sea captain on his bridge. After the survey, he returns to the house and the door closes after him, with finality, and he is seen no more that night. I have watched him go through this often and it seems to me he never varies the routine by a step or a second.

Mrs. Von Manheim has her own idiosyncrasies though of a more active land. She has a maid, a Mexican girl, and together they are forever cleaning the house, decorating, and redecorating, painting and repainting, polishing and repolishing, upholstering and reupholstering, week in week out, year in year out. It is all done according to schedule, room by room, and immediately the last room is finished, the first is begun again.

The maid and the workmen are constantly urged to more and more expedition by Mrs. Von Manheim with the exhortation that the work must be done "before the company comes." But no company ever comes. No friend ever sees the perfect decor and fresh cleanliness of the house. For Mrs. Von Manheim has no friends, no visitors. She has no time for friends or visitors for the simple if strange reason she is much too busy getting the house ready for their coming.

The two houses, as I watch them looking out in their white and red at sand and sea and sky, mask their secrets prettily and well. They are, I think, good instances of what I might call the artistry of our town.

Not all our houses, I must admit, are as innocently faced as the Von Manheim houses or the Ellerton house. Take that somber pile, built of gray stone and turreted like a castle, off in the distance dominating the Point—the promontory that rides out into the sea at the far western sweep of the bay. At the end of day, when the Point is like a black dagger plunged into the blood of the sunset and the windows of the gray-stone buildings are aflame with the reflections of the level light, there is a feeling of otherworldliness in the western sky and one would not be too much surprised to look out and discover the Ancient Mariner on his ill-fated skeleton of a brigantine drifting ghostily into the bay. The turreted house then looks truly like a castle, a castle out of some dark, occult, olden land, and to the discerning eye searching the sunset, our town ceases to appear naively normal and takes on a darkly subtle air and becomes a place of strangeness, of other dimensions, and gives, if only mistily and for only a few moments, hints of a hidden character.

The turreted house is the home of Dr. Thane, the town's only physician but hardly what could be called the town's physician. Dr. Thane might be described as another instance of what I have called our town's artistry. He maintains a practice of sorts and comes into his office two or three days a week, as it pleases him, but his interest is not in the ailments of the community. His interest is in poisons. He is considered one of the West's greatest authorities on poisons.

Dr. Thane, a tall, angular man with a small black goatee, is a widower and lives alone in his house on the Point and it is thus easy to understand how, especially with his dedication to poisons, a legend has grown that he is a necromancer, a sorcerer deep in black magic.

I know the doctor about as well as someone not in his

inner circle can get to know a man of his aloofness (he deigns now and then to treat me for my gout) and I have a suspicion the rumors about him are inventions, inventions such as our town is given to, though usually, I must say, with a much happier theme. The doctor, it could be, has had a legend thrust upon him.

Mann Timothy, who was probably the doctors only close friend, was inclined to believe the doctor invented the legend himself, invented, at least, its beginning. His somber castle on the Point, his saturnine manner, his devotion to poisons, were all, Mann suggested, parts of a picture of a man hungry for mystery.

It could very well be that Mann, in spite of his inclination to discover all sorts of significances in everyone and everything, was right about Dr. Thane. And that brings up a most interesting contrast between Dr. Thane and Bill Ellerton. Dr. Thane's house has, as I've said, a mephistophelian air while Bill Ellerton's house stands out as pretty and innocent as any house on the beach.

Yet, it turned out, it was Bill Ellerton's house, not Dr. Thane's, that actually masked characters and happenings not merely eccentric but sinister and even worse.

6.

The Ellertons played no essential part in Mann's story and yet they were to serve importantly in a revelation of Mann's extraordinary character or, as some would say, of his extraordinary idiosyncrasies. Perhaps, therefore, a few words about the Ellertons would not be altogether amiss here.

I first met Bill Ellerton and his wife, Grace, when they dropped in on me one sunny Sunday afternoon soon after my arrival in Seaview to make inquiries about purchasing some property I had bought between their house and mine. They struck me at the time, I must admit, as a well-mated, amiable, more than conventionally charming couple.

Grace seemed on the serious side, especially for a pretty lady in her early thirties, but she was very feminine, quite delicately so, and she wore a colorful little hat that looked as if it had floated down and come to rest on her head. She was very quiet. Her husband did almost all the talking.

Bill Ellerton was in his middle forties, tall and sandy-haired. He wore young, gay, rather collegiate clothes. I could understand why he was considered by the ladies in the town to be very good looking. He was civic minded and his casual talk tended toward social problems or, perhaps it would be better to put it, toward sociological problems. I had noted he wrote long letters to the *Courier*, most of which were pleas for better living quarters and better wages for our small Mexican population. Bill had a high standing in the town.

He had, before settling in Seaview, been a writer for the films in Hollywood. But in my talk with him it was evident he was not too proud of his past and had a cynically low view of the film capital. He seemed almost to go out of his way to tell me he had invested his money in an importing firm with offices in Mexico City, and spent as much time there as he did in Seaview. He was apparently proud of his venture into business.

The Ellertons were generally considered what is called musical and had a reputation for entertaining many concert artists at their home. I had observed, in my short residence, guests coming and going at all hours, staying overnight and sometimes longer. It was this observation of mine that prompted me to turn down their proposal to buy my

property though I could have made a good profit. I had come
to Seaview for peace and I did not want the busy life the
Ellertons lived any nearer to me than it was.

We parted in the most amiable of spirits. It seemed to
me as we said good-bye in the sunlight at my door that Mrs.
Ellerton was even prettier than I had judged her and her
husband more personable and more handsome, and that they
made an even more charming couple than I had thought
them when first we met.

I saw them many times after that and my impression
was much the same. No one could have told me on that first
meeting or, for that matter, on any of our subsequent pleasant meetings that one night I would look out across the several hundred feet that separated us and discover the blue and
white idyllic Ellerton house the scene of two of the strangest
murders in the history of the West.

7.

Soon, after my first meeting with Mann, I took to going
up to his house to visit him, at first on invitation but later,
on my own impulse which, I must confess, was quite often.
I found Mann as unique as the town had long found him,
and I also discovered he was extremely stimulating though
sometimes, I should say, disturbing. I soon could understand
why the townspeople spoke of him with the respect they did,
calling him The Mann Timothy, saying, for example, when
they quoted him, "The Mann Timothy said," or, in announcing his approach, saying, "Here comes The Mann Timothy,"
and so on.

Mann Timothy lived on some four acres in the ranch
country a mile or so north of the Arcade on the inland side

of the Highway. His acreage was quite high up in the hills, but flat, without trees and covered, except where Mann had cultivated the ground, with tall brownish, weeds veined here and there with pale green ice plant. The acres by themselves formed a small plateau against a backdrop of tall brown hills and commanded a wide view of the ocean. Mann had, when I first knew him, about a year's payments to make before the land would belong completely to him.

The earth near the hills was adobe clay. Out of this clay, Mann had made brown adobe bricks, huge bricks a yard long and two feet thick, and out of these bricks he had built his own house, a U-shaped, one-story, low building with a patio. Mann (much to my surprise) had six children and as each child arrived he added a room to the house and these rather irregular additions gave it an attractive haphazard look. In the patio was a rock and cactus garden that seemed very much a part of the adobe brick house.

The dirt road leading to Mann's place climbed first into the hills and then sloped easily down to the plateau so that the first sight of Mann's house and grounds was from an elevation. The brown adobe brick house and the patio with the rocks and cactus, set out flatly under the vast emptiness of sky and against the backdrop of the blue sea, were blended into the dappled, mustard-brown landscape so naturally and casually as to make you feel all had grown there together out of the earth and had been there unchanged for centuries. It struck me that Mann, in this establishment of his, had expressed himself very well.

As you descended to the plateau you would probably observe—according to the day and time of day—a couple of cows nibbling as they wished, near or far, three or four nondescript dogs chasing about, hens and chickens minding

their own business, an ancient horse diligently seeking out
grass in the brown weeds, a girl of about fifteen hanging out a
colorful wash, a youth varnishing a surfboard, another young
man caulking the hull of a catboat—you might even catch
Mrs. Timothy sitting out in the sunlight of the patio turning
the collars and cuffs of a shirt and looking very young and at
ease, and see Mann Timothy himself stripped to his dunga-
rees, brown and wiry, working in the small vegetable garden
or, in his well-beaten jeep, banging down the dirt road on his
way to a job in town, driving recklessly, singing, swaying, like
some happy soldier of fortune riding off to a new adventure.

Mann Timothy's family was, as I have said, a considerable surprise to me. First of all, I did not expect to find him
with a family at all. I know, at our first meeting after the
incident out on the water, he chided me about my not having
some sort of family but it seemed to me what he judged selfish or cowardly in me he might consider ascetical in himself.

Mann spoke of his wife, Anne, as his "oldest girl," or his
"littlest girl," this latter being in relation to his two daughters, Elizabeth and Mary, who both were taller than their
mother, something not very difficult to be, inasmuch as Mrs.
Timothy was not too much more than five feet tall.

She was an unforgettable woman with level, intuitive
hazel eyes, a slender, symmetrical body that moved with
extraordinary grace, and a voice as soft and modulated and
still as commanding in its own way as any voice I had ever
heard. Like Mann, she seemed very young and like him also,
she had the qualities of simplicity and constant discovery
that are the endowments of happy children.

The two girls were lovely too, though they bore little
resemblance to Mann or their mother. The older girl, Elizabeth, was tall, blessed with what is sometimes described

as Irish-Spanish beauty—flowing brown-black hair, flashing black-brown eyes, a skin, luminous and naturally sunbrowned, and a full, red arresting mouth. Elizabeth was without subtlety. She looked directly at you, spoke directly to you, moved in straight lines—a strong, softly radiant personality, overcoming you, always it seemed, in a glow of subdued, rather dark laughter.

Mary was more delicately cast. She was slender, quaintly brunette, with a responsive, fine mouth, a slightly pale, esthetic face, a little narrower and a little longer than her sister's, and a beautifully drawn forehead that bulged ever so little just above the space between her slightly arched eyebrows, an almost sure mark, in my experience, of creative imagination.

Mary was given to many shadings, little side looks, shadowy smiles, subtle glances from under slightly lowered lids. Her hands were sensitive, and, unconsciously and at all times, struck the most melodious of movements and poses. Indeed, her pliant body seemed always to be moving to some inner music.

Her dream in life was to be a great ballerina and she took dancing lessons from a retired ballerina who lived in town. I know little of the ballet but she seemed to me to have a real predisposition for it. When happily surprised, for example, as by an unexpected gift, she spontaneously moved into dance steps, speaking her pleasure and gratefulness in the classic dance steps of the ballet. Thus did she most naturally express herself.

Mary gave me the feeling she was always dancing, usually with joy, but sometimes wistfully, in delicate shadowy rhythms, as if she, even at her young age, and alone in Mann's household, had some misty sensing of the sorrow in the heart of the world.

Mann's boys, named, understandably enough, Matthew, Mark, Luke and John, were tall, the shortest being certainly six feet two, everlastingly sun-tanned, naturally courteous, almost always laughing or smiling and, young though they were, they were, like their father, still young for their years.

Outside of their simplicity and youthfulness, they, like the girls, did not particularly resemble their father or mother. I must say their faces had sensitivity and character, and it might well have been that superiority of achievement, and even greatness, was in their future but, at the time I knew them, they appeared to be very much like most other extroverted, exuberant Southern California youths, especially like those who live by the sea.

It seemed to me that Mann's boys were always in and out of the sea—working on the fishing boats or as lifeguards, sailing, surfing, fishing, swimming, skin-diving, and, watching them and their fellows, it often occurred to me that they, given a youth long enough, might in time sprout fins like the green rubber ones they wore, and become a new race of men, a cleaner, kinder and more candid type of man than the world had yet seen.

Mann, like any good father, treated all his children impartially but I had the idea on my first visit to his home, an idea that further acquaintance strengthened, that in feeling he was closest to his youngest, Mary. This could have been due, of course, to her being the youngest and a girl, but I thought then, and I think more surely how, this closeness was due to his occasional awareness of her innate wistfulness, her sensitive, shadowy sense of the tragic in life, a sense which he, I know, had had in full measure when he was very young but which had now almost completely gone from him.

Mann's house and grounds seemed always to be in a

constant, happy ferment of singing, hammering, sawing, digging, dancing, shouting, of comings and goings—a colorful, busy world all of its own. Dinner was such an event that you felt it could happen only once, but it happened, as I had occasion to observe, night after night after night.

Everybody, with the exception of the mother and the guests waited on himself or herself. Each one had different tastes and, while the food was of the simplest sort, each had all sorts of ideas about it—one wanted plain bread, say, one wanted the bread toasted on one side, one wanted the bread toasted on both sides, one wouldn't eat bread and wanted crackers, one wanted bread with jam, one with peanut butter—and so it went with all of them, on and on, with all the food, in and out of the kitchen, up and down, this way and that, with no more than two or three seated at the table at one time and, except for the reverently quiet moment before the meal and after it when Mann said grace, no peace, no silence, only laughter and banter and endless motion.

At my first dinner, it was like bedlam to me, and I grew nervous and worried about my gout and about the possibility of a dormant ulcer catching fire again, but on my second visit I took the old advice, if you can't beat them, join them, and I ceased to be the guest and went up and down, and in and out of the kitchen with Mann and the rest of them, and adapted things as best I could to suit my taste, and talked and laughed in tune with all of them.

Mann remonstrated with me but I knew if I was to survive I must do as I was doing, and do it I did. After a while I found dining in that extraordinary manner not altogether unenjoyable and, curious though it may sound, of some aid to digestion. You had no time to count your chews or your swallows (or your burps, for that matter) and this may have had something to do with the improvement in my digestion. I do know that when the tumult was over and I sat in the little living room with my coffee, and Mann and I talked, or Mary danced, or Elizabeth played the piano, I had the wonderful feeling of satisfaction of having finally made port after a turbulent (and exciting) voyage.

Mann had many friends, and they came and went at his house at all hours. Although he no longer practiced law, he still acted as father and counselor to many in town, especially to the Mexican laborers and farmhands in the community. The sheriff's patrol car would be seen occasionally up outside of the brown adobe house, as Sergeant David or others came for consultation.

On one occasion, as the sergeant drove away, I said, "You really are established as a sleuth, aren't you?"

"If I've achieved anything at any time, it's a whim of the Holy Spirit's, I assure you," he replied.

I could not help being amused. It was a windy, sunlit realistic day up on the dappled mustard-brown plateau. The sea to the west was a cool dark blue. The brown hills looked down on Mann and me in a solemn sort of sternness. Many of Mann's religious comments struck me as being rather odd and farfetched but on this cool, realistic day this particular remark about the Holy Spirit seemed to be so—well, so inapplicable, I suppose is as good a way to put it as any, that I did have to smile.

He saw my smile. "I might as well warn you, Tom," he said, "I'm praying for you."

"By the way, speaking of prayer and the Holy Spirit," I asked him, taking advantage of the drift of the conversation, "whatever happened to your walking-on-water project? Give it up?"

"Oh, no," he replied gravely. "I am waiting until my faith is strong enough. I need a new, transcendent faith. I do not want to falter again." Then he added meditatively, "It is hard to increase one's faith. Taking thought or increasing one's resolution doesn't seem to help. It's like lifting yourself up by your bootstraps."

His gravity about his fantastic project was so profound I kept my peace.

Two of Mann's closest friends were from the local Mexican colony. One was a roly-poly, ruddy-faced little man known as Tomato to everyone but called Joseph by Mann. Tomato was one of the Mexicans who worked as gardeners around town. He was dedicated to the wine bottle and had some six or seven arrests against him for drunkenness and disturbing the peace.

The second of Mann's close friends was a gnome-like little man known everywhere as Mig, a crude abbreviation of his name, Miguel, but called Michael by Mann. Mig was Tomato's constant companion but, curiously enough, except on Christmas, he did not touch wine.

Often, on my visits to Mann's place, I would find the spidery Mig and the pudgy Tomato helping Mann in his vegetable garden or with his flowers. Sometimes, if my visits were in the evening, I would find them sitting in the patio, Tomato with his wine bottle, singing, while Mig strummed away on an ancient guitar. The Timothys, with the exception of Mary, paid no particular attention to them, they being obviously considered members of the family.

Mary was their best audience and, time and again, I would see her in the shadows of the roofed walk that edged the patio, dancing to their music and song, dancing, as she always did, with her delicate and wistful special grace.

Indeed, Tomato, Mig and Mary seemed to make a natural trio, they all being so young and all with a faint quality of pathos. And the three, it struck me, had a subtle common enjoyment of their pathos, each expressing it in his or her own way: Mig with his ancient guitar. Tomato with his singing, Mary with her dancing. There was no doubt in my observation the three were close and dear to one another.

8.

It must not be thought from my description of Mann's acres and home and the excitement thereon and therein that Mann was a man of any special means. The land was worth little and the house crude and primitive. It is true that in the spirit in which Mann and his family lived, they were rich indeed, for they were richly happy and it can be maintained to some degree, I suppose, that being happy makes one far richer than stocks and bonds and a million in the vault.

Nor must it be thought, as I have pointed out before, that Mann's every hour was lived in smiling exuberance. He was a happy man, the happiest I've ever known, but he had his shaded moments too.

One evening after dinner when we were watching his Mary in one of her improvised dances—one of her shadowy, sad little dances—he said, kindly as always, but very quietly, "You have your Rodin and your Rembrandt, Tom, to remind you of your opulence. I have my Mary to remind me that time passes and then there is forever."

Now, he did not in any way say this to point up my having no children, nor was his the inane vanity with which many fathers speak of a talented child. No. He said this as if out of some subtle mood inspired by the elusive and delicate sadness of his Mary's dance, as if she, with her natural art-istry, was sharing with him her wistful, intuitive sense of the sorrow of life, reminding him of what he, in his high excite-ment about living, would not ordinarily remember.

I enjoyed my many visits to Mann's house and I think I benefited by them. I do know whenever dividends were off and my gout was acting up and I felt depressed I could always go to Mann's for what I called the Cure. The madness, the courage of Mann's household, and, especially, Mann's extraordinary philosophy, his glowing belief in the incom-prehensible and the impossible, would take the burdens off my back and send them flying, and would stir me, who am tone deaf, to raise my voice in song.

In appreciation, I used to bring to the house on occa-sions a little gift, usually a box of candy. Often I noted the prior box would still be on the sideboard unemptied when I brought the new one, but I tried not to let that disturb me. Most of the candy from Murphy's Drug Store where I trad-ed is on the cheap side, and I could hardly call it tempting, still I made the effort to show my gratitude, and so I let it be. I am, and always have been, a frugal man.

I must also say that Mann and his family never did go in for encouraging gift giving. Mann considered poverty a blessing and I did not want to run any risk of hurting his feelings. They liked people, all sorts of people, and I think they liked me—certainly they never showed any coldness toward me—and, at the risk of being accused of being parsi-monious (as I sometimes am) I must declare I hold a man's best gift to be himself.

Mary often spoke of wanting a ballet costume and toe shoes, a real ballerina's toe shoes, as she would say, and I swore time and time again that on one of my trips to Los

Angeles I would get her the costume and the shoes. But I never did get around to getting them. It was always uncomfortable for me when I would return from Los Angeles and visit Mann's and not have the costume or, especially, the toe shoes. I would have a box of candy with me on that first visit so it was not too bad but, unfortunately, I had once mentioned the toe shoes to Mary and I could see her watching me keenly as I stepped out of the car. Her heart was set on the toe shoes.

But I would joke with her and make a special point of giving her the candy and she would be grateful and that would ease my discomfort and soon I would be caught up in the excitement of life on the plateau and all would be forgotten.

I must say, in my defense, I am persuaded there is more truth than cynicism in the old saying that no one has as little time to think of others as a bachelor. Sometimes, I'm afraid, the bachelor is not charitably understood. Mann Timothy put it very well, though with a different approach, when he once said, "A large family is a great blessing. You have no time to worry about yourself." A good argument, surely.

Yes, I enjoyed my visits to Mann's house and it became so that often, coming back to my own place at the beach, I would feel a cold emptiness, an emptiness not even my Rembrandt and Rodin and books could fill.

One Saturday night, however, the night of the tragedy I mentioned earlier, there was anything but emptiness. I had just opened the door to my house and was extracting the key from the lock, when the silence was suddenly ripped apart by a series of sharp explosions that seemed to be right at my ear.

I rushed into the house, shut the door tightly behind me and, not turning on any light, hurried to the window that

faced north, the direction from which the explosive sounds
had come. As I reached the window, the back porch light of
the Ellerton house flashed on and I could suddenly see Bill
Ellerton, a small black automatic in his hand, standing on
the top of the back steps under the light looking down the
steps. Across the steps was sprawled the body of a woman,
head down. At the foot of the steps was crumpled the body
of a man.

It was a strange tableau under the porch light, Ellerton,
stockstill, with the pistol in his hand, the two sprawled bodies, and no one else, and beyond them darkness, and over
all the deep late-night silence. I remember, at first, looking
on the scene impersonally, without any emotion. I remember
saying to myself it could never be that the explosions I heard
had come from the small black pistol in Ellerton's hand. It
was all curiously unreal.

Then the frightened, furtive face of Ellerton's Negro
maid peered out through the narrowly opening back door. It
was she, I decided, who had switched on the overhead light.
Then I saw the figure of Major Von Manheim, his right hand
thrust into his coat, coming carefully but erectly through the
dark beyond the Ellerton house. The sight of the major away
from his house startled me and brought me back to reality.

I hurried out of the house and over to the Ellertons'.
I got there about the same time the major did. The major
leaned over and gave a slow, scrutinizing look at the woman
on the steps and then a similar look at the man at the foot
of the steps.

The woman was Grace Ellerton, Bill Ellerton's wife. The
man was Mann Timothy's Mexican friend, Tomato.

The major addressed Ellerton. "I think, sir," he said stiffly, "it will be good if you call the police."

9.

Bill Ellerton gave a straightforward account of the double killing.

He and his wife, Grace, had gone to the Majestic, our small local motion picture theater, and had returned after the show and put the car in the garage and were entering the house by the rear door, as was their custom, when the Mexican appeared in the dark and, brandishing a pistol, demanded money. He was drunk and menacing.

Bill took out his wallet to give to him, and the Mexican, grabbing excitedly for the wallet, teetered and Bill, thinking him helpless, seized his wrist to grab the pistol. The Mexican began firing wildly. One wild shot struck Mrs. Ellerton. Bill struggled to wrest the pistol from the Mexican and in the struggle the Mexican was killed.

Bill was not held by the police. Later, at the inquest, the coroner's jury absolved Bill completely from any implication in the crime. The *Courier*, in an editorial lamenting the loss of Mrs. Ellerton, commended Bill on his courage.

There was no doubt of Bill Ellerton's standing in the community.

Tomato, the Mexican, was, on the other hand, universally accepted as a disreputable character and a considerable nuisance. He had, as I have noted before, quite a few arrests for drunkenness and for disturbing the peace, and nobody was inclined to regard him in any way as an honorable citizen.

The community, though deep in grief at the death of Grace Ellerton, looked upon Tomato as well gone.

Mann Timothy alone did not accept Bill Ellerton's account.

"Joseph is innocent. He was my friend and he was, in his own childlike way, a saint." He spoke with a deep intensity. "I shall clear his name if it's the last thing I do on earth."

It was about a week after the killings and Mann was standing in the morning light in my living room, his eyes burning as he faced the window looking out on the Ellerton house.

"I know Bill Ellerton," Mann continued. "I have known him since he first moved here six years ago and I built bookcases for him in his den. I am able to characterize him very well. I saw his books and among them was not one book of the spirit. Voltaire, Marx, Engels, Hobbes, Renan, Nietzsche, they were all there, all the stock skeptics and materialists. There were the moderns there too—John Dewey and Justice Holmes and Bertrand Russell and, whatever their talents, these, likewise, nobody could ever accurately describe as defenders of the spirit. Naturally, there were Rabelais and Shakespeare and the like for cultural appearances but nowhere a sign of Plato or Laotze or Augustine or à Kempis or any of the books of the aspirations of man, neither the Vedas nor the Upanishads nor the Koran nor the Old Testament nor the New. There, in those bookcases, was the picture of Bill Ellerton's mind. There, was the declaration of his philosophy. There, was the credo of a man for whom murder, as Justice Holmes would have maintained, is an offence against the state and nothing more—an offence against neither the natural nor the divine law, for such laws do not exist for them, and the only guilt is in being found out."

I was naturally a little startled. "You believe Bill Ellerton killed his wife?"

"At this moment, I have my hypothesis but I am sure of nothing except that my friend Joseph did not do the killing," he replied, not taking his eyes off of the Ellerton house, a placid and sunny blue-and-white picture framed by the window. "For all I'm sure of right now, you may have killed Joseph and Mrs. Ellerton." He did not smile as he said this. There was silence and he continued to look at the Ellerton house. I could not but feel a little uncomfortable.

"You have watched the Ellertons and their guests coming and going, I'm sure," he said after a moment. "Did the guests look a little strange—a little offbeat to you?"

"I can't speak for all of them," I said, "but there were quite a few longhairs in the lot."

He nodded. "The Ellertons were supposed to be artistic with many concert artists for friends. Most concert artists would fit your description. Wouldn't you say so?"

"If all their guests, or even half of them, were concert artists," I said, "then there are a lot more concert artists in the world than there are concerts."

He gave me a quick look and it seemed for a moment there was a twinkle in his eyes. "Tom," he said, "sometimes you surprise me."

"It strikes me it was quite an ordinary observation." I was annoyed. "Hardly anything to be surprised at."

His eyes went back to the Ellerton house. "Bill Ellerton, with his campus clothes, may be trying to look the Young Alumnus but he is far from being the simple person he appears. He is quite complex indeed."

"And that proves what?"

"Nothing much perhaps. Only that people sometimes are not what they seem to be. There is a type of humanitarian who loves the poor but wouldn't give them a lead nickel.

"Take his letters to the *Courier* on our little Mexican settlement, for example. Mr. Ellerton pleads for the downtrodden. It is curious he never goes down to the railroad tracks and mingles with them. He would, I'm afraid, shrink from any such close association with them. Nor has he ever contributed a loaf of bread to appease the hunger he so vividly pictures there."

This Mexican colony was very much a subject of concern in our town. Its members dwelt in dilapidated wooden shacks near the railroad tracks not far from the station. The shacks were what was left of a row of little houses that had many years ago housed a railroad maintenance gang, but the gang had long been gone and the houses with the passing of time had become little more than skeletal boxes providing shade against the sun and, where the sides were tar-papered, some small protection against the wind and even less against the rain.

They were a merry people, it seemed to me, given over to music, to singing and dancing—and gambling and carousing—and were really only transients here, waiting till they had earned enough money to permit them to return with filled pockets to their beloved and more colorful and friendly homeland to the south. They were all adult males, and therefore without the usual adolescent troublemakers, and worked mostly at the nearby ranches, picking fruit and vegetables—lemons, oranges, avocados, lettuce, tomatoes and so on—in their season, although a few worked at odd jobs in town, at the gasoline stations or at gardening which in Seaview is mostly a matter of cutting grass and raking up leaves.

"They are children with the gift of faith and they are happy," Mann said to me once when I was talking of the colony. "What more can one ask for in this world?"

I was, of course, well aware of Mann's fondness for these people and therefore when I spoke to him, standing there in my living room defending his friend, Joseph, I tried to put my objection as delicately as possible.

"These Mexicans in the colony, are, I'm sure," I said, "wonderful people but how, Mann, does that make Bill Ellerton evil?"

"I'm just trying to develop the characterization," he said. "The rich and miserly humanitarian is far more complicated a character than is immediately apparent. Bill Ellerton underpays his help, and has never been able to keep a servant more than two or three months. He has, by the way, still to pay me for those bookcases I made for him. When first I heard of the killings at his house, I had a wild thought Joseph had gone there that night to collect wages due him. He had been doing some gardening for the Ellertons lately."

"There's the motive then!" I exclaimed.

Mann shook his head. "Joseph thought too little of money to kill a man for it."

All this seemed a little too much to me. "Mann," I said with all the vigor I was capable of, "friendship is all right. Friendship is fine. It has a power, I know. But facts are fine too and, it seems to me, they have a greater power. Bill Ellerton owed Tomato money for his work as a gardener. There is the motive.

"But what motive would Bill Ellerton have? To all appearances he loved his wife. If he didn't, he would have had no hesitation about getting a divorce. A man with his philosophy, with the philosophy you attribute to him, certainly would have no scruples—"

"Especially no scruples about murder."

I became a little impatient. "Mann, your great affection for Tomato has blinded you. Tomato was drunk. He was a Mexican and Mexicans, especially when drunk, have little regard for life. He was in the dark in the rear of the Ellertons' home when they came back from the show. There is no doubt about that. He had a motive. Money. His wages. He had a pistol—of Mexican make, by the way…"

"Are you sure the type of pistol they found on Joseph is manufactured in Mexico?"

"Now you're splitting hairs. Mann, you're the only one in Seaview who does not know that Tomato killed Grace Ellerton before he was killed himself."

I had had my say and was glad I had finally spoken out.

Mann sat down but he sat in a chair that faced the window looking out on the Ellerton house.

There was a little silence, then Mann said, "Yes, Joseph drank, and drank far too much, and he was arrested a half dozen times for disturbing the peace. And he did sing when he was drinking, as I have said, and sing exuberantly, and he, being a Mexican, might well have bothered some of the more proper and patriotic of our Seaviewites.

"But, believe me, Joseph was not mean and vicious when he was drinking. He was naturally kind, but when drinking he was so generous he would give you his life. Drinking made him uncommon. In his cups he was no longer plain. He grew in courtliness, in graciousness. He seemed closer to the Original Innocence when he was in wine. He was one of those pathetic but thoroughly understandable souls who, unsatisfied with their ordinary humanity, go searching for their lost kingship in a glass."

All this about poor Tomato! Mann saw my smile.

"Please believe me, Tom," he said. "Joseph was a bewildered but saintly child. I remember clearly the first day I met him. It was Sunday morning and I was going to Mass—"

"You actually go to Mass?" I asked him in surprise. "I would never have guessed that."

It was his turn to be surprised. "Why not?"

"You're such an individualist," I said, "a man of such audacity and independence, I can hardly picture you as—as, well, regimented, let's put it that way."

He answered me in a sort of weariness. "Tom, when you get around to reading those books, you will be surprised, I think, to find the New Testament tells you there is more to faith than the New Testament.

"You will learn of a Citadel that is built on a Rock. And there, in that Citadel, Tom, you will find peace and security—a peace and a security that allow you an almost reckless liberty. There the individual is at home in all his importance. There, truly, he is an adventurer, audacious and free."

He paused as if waiting for me to say something, and when I did not—what could I say that would not offend him?—he went on. "The morning I mention, I was entering church and there was Joseph entering church also. He had very obviously had a long Saturday night. His face was ruddier even than usual and he swayed a little, and an usher saw him and turned him around to steer him out of church, telling him he should be ashamed of himself. But I stopped the usher.

"I pointed out to the usher that others, many millions of others with far clearer heads and far less in need of sleep than Joseph, had forgotten their Maker and he had remembered. I took him to our pew with the family and he knelt there and from then on he was very much a member of the family until..."

He waved gently over to the Ellerton house. He could not go on speaking. His emotion had got the better of him.

After a long moment, he spoke again and now his voice was quite well controlled. "Last night I went down to visit Michael in the little lean-to near the tracks where he and

Joseph lived. Michael was still weeping over the loss of his friend. A candle burned before a worn picture of Our Lady of Guadalupe. The candle was stuck in a wine bottle, a white candle in a red wine bottle, and the red wine bottle with the white candle glowing in it was, in one way, such a vivid symbolic representation of my friend, Joseph, that for a moment he seemed to be back in the little home with us.

"I had been to their home many times but I had never noticed how few possessions Joseph really had—a bed, a chair, a small oil-burning stove, a section of a roof, a section of a wall, the clothes he wore and little else. Even his bitterest accusers could not say of him that he was corrupted with luxury, nor that the world was too much with him. Lady Poverty had blessed him indeed. True, he had his faith and his happiness, and his friends, and his singing, and the sun and the stars—the whole world was his, really—but I don't think his accusers were aware of this wealth and thus could hardly bring it up against him.

"Michael and I talked of our friend and especially of the great store he put by friendship. And Michael told me something I found most interesting. On Saturday night, Joseph had been drinking, and he and Michael had been sitting out in front of their little home singing, Michael with his guitar as always. Joseph had been very much himself, very affectionate, very gay.

"Then Joseph had gotten to his feet and put his wine away. 'I shall be back in a little while, friend,' he had said, 'and tomorrow we shall have much wine and we shall have a big feast for everybody.'

"As he was putting on his coat, Michael, puzzled, asked him if he would like him to go with him but Joseph shook his head. 'It is a big secret,' he said."

Mann paused and looked over at the Ellerton house. Bill Ellerton and a tall man in a black Homburg, a strange head-piece in the California sun, were leaving the house by the rear door. As we watched, they moved through the sunlight toward the garage. The man had a long, severe, high-cheek-boned face. Bill was smiling.

"Pray for him," Mann said quietly.

Mann was silent. Perhaps he was praying. I did not know.

"Mig's testimony seems conclusive," I said after a moment. "Saturday night, Tomato, in his wine, went off mysteriously to get money—his wages, if you wish—for a big feast. If Tomato were alive, Mig's testimony alone would be almost enough to convict him."

Mann looked at me with all his youth shining on his face. "There is a little more to tell," he said softly. "Just before Joseph left, he decided he should have another drink of wine. As he drank, he said to Michael with a great show of happiness, 'Tonight I am going to do a favor for a friend.' He put his finger to his lip. 'Remember, it is a big secret,' he said.

"Then he went gaily away. Michael was not to see him again alive."

Bill and his guest backed out of the garage in Bill's beautiful white Cadillac convertible. Bill turned the car around in the courtyard and they drove off, the car shining in the sunlight.

Mann waited a moment and went on, "Bill Ellerton is a writer of films. At least, he was. Not too good a writer, as I understand it, but an ingenious composer of plots, which is more profitable than being a good writer. I can see him devising a plot to suit his purposes.

"The plot in this case would not be difficult for him. It

could have been suggested by cases in police files, cases very probably known to a writer of plots.

"With Bill Ellerton it would run something like this: A wealthy and personable gentleman wishes to rid himself of his wife, not merely to divorce her but, for some special reason, to eliminate her immediately and forever. He goes to his Mexican gardener. He knows his gardener well, knows him as a romantic, simple-minded man who loves his fellows.

"'Friend,' he says to the gardener, 'would you do me the greatest of favors? Here is a gun. Tonight, my wife and I will arrive home from the movies about eleven o'clock. You stand in the rear of the house. There will be no light on. It will be dark. No one will see you or know who you are. When you see us, point the gun at us and demand my money, and my wife's jewels. I will refuse. I will grab you and take the gun away from you. You will run away in fright and my wife will embrace me. I will have become a hero to her. It will only take a few minutes and I will see you have plenty of wine for it. Would you do me this favor, friend?'"

Mann stared out at the empty courtyard in the rear of the Ellerton house. "It is an ingenious plot, don't you think?" he asked me in a faraway voice that seemed to say he did not care much if I answered the question or not. "He takes the gun and turns it on his friend and on his wife. Who would ever accuse him when this drunken Mexican is dead at his feet?"

"Why on earth," I asked, "should Bill Ellerton want to be a hero? And why, further, should he expect your Joseph to fall in with such a farfetched—such, I might say, a fantastic idea?"

"Bill Ellerton was inventive, for one thing, and he knew Joseph very well, for another. He probably intimated to

Joseph that his wife considered him a coward and he knew
this was the sort of romantic idea that would appeal to my
childlike friend. He knew the more poetry—the more chiv-
alry, indeed—the idea had, the more strongly Joseph would
be moved by it."

"Of course, this is only a hypothesis," I, still incredulous,
said. "You are not making any claim for it in fact, are you?"

Mann smiled slightly. "I was merely outlining a plot for a
film, you may recall—a film that might have been written by
Bill Ellerton." Then, he added gravely, "If it sounds extraordinary to you, and I can understand why very well, I would like
to point out that only an extraordinary explanation would
ever explain Joseph's curious remark to his friend, Michael,
on the night of his death, 'Tonight I am going to do a favor
for a friend.'"

I pondered Mann's hypothesis. It was ingenious, as he
said. But it seemed to be too unreal—too original, perhaps
I should say.

"Suppose, Mann," I said, "I accepted this entertaining
fiction—this plot for a film. It still doesn't solve the biggest
problem in your hypothesis—Bill Ellerton's motive. Why
should he want to kill his wife?"

He got slowly to his feet. "I'm groping my way toward
that. There is still for me one unknown factor in the plot—
Mrs. Ellerton's characterization. That I will have to know.
Indeed, one reason I came here to visit you today, Tom,
was to find out if you knew anything about her—about her
beliefs or loyalties or ways of thinking."

"I don't go in much for people's philosophies, as I think
you know," I said.

"But didn't you have any opinions about her? Was she
harsh or gentle, unkind or kind?"

I shrugged. "She was attractive and, so far as I could see, a happy woman, that's about all I can tell you. My chief observation about her was that she chose very pretty hats and they suited her and she wore them very well."

He nodded slowly. "Very interesting. She chose pretty hats and wore them very well."

He was meditative a moment, then turned toward the door. At the door he stopped and turned back toward me.

"There's one thing I should tell you, Tom, in case you should want to meditate on this matter," he said, "and that is, the pistol used in the killing was an automatic of Spanish make, not Mexican, and not common."

"But the motive?" I had been an attorney too long to be troubled about being insistent. "What about the motive?"

He looked at me for what seemed like a full minute. "Your observation about the pretty hats has given me the beginning of an idea," he said levelly.

Having said that, he turned and went on out through the door.

10.

Mann left me with quite a bit to meditate on, to use his phrase, and meditate on it I did, especially during my own quiet waking hours in the deep of night. The plot, as Mann called it, especially held my imagination.

The idea of a wealthy husband, wanting to get rid of his wife, hiring a drunken jailbird to pose as a holdup man, ostensibly to prove the husband's courage, and then to swing it so the unwanted wife is slain, and the poor dupe as well, and the husband emerges as a man not only of innocence and of courage, but as a hero—that idea fascinated me.

If Mann's invention were true, then Bill Ellerton was a man of exceptional daring and talent, and of diabolical ruthlessness, and a man to be feared. There were moments in the dark of night when I looked over at Ellerton's house and imagined I saw him at a window looking out at me, and at those moments I would go cold with fear.

These moments of fear were very brief, however, for I would soon come to my senses and realize that the plot almost certainly had to be a product of Mann's imagination. It was much too fantastic, much too perfect, indeed, to be true.

The more I thought of the crime, the more I realized Tomato could never be a murderer to Mann; no more than, despite his police record, he could ever be a drunkard to him. His drinking was merely the searching for his lost kingship in glass!

Mann was addicted to sentiment. He was as romantically devoted to his wife as if he were still courting her. His daughters he treated with unfailing courtesy and a constant show of affection. He loved his friends and was invariably affectionate with all he knew, even with me whom, I suspected, he considered dull and, possibly, a bore.

Once I was up at Mann's when Tomato, just after a short stretch in jail, came up to visit him. Tomato was unshaven and untidier than usual, and, though it was daylight, he had a strong smell of wine on his breath. But to Mann he could have been an angel in white garments. When Mann first saw him coming through the sunlight of the patio, he shouted a greeting and when they came together, he embraced him.

It was an inordinately happy meeting, one you might not reasonably expect even in old comrades separated for many years, and the show of affection, especially the embrace, made me feel a little uncomfortable. I slipped into the house as unobtrusively as I could.

Mann must have observed my embarrassment for later, when we were alone, he, without making any special point of it, said, "Tom, if, by some miracle, you ever get around to reading the New Testament, you'd find, among a thousand beautiful moments, many beautiful moments when men, unabashed, showed their affection for one another. They might seem a little extravagant to you, some of those moments, but I have an idea you'd admit they are moving.

"These men, and they were rugged men, embraced each other, and laughed and wept together. They happily went to death together. Little wonder is it that their enemies, in admiration, said, 'See how they love one another.'

"Very primitive, I know. I'm afraid they would never have been able to make the Blue Book or the society section of our newspapers. It is very doubtful if they would have been able to make the religion section, for that matter. Yet, yet this generosity in affection marked them as superior men. Socrates would have called them gods.

"The truth is the truth, Tom," he added with finality. "Christ, you might say, died on the Cross out of sentiment."

I thought it best to make no comment, so sensitive was he on the subject, though like most sensible people, I preferred to see things in the cool light of reality. I liked the solid feeling of a fact. I wanted to look directly at life and see it as it is. And sentiment, I believed, blurred and distorted. It vitiated purpose, inflamed the imagination. It screened reality like a gauze. I wanted no part of it.

It must be clear then why it was just not reasonable for me to expect Mann, with, as I say, his addiction to sentiment, to view Tomato's part in the killings at Ellertons' with any clarity of thought or coolness of detachment.

Several days went by after that morning in my living room, when Mann defended Tomato and advanced the possibility of Bill Ellerton's guilt, before I saw him again. I was on my way to Mr. Bosdick's barber shop and came upon him coming out from Dr. Thane's office into the sunlight.

"I think I have news about Joseph," he said. "Small news but significant. Thanks to you, I got the idea that an attractive woman with a philosophy of pretty hats could hardly be happily mated to a man of Bill Ellerton's philosophy. Women who share, who really share with their husbands, Bill Ellerton's particular kind of fanaticism are almost always plain or drab, and sometimes dowdy. They certainly never go in enthusiastically for pretty hats, and should they ever have one thrust on them they would not know how to wear it. I had a feeling something was out of joint."

He nodded toward Dr. Thane's office. "Grace Ellerton had lately been going to see my friend. Dr. Thane. She was nervous and depressed. She was worried about her husband. She found, she said, she had married a stranger.

"The doctor suggested she try a temporary separation from her husband. This was impossible, she objected. And when the doctor pressed her for a reason, all she would say was that there were circumstances that would never permit it."

Mann grabbed my arm. "It is small, as I say, but it is significant." His eyes shone even more than usual. "Joseph's honor will be vindicated!" he said triumphantly. "You'll see!"

It was a bright, young morning and very much suited to Mann's mood, so it was with reluctance I said, "But, Mann, there is still no motive."

He laughed his quiet laugh. "The characterizations first, Tom. The plot will follow."

At that moment, Bill Ellerton, bareheaded, the top down on his white Cadillac convertible, drove swiftly along the highway before the Arcade. He wore a careless brown tweed coat and a pale green sport shirt open at the neck and, in the happy sunlight, looked very much what Mann called the Young Alumnus. On the seat of the car beside him, was a bag of golf clubs.

We both watched the car until it was out of sight.

"Pray for him," Mann said, as he had said before.

11.

I was in san francisco when I read in the newspapers of Bill Ellerton's arrest.

The day after the day I talked to Mann outside Dr. Thane's office, I had received a telegram telling me oil had been found on some property I owned in Nevada. It came as a complete surprise to me, this announcement of the discovery of the oil, for the four hundred acres I owned I had written off as a bad investment.

A few years before, when the great search for uranium was first on, I had been persuaded by a real estate agent that there was uranium to be found here and there in certain areas in Nevada and, after tests had proved him right, I bought four hundred acres. There was uranium there all right, but it turned out to be of such small quantity and of such low potency as not to be worth the trouble of digging out. The acreage was thus of no value, and try though I did, I was unable to sell it off. There were some weather-worn ranch buildings on the property and these I rented out to an old couple who lived there and wrote to me now and then, telling me mostly about the weather. I had looked upon my

purchase as the only real mistake in business matters I had
ever made.

Now, it was found rich in oil. It was my tenants, the old
couple, who had made the discovery. I flew to Nevada to see
for myself. The oil was actually bubbling up out of the earth
in several places. No survey had been made of that section of
the state, nor had the existence of oil been suspected there,
and thus I had not been approached by any petroleum company with even tentative terms for a lease or sale. I accordingly had no commitment of any sort and was in an excellent
position to make a most profitable deal. I was deluged with
offers by mail and telephone and telegraph, and besieged by
representatives of the petroleum companies, and all sorts of
go-betweens and entrepreneurs, but I took my time until I
had an offer of the best possible terms. I went from Nevada
to San Francisco to the offices of the petroleum company to
close the deal.

I had considered myself reasonably wealthy before the
finding of the oil. But now I was rich beyond my craziest
dreams. Now anything I wanted was mine to buy—an apartment in Paris, a villa in Rome, a penthouse on Park Avenue,
an ocean-going yacht, a private airplane with my own pilot,
on and on, anything, anything.

On signing the papers in San Francisco, one of my first
thoughts was of Mann Timothy, and I went to a shop and
bought for Mary the finest ballet costume and the finest toe
shoes money could buy. This time I was not going to fail
Mary or the Timothys. I could for once dare not to be frugal.

It was then, when I was leaving the shop with my purchase, that I saw the newspaper headlines telling of Bill
Ellerton's arrest. I bought a paper and standing there on the
sidewalk, with my packages under my arm, I read the news

story from the first word to the last.

Mann Timothy was not mentioned. The Seaview police were, understandably enough, given the credit. The police in Mexico City, at the request of our local sheriff station, had traced the purchase of the small Spanish automatic, which had been used in the killings, to a little shop in that city. Bill Ellerton had been identified as the purchaser. He had bought the pistol only two days before the crime.

Ellerton had somehow got wind of the undercover investigation and had reserved accommodations on a plane for New York and Lisbon. He was seized as he was about to board the plane at the International Airport in Los Angeles.

As Mann Timothy, in his evaluation of philosophies, had so wisely suspected, there was far more to Bill Ellerton than was apparent. His home in Seaview—that chaste blue and white house I used to like to look upon as it sat prettily like a gift box in the sunlight—was a key place in the underground for undesirable aliens, many of them subversives, illegally on their way into the United States through Mexico. The traffic at the time was considerable and Bill Ellerton was an important figure in it.

The authorities, local and federal, had had a suspicion of such a place somewhere in or near Seaview, a suspicion I'm sure Mann was familiar with. In the investigation after Bill Ellerton's arrest, it was found that he was an importer only in that he imported these undesirables. Bill Ellerton was, as Mann had intimated, a sham humanitarian and a sham intellectual with no sense whatsoever of the ancient loyalties.

And the motive for the killing of Grace Ellerton, the motive I had so earnestly insisted on?

Mann's study of the philosophy of a woman with pretty hats had come to a most accurate conclusion. The Ellertons

were far from being the happily mated couple they were supposed to be. After Bill Ellerton's arrest, the Negro maid—
whom the police had hardly bothered to question after the
crime, so obvious had it seemed to them that Joseph was
guilty—described Mrs. Ellerton as a much-worried woman,
and told of loud arguments between the Ellertons, and of
one very bitter argument a few evenings before Mrs. Ellerton's death, when she had heard Mrs. Ellerton scream, "I'm
sick of it! I'm frightened! I wish we could wash our hands of
the whole business!"

After that, the maid reported, Mr. Ellerton spoke very
quietly and very nicely to Mrs. Ellerton and evidently quiet-
ed her for she overheard no more. Mr. Ellerton ordered wine
chilled for dinner and they seemed to have made up, and
both were very amiable that night. Mr. Ellerton was even
nice to her, the maid said.

I folded up the newspaper. The plot was very much as
Mann had worked it out, a plot that might have been suggested originally by a case in the police files. Bill Ellerton
had a very good reason for the killing of his wife—fear, fear
for himself, fear for exposure of his activities. Divorce would
have given him no security. But there was no mention of
Mann in the paper. He would not have wanted any mention.
But I was sure it was he who had had the purchase of the
pistol investigated by the sheriff station. His was the accomplishment but not his the glory.

I was certain he was happy that day. He had stood alone
in his faith in his friend's innocence. Now the name of his
friend had been cleared. I could see the happiness up in the
little adobe house on the dappled mustard-brown plateau.

12.

It turned out, when I got back to Seaview, I found anything but the happiness I had expected to find in Mann's little adobe house.

On the way home from San Francisco, I stopped over for a few days in Los Angeles to buy a new car, and thus it was, with the time spent in Nevada and San Francisco, some three weeks that I had been away from Seaview. The afternoon of the day I returned, I took the ballet costume and the toe shoes I had for Mary and drove up into the hills to visit Mann. I was in high spirits, as may be imagined. I could not wait to congratulate Mann on the Ellerton business. But, even more than that, I was pleased with myself that this time I was not going up to the house with my usual parsimonious box of cheap candy from Murphy's Drug Store.

In the hills, the moment I turned the bend in the dirt road that looks down on the plateau, I could see a change had come over the little settlement. There were no noisy comings and goings, no singing or laughing, no hammering or shouting, none of that happy dissonance in which Mann and his family seemed always to live.

This was not natural, this quiet and emptiness. As I drove, I had a presentiment this was not accidental and I would not find Mann and his family as I had always found them before. The presentiment grew as I neared the empty patio and the lifeless house, and the sunlight seemed to vanish from the day.

I drove up to the place where I usually stopped, just alongside the patio. As I got out of the car with my package, I heard the sound of a low, melancholy voice in a sort of chant accompanied by a forlorn tinkling of a guitar. The language of the mournful chant was Mexican Indian

of some sort, and I had no knowledge of it, but there was
no misunderstanding its meaning. It was a lament, ancient
and primitive, such a lament as one might hear moaning
through the dark of the deeply wooded jungles of Tobas-
co or undulating across the ghostly silence of the moonlit
deserts of Sonora.

The door of the main house was open, and, as I approached, it became apparent the lament was coming from the
living room. Then, entering through the open door, I saw
Tomato's friend, Mig, smaller and more gnomish than ever,
it seemed, squatted on a little, cushioned seat, beneath a window that opened out to the west and squared a patch of misted blue sky and dark blue sea. He wore soiled, frayed, brown
corduroy pants and jacket and a red cotton shirt. Around
his neck a black handkerchief was loosely tied. His wizened,
small stockingless feet showed through his heavy coarse san-
dals. His head hardly came to the window sill.

He looked up at me with red-rimmed dry little eyes but
did not cease for a moment in his lamentation nor in the
mournful tinkling of his ancient guitar.

I waited for him to put an end to his chant, but, after a
few moments, when it was clear he had no idea of doing so,
I spoke over his singing and asked him what had happened
and where everybody was.

He continued to moan on as before, his face expression-
less, as if he had not heard me. I decided the chant was rit-
ualistic in one way or another and would not be ended until
the prescribed moment for it to be ended had come, so I sat
down in a deep easy chair which Mann had made himself,
and prepared to wait.

It was a strange experience, sitting there in the house
that once had overflowed with living and now, in contrast,

seemed desolate. The empty house with its heavy lifelessness was disturbing enough by itself but this odd little child of a man, squatted under the window intoning what seemed like the last rites over an invisible grave, added an eerie quality that was unnerving.

So, I sat there with my package for Mary in my lap while he chanted, and waited, growing more and more strained and ill at ease with every moment. The chant seemed interminable, moaning on and on in an agonizing repetitious sort of rondo movement, and finally I reached my resolution's end and had about decided to jump up and rush across to the little man and throttle him when suddenly he stopped. He stopped in the middle of a measure and left the chant on a note up in the air, but, apparently, that was the way it was meant to be, for the moment he finished, there was an obvious finality about the way he put the guitar aside and folded his hands and bowed his head.

I waited until I was sure of the silence and then I asked him again what had happened and where Mann and his family were.

He answered in Spanish. I knew the words but I could not put them together to make sense. I told him so.

"Our Lady," he repeated in English, "she has taken the little dancer. She has taken her for herself."

Then, I knew. Then, I understood Mig's grief and the lifelessness of the house and grounds. Sometime, in the three weeks or so I had been away, Mann's little girl, Mary, had died. The shadowy, wistful little dancer, who seemed to know intuitively and express delicately the secrets of the dance of life, no longer had life to dance to.

The package with the ballerina costume and the toe shoes became intolerably heavy in my lap.

Beauty had been here in this house, in this child, had lived here some of its immortal moments in the shadowy but exquisitely defined ballet steps of a sensitive and spontaneous artist. The childhood and the beauty had been destroyed at one stroke. The thought of Death coming to Mann's house, that house of life and living faith, was difficult for me to accept. But the thought of Death coming to Mary, to this child of grace, was almost beyond acceptance.

It occurred to me it might all be a fiction of this strange little creature squatting on the window seat and staring at me with his red-rimmed dry eyes.

But I remembered the emptiness and the lamentation that had greeted me, and I knew it was not a fiction. Then, as I became aware again of the burden of the ballet costume and the toe shoes in my lap, I remembered the intimations of mortality I had discerned in the little girl's dancing, the wistful, shadowy rhythms that whispered of sorrow and, even, of death. Then I knew for a truth this child of grace, as I described her, was dead.

I questioned Mig about the circumstances of her going and, by diligently putting the little man's words together, I learned that one evening she was dancing and then, suddenly, her slender, small legs would dance no more. In tragic cynicism, paralysis stilled the little body that had been so lyric with motion. It came from some grave disease of the spine and in three or four days she was dead. She was buried in a cemetery near San Diego. Mann and his family had gone on to San Diego and were not returning to the plateau.

"Shadows," Mig whispered, when I asked why they were not returning to the house.

His little eyes searched cautiously, timidly into the shadows the late afternoon sunlight made in the house and in the patio, seen through the open door, and he whispered again, "Shadows."

He spoke as if the English word, shadows, were a very strange word and had a deep meaning for him—memories, ghosts, possibly demons—and told all that was in his mind.

He picked up his worn guitar and held it up for me to see. "Try send 'way shadows," he said, peering out into the room and the patio again with his cautious, timid eyes, "but shadows won't go 'way."

Mann and his family, I gathered from further questioning, were never coming back. They were going to buy a boat and sail northward. Mig mentioned San Francisco and Vancouver and Victoria but it was all very vague except the sailing northward.

I was heartbroken. I realized in those few moments, sitting there in Mann's once teeming, now desolate living room how much Mann and his family had come to mean to me. More, I knew then, than my Rembrandt and my Rodin, more indeed than my oil in Nevada and all it could buy.

Mig and I stared at each other in a long, significant silence. Then, he picked up the guitar and began again his strangely intoned chant with its mournful accompaniment, the eerie incantation that he hoped would drive away the shadows.

But I got to my feet. I took the package with the ballet costume and toe shoes and left the house.

I knew the shadows would not be driven away.

13.

For days after my visit to Mann's empty house, I had the feeling I would never see him again. Mann was a man of absolutes, to use an expression of his, and I was sure once he had made a decision not to return to his home, he would not return. Nor did he. But he did return to Seaview. And I did meet with him again, though it was briefly, and only to say farewell.

But in those days and, especially, in those nights before I saw him again, I spent many hours thinking about him and Mary and the family and what they had come to mean to me. Curiously enough, I was not alone in the town in my way of thinking. The newspapers in Los Angeles and San Diego were giving a big play to the Ellerton story and the town was thronged with strangers, not only newsmen and photographers and the like, but the usual psychotics who are drawn by their love of the macabre to the scenes of crime. Bill Ellerton had become big news, not only in the West but across the country and throughout the world. But to most of us in Seaview the important story was little Mary's death and Mann Timothy's leaving our town.

Mr. Bosdick's barber shop was a subdued place during those days. Mann had managed to get himself loved, there was no question about that. The little Mexican colony was in mourning. But so, in one way or another, was about everybody else. Even the isolates, as I used to call those who lived in the town but were never a part of it, were affected.

One evening, just after the coming of dark, I was walking the beach and I passed Major Von Manheim's house at the time he, glass in hand, was coming out to the bulkhead to indulge in his routine scrutiny of sea and sky.

I greeted him and was astonished when he returned the greeting. He raised up his free arm stiffly and erectly, like a general summoning a mere private, and I knew he wanted to talk to me.

He spoke as a man unaccustomed to speech, uncomfortably groping for the right words. But he made his point clearly enough. He wanted, he said—commanded, in a fashion—me and others like me, friends of Mann, to form a committee and find Mann and insist on his coming back. We would make him burgomaster, he declared. We would pay him a salary so he could retire for life.

I knew Mann was the major's only friend in town and, with the exception of Mr. Bosdick and occasional tradesmen and workmen, the only visitor to his home, but I could see that the major did not know Mann very well. If there was anything Mann would like less than being mayor, honorary or otherwise, it would be to be retired for life. I did not mention this to the major, however. I simply said that Mann, for all his gentleness, lived his own life completely in accordance with his own design and no one could change him.

The major turned his back abruptly on me after I had said this and marched stiffly into his house.

I knew he considered me as failing Mann and the affection Mann bore us.

Those days and nights immediately after I had visited the empty house on the plateau and learned of the tragedy from Mig, were the emptiest I had ever known. I realized more and more how dependent on Mann and his family my happiness had become. It had been a subtle process, beginning first with my amusement at Mann and his madness, but growing into an admiration for his courage and, finally, to use the words he would use, into a love of him. I had not realized it until I sat that late afternoon in the living room of the tragically desolate little adobe house that once had been overflowing with life.

Grief is usually selfish but mine, it seemed to me, was more than ordinarily selfish. As a bachelor, I was able at Mann's to enjoy, in a vicarious sort of way, a happy, colorful, family life. But more than that, the sight of him and his sure and audacious way of living was not only a pleasure but a sort of inspiration for me. Not that I ever acted on the inspiration. It was, I'm afraid, as with the family life, vicarious, the enjoyment of audacity without any risk, or, to put it more honestly, as I used to do in the meditative hours of the night, it was caution basking in courage.

Yes, it is true, I thought of myself first, as I (and most veteran bachelors, I'm sure) am accustomed to doing, but, I think to my credit, I also thought of Mann. I knew how he loved his Mary and I understood why he could not return to the adobe house where she had lived. She would still be dancing for him there, a shadowy wraith gliding delicately, wistfully through the shadows. The illusion would be unendurable even for a man of Mann's faith and philosophy.

I wondered, in those hours in the deep of night, just how this faith and philosophy of Mann's had endured the merciless reality of death. Mann was so much in love with life he seemed to be unaware of life's indissoluble partnership with dissolution. Only once had I ever heard him speak of anything connected with death, and that was when, as I have already written, he said he had his Mary "to remind him that time passes and then there is forever."

His extraordinary youth and happiness seemed to be so essentially sprung from his gratitude for life, it was hard for me to see him other than struck down, broken indeed, by the tragic death of his beloved Mary. In addition to the pain of loss, the senselessness, the reasonlessness of the sacrifice of one so young and blameless would, it seemed to me, grieve him beyond all faith and fortitude. No one, I was certain, not even Mann, could find any cause for gratitude in so cruelly useless, so cruelly incomprehensible a death.

I was sure the deep hurt of his loss had changed him radically, though possibly not as much as it would have other men. Life would have grown gray for him, and he would have become impassive with despondency if not with disillusion.

I was to find the answer to my speculations in Mann himself.

Some three weeks after I had returned to Seaview, and at a time when I had decided neither I nor any of his friends would see him again, Mann appeared at my door.

It was quite late at night and I was reading and having coffee by myself in my living room when I heard his knock. He never pressed the door buzzer. He always knocked. And his knock had its own particular character to it, being hushed and always of the same pattern as if he were tapping out the notes of some brief musical phrase. When first in our acquittance at Seaview, I heard his knock and opened the door I expected to find a child there. It was a child there, in a fashion, I know now, but I was not acquainted with Mann then.

This night again I knew it was Mann at the door but still I could not realize it. Only that morning I had driven up to the plateau to see if there might possibly be some sign of him or his family, and I had found the place already had been sold. Indeed, the new owners were already moved in, a gaunt, suspicious couple who looked as if they might have been farmers from the Great Plains.

I rushed to the door. I put my hand out in greeting but he ignored the hand and embraced me as he had his friend, Joseph, and as he did his friends. I was taken unawares and embarrassed but I must admit I felt honored. He had never done this before. I knew then he had changed, though not as I expected.

He looked the same: young, challenging. He was not smiling and there was an intensity about him that was not usual. But still, he was no more intense than he had been when he learned of Tomato's death and the unjust charges against him.

He looked the same, as I say, and yet I was sure he had changed. His love of his fellows, always great, had now to be greater. For now it actively included me. Had he not embraced me?

He apologized for coming at so late an hour. He had been making the rounds, he said, saying goodbye to his friends. He spoke rather casually as if he had no idea how deeply moved I was at the sight of him.

I poured him a cup of coffee and we talked over our cups much as we did that extraordinary morning when I first discovered him trying to walk on the sea. He talked a great deal as he always did. But I was not able to hold up my end. I fell into deep silences and could not speak. I was too keenly aware of the finality of this last meeting. I knew it was farewell. And I, I who so long had been against sentiment of any sort, was saddened, more saddened than I had ever been since my childhood.

It occurred to me I too had changed. I more fully understood or, to put it better, perhaps, more fully felt what Mann had meant when he said time passes and then there is forever. I had a strange feeling of forever.

At first, the talk was quite matter-of-fact and there was no even slight reference to Mary. In San Diego, with the money from the sale of all he owned on the plateau, he had bought a yawl that would sleep him and his family. He had it fitted out completely and all were going to live aboard. It was at that moment moored out near our pier. They planned to sail the yawl leisurely up the coast, under canvas or power, or both. They would put in at this town or that as pleased them, and when they found a town to their liking, they would put in there for good or, at least, till all the youngsters were through school.

"All my boys are sailormen, and the boat should be a beautiful experience," he said levelly, as if there were no other thought in his heart, "one every family should have. It has long been a dream of mine."

Then, as he spoke, he noticed the pair of toe shoes I had bought for Mary on top of a bookcase where I had put them as a remembrance of the child. He stared at them as if trying to place them. Then he drained his coffee cup and got to his feet and went to the bookcase. He picked up the shoes, one in each hand, and looked at them.

"I got them in San Francisco," I said, wanting in spite of the sorrow of the moment to win some credit for my thoughtfulness, but no sooner had I begun my speech than I knew I could not finish it. I stopped and sat in foolish silence.

He seemed not to have heard me and yet he apparently understood the shoes had been for Mary for a little smile came on his face as if at some memory. It was his first smile since his coming.

There was a deep silence. Then looking down at the shoes he said, still with his little smile, "What a heart for breaking my Mary had. Now it will never be broken."

He gently put the shoes back on the bookcase.

After a moment he turned back to me. "I've learned a lesson, Tom," he said quietly. "Death, not life, is the test of faith."

He came back to his chair but did not sit down. I got up from my chair.

"Yes, Tom," he, his eyes bright, went on with his overwhelming simplicity, "as you are sure to have imagined, I went down into the depths. Like Thomas, I doubted. Like Peter, I denied. I had been too happy too long searching and enjoying the incomprehensibility of life. I had to learn to suffer and overcome the incomprehensibility of death."

He turned to the great window and looked out into the dark where the white surging of the breakers could be seen against the black of the sea.

After a long moment, he said, not turning from the window, "There is a cross you take up yourself, Tom, and there is a cross that is thrust on you as a cross was thrust on Simon of Cyrene. The cross that is thrust on you is the heavier, at first, and the harder, but if you carry it well, it grows light and can become even happy for you in the end."

He turned away from the window. "The lesson I learned, I was too blind with the radiance of living to learn before. No, Tom. Not life, as I had thought in my love of it, is the test of faith. Death is the test of faith."

It seemed to me, as he talked, the faith he had sought, the new transcendent faith was glowing in his eyes.

He came toward me and quickly embraced me.

"Goodbye, Tom," he said, "I love you."

I was aware of the door opening and closing. Much later, I was aware he was gone.

14.

That was, as I have said, my last meeting with Mann. But I have an idea I saw him once again.

Ordinarily the night hours with their beautiful stillness and challenging secrecy are much too short for me. But this night, after Mann's going, the hours were long and empty.

It would have been better in some ways, I tried to tell myself as I paced the house, if Mann had not come back at all. True, since seeing him, my concern for him had gone. He had not only accepted the death of his Mary without recrimination but had seemed inspired by the tragic experience, had seemed to have found in it new powers and new perceptions.

It was this new richness, this new largeness of spirit, that made my sense of loss at his going even deeper than it ordinarily would have been. Before the visit that evening, I had considered him an extraordinary person. But now, after he had gone, in a house made desolate by his having been there, I had a feeling I had been in the presence of greatness, genuine greatness. And this made my feeling of emptiness more profound. It is not easy to give up a friend of that stature.

Nor did his new affection for me, born, I'm sure, of the new charity that had come out of his heartbreak and his conquest of despair, make it any easier for me. His last embrace and his last words had inspired me, for the moment certainly, with some of his greatness. I felt suddenly as if I were of heroic cast and had depths of courage and affection I had never dreamed of. I seemed, for that moment anyway, to have been lifted up to some towering height and there shared with him his vision of a world where, as he would have put it, the incomprehensible was clear and the impossible possible, and audacity and affection inspired the hearts of men, and where the haters, for all their enmity, were in wonderment saying as they once had said, "See how they love one another."

But the moment was gone with his going, and I felt as if I had been dropped into a great deep of futility and loneliness. I waited impatiently, I begged for daybreak to come. At the first light, I told myself, I would walk the beach to the pier, take over a skiff and go out to the yawl and see Mann once again.

Daybreak finally came, but a fog, not unexpected since this was spring, had rolled in during the night and the morning was blurred and gray. Even in the fog, I felt some of the excitement I always felt with the coming of day, and, though from the bulkhead I could not see the yawl, I decided I would walk along toward the pier in the hope the fog would be lifting by the time I got there.

But the fog did not lift. It grew heavier as I walked. I could not only not see the yawl, I could not even see the pier. I could see nothing, indeed, except the white breaking of the surf and the white moving patterns it made on the sand.

I was sure Mann would not have put out to sea in such weather, so I found a seat on a heavy stump of driftwood on the beach by the pier and waited for a break in the fog.

Then, as I sat there, I thought I heard the distant, muffled grating sound of oarlocks and of oars in them. The sound seemed slow, leisurely, as if the rower were indolently at ease. As I listened intently, the sound faded and I persuaded myself I had been mistaken and there had been no such sound at all. Gulls, perhaps. Or some movement of boat gear on the invisible pier.

A few minutes passed, and then I heard the sound of leisurely rowing again. There was no doubt about it this time. It was nearer and, as I listened, came nearer still. Suddenly I had a curious feeling of excitement. I remembered it was on such a morning about a year before, and under very much the same circumstances, I had had my first meeting with Mann Timothy in Seaview.

I got to my feet and went down to the edge of the surf.

The fog began to lift a little here and there, and I was sure presently I would see the rowboat and whoever was rowing it. But the fog settled again and there was only the slow, lazy sound of the oars and the oarlocks leisurely coming nearer. Soon it was so near, I could make out the soft splashing of the oars in the water.

Then, at a moment when I waited tensely for the boat to come into view, the sound stopped abruptly and completely. I was exasperated. So on edge had I been with excitement and, even, with expectancy, that now I felt I had been meanly tricked and, as the silence continued, I grew angry at it and at the deep curtain of fog as well. I waded, loafers and all, out into the surf to be nearer to the boat I knew had to be not more than fifty or sixty yards away.

As I stood in the surf, the fog began to separate here and there. Then, suddenly in a little rift in the fog, I could make out an empty rowboat, the oars pulled in and at rest in the boat. But, as I intently searched the small, misted patch of water visible near the boat for sight of a human figure, the fog closed in again.

The outline of the boat became a blur, and slowly, as the fog deepened, even the blur vanished but, as it did, I saw for an instant, or thought I saw, a fragment of a gray spectral figure approaching the boat on the water. It could have been an illusion, it could have been a wisp of vapor among vapors, but in that instant, I was sure I saw a ghostly coat sleeve and a ghostly hand carrying a walking stick.

The sight, or the illusion, vanished as the blur of the boat vanished.

Again there was only the deep gray fog and the silence.

I was desperate. Had I seen what I thought I had seen?

I knew I did not have time to run back to my house to get my small flat-bottomed rowboat. I turned and raced back to the dry sand. I kicked off my loafers. I would swim out beyond the breakers and find out.

Then, as I was pulling off my sweat shirt, I heard the grating sound of oars in oarlocks again. But this time the sound was not the slow, lazy sound of the rowing of a leisurely rower. It was brisk, the sound of excitement.

The boat began to move away quickly and, in no time at all, the sound of rowing could be no longer heard.

It was late afternoon before the fog began to lift. I had returned to the house but at the first break in the fog I started back toward the pier. I was far more excited, as may be guessed, than I had been even on my early morning walk.

I had gone only a little distance when an offshore wind came up and blew the fog away completely. I stopped and searched the bay where the mooring buoys floated and bobbed beyond the pier. Mann's yawl was nowhere to be seen.

Then, looking off toward the horizon, I saw the yawl already standing out to sea. Her mainsail and a single jib were whitely burgeoning in the new wind and the boat, leaning slightly before the wind, cut cleanly into the serene blue water.

I stood on the beach and watched the boat grow smaller and smaller against the western sky. It was the beginning of the sunset, and it seemed to me the audacious little boat, alone on the horizon under the great arch of gathering sunset colors, was more expressive of Mann than had been his brown adobe home high up on his dappled mustard-brown plateau. That had been brave enough, but this new adventure was braver still, and struck me as being a finely proper expression of his new transcendent faith.

I stood and watched until the boat was lost to view, a speck fading at last into the merging sea and sky. I still stood and watched the vast emptiness after the boat was gone, and again I had the strange feeling I had had at Mann's farewell visit the night before, but more profoundly now, the feeling of forever.

JOHN MARTIN

*If Dennis and Mann Timothy, in their adventures, were lacking in good
common sense, as has been noted, then it might be said that John Martin
had no common sense at all. He would have agreed, I'm sure, and would
have boasted his great endowment was uncommon sense. Whatever the
truth, it must be pointed out his explorations were in a nether world.
In the darkness, he was, it could be maintained, very much in need of a
special endowment.*

1.

He sat on the edge of the bed and watched the woman in
the pale yellow robe seated at the mirror brushing her blond
hair, brushing it slowly, rhythmically, and he said to himself,
I'm going to kill this woman and I have no feeling of dread
or guilt or any feeling much except perhaps a feeling of inevitably drawing near the end of an intolerably futile and
wretched journey, an end for me as well as for her.

He hunched forward on the bed and took a long drink
of straight whiskey from the glass he held in his two hands,
not taking his eyes off the woman at the mirror brushing
her hair. In one panel of the three-paneled mirror, beside
her image he could see his own. He looked very much as he
had always looked except that a strand of hair fallen down
his forehead tended to point up the paleness of his face. But
his face had been pale of late, and that particular strand of
hair had quite often fallen down over his right forehead so

really there was hardly any difference at all. Certainly his face looked no more a murderer's face than it ever had.

His hands gripping the glass were white but that was not from any tension. His hands had always been like that when they gripped a glass. He raised a hand to loosen further the opened collar of his gray shirt and his hand shook but that was not from tension, either. That was from drinking, too much drinking. That was why he held the whiskey glass with both of his hands, to keep them from shaking.

She was older than he, seven or eight years older. He was twenty-six and she was thirty-three or thirty-four. Her being older had been part of her attraction for him. Not that he had wanted to be mothered. It wasn't that. She was the last woman one would turn to for mothering. Her maturity had attracted him because he was immature. He knew he was immature. But what was wrong with that? Nothing except that when you suffered you suffered more than did emotionally mature people. When you were happy, you were extraordinarily happy, yes. But when you were unhappy, when you were lonely, for example, you were lonely with the deepest loneliness in the world.

Geniuses were often immature, were they not? One had to consider that. How else would they be able to see the world with a child's eyes, see all its innocence and all its evil. If they weren't immature, they would follow their reason instead of their instinct and the best they could ever be would be men of talent. Instinct is genius. Instinct is the genius of the artist just as instinct is the genius of the insect.

The woman stopped brushing to separate several tangled strands of hair. Now, with the distraction of the rhythmic brushing of her hair gone, he became more aware of the reality of the storm outside.

It had been raining monotonously all afternoon but with
the coming of dark a gale had sprung up in the west and
was now furiously driving the storm in from the wide bay,
lashing the Coast Highway and the hills beyond it. Now and
then a particular gust of wind and rain would strike at the
little house and swirl fiercely around it, as if in some personal
animosity, slapping angrily at the doors and windows, bow-
ing down the tall, proud eucalyptus trees behind it, whirling
their leaves from their branches and making them whimper.
He listened to the fury of the storm and found it good. It
fitted into his plan, this storm.

The woman at the mirror began again to brush her hair.
She had not looked at him, had not even given him the least
glance in the mirror. He was not surprised. He knew she
would not look him in the eyes. He knew she could not look
him in the eyes. It was just as well. If she had looked at him,
had turned and come to him, holding him with her eyes, he
might have lost his resolution and given up the thought of
killing her, and then there would be nothing for him but
more failure and more despair. But he was not concerned. He
knew she could not look at him.

She did not look at him but he could hardly take his
eyes off her.

She is common, but singularly common. Her hair flows
heavily to her shoulders, more heavily than hair should. It
has weight and a physical quality, her hair. It is intemperate,
that is the only word for it. Look at her mouth. It is large.
It is intemperate, too. Her brown eyes, darker because of the
blond hair, they too are physical. They are a little more deeply
set than they should be, and a little more widely apart.

Yes, she is common, singularly common, this woman. So,
that very first night when he saw her in Sicilia's, the tawdry

café off Main Street, had she appealed to him. I, he had said, I, volatile, complex, uncommon, I shall find fulfillment in you, and I shall become strong and complete, and the ordinance condemning me to frustration and failure will operate no longer.

He watched her brush her hair. How fatuous, how completely silly this all sounded now.

He had told her of his resolution at their first meeting. He had told her passionately and with complete conviction. In you, he had told her, I will renew myself, and my triumph will be inevitable and the glory will be yours. But she had had only the vaguest idea of what he was talking about. Glory, talking to her of glory, what a waste of breath that had been. She thought, when she thought at all, only in prose, the plainest, most prosaic of prose.

A sudden attack of the storm shook the little house. He lifted the glass in his two hands to his mouth, slowly sipped the straight whiskey. It is superior, this storm, superior and important as so often are the storms that sweep in from the sea in wild anger at the land and its houses and roads, its trees and its hills. Outside there are size and importance but here inside there is no size or importance. Inside, it is tawdry and petty and inconsequential. Two people, out of two thousand millions of people, in an infinitesimal square box with a cheap pink-and-cream dresser, a vanity dresser they call it, and a pink-and-cream bed with a pink, quilted headboard and two pink-and-cream chairs and a gas heater smoldering sallowly in the wall and smelling meanly, as it always did, of scorched paint. And the cheap, blue-and-white ceramic madonna on the little shelf on the wall. Don't forget that, the madonna. What a place for a madonna, this bedroom, even for the cheapest of ceramic madonnas!

All was tawdry, inconsequential. Even death, he said to himself, even death with its sublime finality will be inconsequential here.

What would she say, he asked himself, if he told her that death was coming to her that night?

He was not going to tell her. She would never know. Nobody would ever know. It would be the perfect killing as he planned it, simple, easy, without hurt to her and beyond detection. He glanced at the smoldering gas heater set in the wall near the bed.

Sooner or later, she would be finished with the strokes she gave her hair. After that she would go to bed as always, and in bed she would, as always, soon be sound asleep. Nothing ever disturbed her sleep. Relaxed, nerveless, she would sleep nine, ten hours almost without stirring. All he had to do was to sit there and wait until she was well asleep. It would be very simple then, when she was well asleep.

No, he would not tell her, for that might defeat his purpose. Still there was a temptation to tell her, a strange, perverse temptation, merely to hear what she would say. Her reaction might well be singular. She, being she, might simply go on brushing her hair.

Once, on the night when first he discovered her perfidy, he had driven with her madly down a road that led straight to a cliff that dropped abruptly to the ocean. He was going to kill both of them, he had shouted.

She had been quietly smoking a cigarette despite the seventy-miles-an-hour speed of the car. She continued to smoke. She did not stir or cry out. She continued to smoke the cigarette.

It had been this strange, this extraordinary acceptance of the threat of death that had thwarted him that night. How could he kill someone who apparently did not care? There would have been no satisfaction for his frenzy in that. He had brought the car to a stop hardly two car lengths from the rim of the cliff.

But tonight was different. He was calm. He was particularly calm with the thought that the idea of death might very well not shock her. But tonight he would not tell her. Tonight, they were drawing near to the end of the intolerably futile and wretched journey, and there would be no turning back.

There could be no turning back, he felt, even if he had wanted it. All there could ever be would be a delay, a postponement of the end.

For the last year, there had been a strange inevitability to the direction of his life.

It would have made an interesting study for a psychologist, a chronicle of his life. Are there people inevitably destined for failure, no matter how great the efforts of others to help them? Are there people who carry with them, no matter where they are, a condemnation to failure?

2.

He, John Martin, was born twenty-six years ago in Santa Monica, California. So his chronicle would begin.

Then what should be told next? What would there be to tell that belonged in the beginning? His conceit, that should be told, his young conceit that often rose to arrogance and made him unconsciously rude and insolent. His unfounded conceit, for it had then no base in accomplishment. It came out of his instinctive feeling of superiority.

From the beginning, he had had a chronic faith in his

destiny. He would one day be great. How, he did not know. This dream, this faith, they belonged in the beginning.

Always he had been a youth apart; subjective, introverted. He had had none of the normal interests of his contemporaries—gambling, girls, surfing, sailing, tennis. He had been looked upon, not always favorably, as something of a character, and he had been pleased with the classification.

Psychotic, the sophisticated would call him. Mad, perhaps. Shy and bold at once. Silent with antagonisms that thundered in his brain. In the presence of girls, he had been both timid and arrogant. He had felt himself capable of a great passion, a superior passion. But he had never made any move to share his passion with girl or woman. It had seemed to him in his boyhood that his life was somehow dedicated to aloneness. Some of this feeling, he knew now, had been defensive, coming out of his shyness; some of it had led to loneliness. He had been a contradiction, he could see looking back: hungering for affection yet always alone.

His physical appearance was likewise in contradiction to the truth. He was tall and lean, clear-eyed, always apparently fit. Yet he never was fit. He was beset from his early boyhood with petty ailments: nervousness, sleeplessness, palpitation. All of which he considered somehow associated with his genius, his capacity for greatness. Out of good health, he would tell himself, came only platitudes and insensitivity, athletes and beauty-contest winners. His capacity to be ill, to be easily hurt, he considered a sure mark of his superiority.

All this belonged in the beginning.

His mother, she belonged in the beginning, too.

His mother talked, and lived, to a distant music and his ear for that distant music he had inherited from her. She, though hardly what could be called lettered, spoke beautifully, poetically, personalizing almost everything. He, like her, had little interest in the vernacular and sought studiously not to cultivate any further interest for it. An ear for the colloquial and an eye for the contemporary led, he had believed, almost invariably to mediocrity.

Often, when he was young, she, her housework done, would take his hand and walk him from their small conventional stucco house down to the steep palisades that overlooked the wide bay spreading the length of the horizon from Palos Verdes to Point Dume. It was a walk of a mile or so but it led to another world. They would sit on a bench and look out over the water, often for hours, sometimes even until the sunset. Those were times when she was given to silence.

She loved the Pacific and her silence was, in a way, a mark of this affection. She had come a long way to the Pacific, all the way from Concord, New Hampshire, where she was born and where she had married. The West, and the ocean of the sunset, had always been in her dreams and she had prodded his father on across the continent, stage by stage, Albany, Cleveland, Chicago, Omaha, Salt Lake, until at last the land of her dreams was reached. His father, a printer by trade, worked in each city on the long trek, and would have been content to have stayed on in any one of the cities but his mother, with her insistent dream, would not let him rest. Not that she expected any great opportunities in the West, or any change in his father. It was simply the poet in her following the sun.

Those silences of hers on the palisades were a tribute to her affection for the great ocean but there was more to them than that. His mother was a religious woman, and in her silences were meditation and prayer. Many of those prayers were for him he knew, and if they proved useless through the years, as they had, it was not because of any lack of faith on her part. Once when he was older, he came upon her, stopped reverently before the statue of St. Monica on the wide avenue that edges the palisades. He knew she was praying for him then, too. In one way at least, his mother had been blessed: the enigma of the perfect strength of her faith and the complete futility of her prayers never troubled her.

In any chronicle, there would have to be his father also, if for no other reason than that he had been the reason for his writing his play.

His father was a simple, conventional man, at ease in his normality, aspiring to little and envying no man. His English-Scotch parentage had given a plain hardness of fact to him.

Unlike his mother, his father had no religion and was in no way religious. Any awareness of divinity or divine precepts was not in his life. He loved his wife to the fullness of, his nature but he had no interest in her religion. He had no interest in any religion. He viewed her going to Mass with an affectionate, smiling tolerance, but this tolerance came from no particular virtue or philosophy, only from indifference.

Poor mother, how alone in her belief she had been! She had had him baptized in St. Monica's Church, her parish church, but, to her great sorrow, as the years passed he had grown to be like his father, without any religion at all.

His father had been the hero of his play. He was, in his easy normality, about as unheroic as a man could be, unheroic in the stage or storybook sense, and it was this unheroic quality that made him the hero of the play. His play. How that play once had been everything to him, the first accomplishment in the fulfillment of his destiny! Some of his chronicle would have to tell of his play. There was a time when he was sure that his play was a masterwork, a magnificent heretofore-unmade comment on the life of men, and that it would last as long as the life of men would last, growing in glory until the end. How presumptuous that seemed now, how insanely egotistical. The play appeared, was applauded, then disappeared, and now, hardly a year afterwards, was forgotten by all but him.

How well he remembered the evening the play came into being.

That evening, he and his father and mother had had supper as usual together in the kitchen. The spring day had been clear and warm but now a fog was sifting in from the bay. His father got up from the table but instead of going out to his pipe and paper in the living room as he invariably did, he went to the window that looked out on the back yard with its dried-up, crumbling fish pond and its scrubby lantana. After a moment, he said, "The lantana seems to be more purple this year, don't it?" Then he turned to him and his mother who were still at the table and said, "I might as well tell you now. It's as good a time as any. I've got a cancer here in my liver and the docs aren't very enthusiastic about it." He rubbed his hand slowly along his right side below his ribs. "They tell me not to get hopeless about it but I figure if I go another five or six months, I'll be doing fine. There isn't much sense in playing games about this sort of thing. We're all going to have lots of thinking to do, so I thought I'd tell you." He came back to the table and put his arm around his mother's shoulders. "It's that high living, that's what's done it, Mrs. Martin."

She got slowly to her feet. "No, John. No," she whispered. Then she sat slowly down again. She took the hand that was on her shoulder between her two hands. She held his hand tightly. When she spoke again, her voice, though a little higher pitched than usual, was completely controlled. "We'll pray to God, John. We'll pray to God and you'll be all right. You've been a good man. He'll take care of you. The doctors don't know everything."

His father smiled a little smile. "I won't be mad if they're wrong."

He, looking on, was too stunned to speak. Yet, for all of his shock, he saw his father and mother in a curious way. He saw them as a son would see a father and mother he loved facing a great tragedy but at the same time he saw them as actors in a scene. He saw them as a son but he also saw them as an observer. This scene should not be lost, he said to himself. It has a quality of greatness to it.

Two people, a man and wife, individuals with their separate gifts and idiosyncrasies but still only two people of the undistinguished, ordinary millions, greet death as he comes to their home and greet him with extraordinary dignity. His father's dignity came from his easy, natural courage and his mother's from her faith. But his father, for him, was the greater figure. Here he was, an ordinary man without religion or philosophy, without any sustaining power of any sort, accepting the great, dreaded absolute with ease and graciousness. All he had in life was life and all he had to look forward to was life, and here he was having it taken from him, and he could say, seeking to dull the hurt for his wife, "It's that high living, that's what's done it, Mrs. Martin."

Not a great speech, certainly, not even a very good one, but when spoken under the circumstances by an ordinary man without even the ordinary supports and resources of his kind, it took on the quality of greatness. His mother had her faith and its comforts and illusions but his father stood alone in midair. A small figure, yes, but in its gracious acceptance of the inevitable, a great one.

It was not until months after his father died that he thought of writing the play.

As he watched his father die, hardly ever faltering in his gracious acceptance of his dissolution, he grew angry at the senseless forces that were destroying him. His anger brought him near to madness. It was not only the sight of his father's life being wasted that enraged him but, even more, the sight of his graciousness being wasted. It was almost as if he expected death itself to appear and, in appreciation of his father's civility, grant him a reprieve.

At the end, when he saw him dead, he realized that his anger had been as irrational as it had been futile. He learned then that his father's was the finer part, that his graciousness in the acceptance of the inevitable was man's proper and best defiance of the natural powers of darkness and destruction. Only thus could he stand larger than the spinning suns and whirling constellations of infinitude. It was an experience he felt should not be left unrecorded. Thus he came to write his play which he called, *Defiance*.

The setting of the play was the living room of their little stucco house, plain but warm and bright with touches of color, as good a place as any for man to pause in on his way to death. The room in life had dignity, given to it largely by his mother's simple taste and by her graciousness and by his father's quiet presence, but to guarantee this dignity, should the setting ever be seen on the stage, he moved the house nearer to the bay. There, a sweep of the sea could be seen afar from the window, and he worked into the play the moods of the sea, especially as they affected his mother, and he added music from an amusement park on a pier some distance away.

He worked on the play for almost a year, testing each word, each line, acting out each part, and when he had finished, he felt he had written something of great importance.

He had met a writer who lived not far away and wrote for motion pictures and for magazines and he took the play to him. His name was Joseph St. Lawrence, and he would have to be in the chronicle, for he became his closest friend and, finally, his only friend. He knew that on tomorrow's morning St. Lawrence would be the only one on earth to mourn, even a little, his passing.

He had read a magazine story by St. Lawrence and had sent him a note telling him how much he liked it. The story was about the joys and sorrows of a little Negro boy who had been born without rhythm. He had rarely liked fantasies. To him, they were usually derived from ineffectuality and, quite often, were a form of deceit. But this was a good fantasy with roots in reality.

He was surprised some weeks later to get a letter from St. Lawrence in nearby Hollywood thanking him for his note and suggesting that perhaps he would join him at his house for a cocktail some evening. "The bar opens at five-thirty," he had written.

St. Lawrence lived high up in the Hollywood hills in a small cottage that was one of a group of similar cottages set on different levels on graded terraces. His tall living room window and his garden looked down on the great Hollywood plain. That first visit it was dark when he left St. Lawrence's and, for the first time, he saw the plain at night, spreading to the black faraway hills, a vast brocade, beaded and woven with millions of multicolored lights. It was a flat, twinkling immensity of lights that seemed to him to have suddenly appeared and to be about to disappear just as suddenly. He saw the lighted plain many times after that first night and the lights always gave him that same feeling of sudden newness and evanescence. St. Lawrence said they made him think of a fantastic carpet rolled out every night for some fantastic event like the Second Coming of Christ.

Tonight, later, he would see those lights once more and for the last time. It would be hard for him to realize they would be there tomorrow night again and he would not.

Yes, St. Lawrence would have to be in the chronicle. He would put him down as a tall, slender man who looks like an ascetic. He gets quite tipsy every night and recites poetry, and in the morning he is up with the birds and is as gay and clear-headed as any teetotal sunworshiper he'd ever known. If he had any regret tonight, it was that he would not see St. Lawrence again.

St. Lawrence read his play and thought it very fine. He did not stutter in awe as he discussed it but St. Lawrence was a man of superior taste and education and he was gratified by his reaction: St. Lawrence had one reservation. To him, it was a play of frustration and he did not care for plays of frustration. "In life, death always wins out over man," he said. "I'm for giving man a break in art."

He replied that, in writing the play, he had had no thought about giving anyone a break. He had tried to write the drama as he had seen it and for him it was a drama of triumph, not of frustration. His only motivation in writing it was an impelling desire to share his experience with others.

"As good a credo as most," St. Lawrence had said. "I'll send it on to my agent in New York with a letter. The play will be produced sooner or later and will have a fair run, and the New York critics will proclaim it a classic."

What St. Lawrence had predicted was very much what happened. The critics, while not proclaiming the play a classic, unanimously greeted it as an important event in the American theater. He was hailed as a genius out of the West.

"A genius out of the West," he repeated grimly to himself. Such was the golden promise. And what the fulfillment? I sit in this tawdry room, unremembered, unknown, waiting to kill this common woman.

3.

He continued to watch her brushing her hair.

She has brushed it more than a hundred strokes tonight, he said to himself. Could it be she wanted him to leave? She could be thinking that. It was curious, this long, long brushing of her hair. Still, she had never wanted him to go before.

It could also be that time, for him sitting there with his mind wandering into the past, had been drawn out and that she had been brushing her hair no longer than usual. Yes, that could very well be. She had never wanted him to go before.

The past was very much with him, there was no question about that. No playwright, he was sure, had ever had a success story such as his. He had had no training in writing for the stage, no experience in or with the theater, had hardly had any experience in life for that matter. And there he was, the darling of the critics and the theater crowd, a celebrity about town, a celebrity certainly about the expensive and affectedly exclusive cafés.

He liked Manhattan. He liked to walk the floors of its

great stone ravines, especially in the early morning before the city was awake. He liked the sights and sounds of its two wide rivers, gracefully carrying their burdens to the sea. He liked particularly the night sound of ships' whistles and fog-horns coming to him high in his hotel room twenty-two stories up in the dark. He liked Manhattan at dusk, too, when its lights, its million starred windows, seemed to sublimate it, seemed to lift the island into the sky like a mirage, seemed to set it magically afloat so that he had the feeling it might, at any moment in the mystery of dusk, ease its way out to sea, like one of its ocean liners.

It was autumn when his play opened, and in New York he discovered autumn. He discovered it on Long Island, in Westchester, in Connecticut. He had seen many pictures of autumn landscapes but still he was not prepared for the splendor flooding the hills and valleys. He had read of autumn's mood, of its melancholy, and yet he was in no way prepared for its wistful evocation of the enchantment of the last and endless sleep.

He had never known autumn in California and it had been a real discovery to him. It had, as much as any other influence, made him decide he wanted to stay in New York. But the final decision was not to be his to make.

His mother died in a way that would, he felt, have suited her. She had gone to her six o'clock Mass at St. Monica's Church as usual, had received the sacrament and returned to the dusk of her pew. She had knelt there for a minute, head bowed, praying, praying for his father and him, he was sure. Then she had slumped and died, her knees on the kneeling bench to the end. Cerebral hemorrhage, the doctor said.

He was surprised to see how few there were at her funeral. Not that it was anything to be chagrined at. Her dreams had been her closest acquaintances through her life. And her religious faith had populated the air with hundreds of friends, unreal but nonetheless present and alive to her. He was happy that, in his play if not otherwise, he had justified her confidence in his genius. Fate was kind to have taken her away when it did.

His mother's death had brought him back to California but it was a cinema company that was to keep him there.

When the play had first opened, he was sure it would run for years and years. But Jonquist, the agent, had chilled his enthusiasm. "If it lasts a couple of months," he had said, "we'll be doing fine. It's a critic's play. The best thing is to see if we can't sell it for pictures while it's still hot."

He, himself, had been skeptical about its being sold for a film. "Maybe fifty years from now when it's a classic, it'll be made into a picture," he had said.

"Maybe. Maybe," Jonquist had smiled. "But the best thing for us is to sell it while we're still alive. It'll be tough to sell, I agree with you there. It's an especially tough one to translate from the stage into pictures. But the picture-makers are translators, that is, the best of them are, and this'll be a challenge to them. This clamor by the critics, that'll give it a boost. The real picture-makers, the directors, don't want to make pictures for the public—that is, the best of them don't. They want to make pictures for the critics. Academy Awards aren't given on the basis of grosses. I can sell it. I got a hunch."

It was not, however, anyone in the studio who was responsible for the purchase of the play.

The president of the company in New York had seen the play with his wife. They both had been deeply moved by it. At first, he had no idea of it as a picture. But for days he and his wife found themselves talking about the play as if it had been a real experience.

One evening the wife had said, "We're not intellectuals and we keep talking about the play. It's about death, yes, but it seems as if we can't stop talking about it. Why wouldn't the public, if it was made into a picture, talk about it too?"

Her husband had shrugged. "I talk about it, my dear, because I've got to the age where I always keep a black tie in the top drawer of the dresser."

But the next morning he ordered the purchase of the play.

So, it had seemed at the time, the success story was continuing. He had checked out of his room in the hotel in Beverly Hills and was standing under the carriage porch waiting for a taxi to take him to catch the airport bus—indeed the taxi was already coming up the palm-lined driveway—when a bellboy brought out the telegram from Jonquist. Would twenty-five thousand dollars be a satisfactory price and would a six months' studio writer's contract for him, with options for five years starting at five-hundred dollars a week, be all right? His play could run only a couple of weeks more, Jonquist added as a sort of postscript, urging him to accept the offer.

Twenty-five thousand dollars, five hundred dollars a week. This was riches for him, and riches had, he supposed, a place in his dream of greatness though he hadn't thought much about it. He stood out on the carriage porch reading and rereading the telegram. He should have been jubilant but strangely he wasn't. The doorman waited for him, holding open the door of the cab. He slowly folded up the telegram, and then, suddenly, he had the impulse to get into the cab and go. But he didn't. He tipped the cab driver and the doorman and told them he would not need the cab.

He watched the cab roll down the drive and when it was gone, he felt something had gone with it. His play, perhaps. Manhattan. His future. One or all of them. He did not know. He had no clear thought about it, only a feeling, a vague strange feeling....

He drained his drink, his eyes steadfastly on the girl at the mirror. She, as if for the first time aware of his gaze, drew her robe more closely about her. This was a twist, certainly. She had never had any such self-consciousness before. Still she had been much too careful not looking at him when she drew the robe more closely about her. Could it ever be that the impossible was taking place, that she had somehow changed? That would be a switch to the story.

That might well be a story worth writing. The story of the two of them, the sordid story, with a switch at the end. It might make a play.

He cursed to himself. He was through with writing. Writing was not a man's job. It was an escape from living, writing was. At best, it was living vicariously. Anyway, what difference did it make what writing was? He was through with living. That's what made the difference.

What would have happened if he had taken the cab that day at the hotel? What would have happened if he had refused the studio contract and gone back to New York? All this was idle too. He had not taken the cab. He had gone to the studio.

4.

The studio, how far away that seemed now.

Manhattan was still very real to him, and the theater and his play. But the studio was like a picture, badly drawn in the first place and subsequently blurred. Yet, his months there belonged in the chronicle, not because of anything important that happened in those months but because, on the calendar, they marked the beginning of the long descent.

Two weeks after the telegram from Jonquist, his play closed in New York. The Monday following, he reported to the studio. His misgivings about his new life were as yet as slight as they were strange, and he approached his new career, as he had approached almost every experience in his life, with a determination to explore it for greatness. He had given up his dream of Manhattan and was resolved to become, so far as he temperamentally could, a member of the local community. He bought himself a cottage in the Hollywood Hills on a terrace above St. Lawrence's, a cottage that also looked down on the twinkling vast brocade of the Hollywood plain.

At the studio, a slick-haired, agreeable young man, who insisted on calling him "Mr. Martindale," settled him in an office on the first floor of the main administration building. The building was large, geometric, with long, rigorous corridors indented with many doors. The mood of the building, while hardly inspirational, was not depressing, having, as it did, a metallically bright, practical quality to it. It was the sort of building he associated with a scientific research institute, and as each door opened he expected to see in the room a large, silver-bright, highly complex machine or instrument at work. Instead, he saw men and women, looking very much like men and women everywhere. These, he learned, were writers.

His office was small and furnished for strict utility with two chairs, a desk, a typewriter and a telephone. In a drawer of the desk he found three scripts, left, he presumed, by writers who had been in the office before him.

The first few weeks at the studio he lived in a vacuum of silence. He knew nobody and nobody knew him. He had his lunch brought over by a waiter from the studio commissary and he ate by himself in the office. His telephone did not ring once. His only visitor was a salesman, a former writer who was now selling the Encyclopædia Britannica. He felt like an item filed away in an enormous filing cabinet. To use time, he read and studied the scripts that had been left in the desk.

He studied the scripts to learn what he could about writing for the camera. He invented exterior sequences for use in the filming of the play. One was laid in the amusement park on the pier, the music and sounds from which he had worked into the background of his play. In this sequence the son, his defiance of the callous fate that was so impersonally killing his gracious father reaching the breaking point, went into a frenzy one night in the amusement park on the pier, and savagely sought to destroy the gaudy signs and baubles advertising the tawdry pleasures of the park. The while the son was going berserk in the neon-lighted glitter, the father dozed quietly in his bed, dying.

He decided he would put the sequence down on paper. He telephoned the script department for a stenographer. She was a skinny, brazen, reddish young woman who sat on the corner of his desk and smoked cigarettes and was patronizing toward him.

"I don't like the sequence," she coolly announced to him after she had typed it. "I don't like it at all. It's too sad."

He was embarrassed more by her manner than by her comment. He felt, he answered apologetically, that there was a quality of audacity about the boy in the sequence that was interesting.

She had hardly listened to him. "Nobody in the studio likes your play," she said as if in justification of her opinion. "They think it's too sad."

Through the cigarette smoke, she saw the angry surprise on his face.

"Of course, nobody in the studio likes anything that's bought by the New York office," she said trying to ameliorate the cruelty of her remark.

He controlled himself. He turned deliberately away to the window, stared out at the red hibiscus bush that grew outside the window.

"My, but you writers are sensitive, aren't you?" she went on, and he could feel her voice dripping a smiling intimacy. "I ought to know. Guess I've worked for a hundred of them. I was even married to a writer. I've been here nine—no, let me see—no, I've been here ten years as of last week. How time does fly. Have you met Mr. Gordon yet? He's awful nice. Sometimes I substitute for his secretary when she's sick or on vacation. He calls me 'Miss Studio.' He's really nice."

This can't go on, he said to himself, not daring to let his eyes leave the hibiscus. This can't possibly go on. Fraternity is fine, friendliness is fine, but this is completely out of proportion.

She stopped only for an inhalation of her cigarette. "Are you married, Mr. Martin?" Her voice took on an insinuating quality. "I'm divorced. But I don't sit home and stare at the wall, not me. I keep myself available at all times."

This isn't petty, he groaned to himself, this isn't mere disproportion. This is vulgar.

"You're not as sad as your play, are you, Mr. Martin? Tell me."

He jumped to his feet and strode out of the office.

He walked up and down and around the sun-blistered streets in the neighborhood until evening came.

The three weeks of silence had been difficult enough but to drop into that silence this scene, that, he felt, was too much. He was not going to conclude from this stenographer that a cheap camaraderie was the key to life at the studio, though her presumptuous attitude did indicate that writers there were hardly considered high caste. But he did conclude from her, and from the silence, that the pattern of his life had been changed, had been cheapened. He felt this deeply and was uneasy about it.

He began to think again of the cab that had rolled down the palm-lined driveway and gone away without him.

On a morning, two days later, the telephone in his office rang. The sound of the telephone was so alien to the office, he listened to it ring for several moments before it occurred to him it was his telephone and he should answer it.

It was a Miss Valentine, Mr. Gordon's secretary, pleasant and casual. Would it be convenient for him to be in Mr. Gordon's office at two-thirty that afternoon? The pleasant casualness of the secretary raised his spirits. He responded in kind. He would try, he said, to arrange his affairs and, if humanly possible, he would be in Mr. Gordon's office at two-thirty that afternoon.

At two-thirty he was in Mr. Gordon's office.

Mr. Gordon was affable. He had read his play and he thought, he said, it was beautifully written. "It has rhythm," he said in his literary way. "It has meter." But he had not been in New York since the play opened and had not seen it. He had however, had the play photographed during a performance, and, if he didn't mind, they would go into the projection room now and look at the film together. On the way to the projection room, he remarked that the present plan was to make the play into a prestige picture with a good cast but a rock-bottom production cost.

"This has nothing to do with the quality of your play," he said sensitively. "No one would put a great deal of money into Ibsen's *Wild Duck* or Chekov's *Cherry Orchard*, would they?"

The camera had not been kind to the play. Pictorially, it came through in a dismal gray monotone. And the performances, only adequate to begin with, were now less effective having, through transference to film, been a further degree removed from reality. The somberness of the play, the somberness of death, had become more somber, and the brightness, the brightness of a man's courage, had become dim.

In the silence after the running of the film, he could feel Mr. Gordon's coolness to what he had seen.

"It's the first time I've seen the film," he said finally. "It's very brave, very. But it's going to take a lot of doing to make into a picture. A lot of doing. We're going to have to get it out of that house, for one thing. Move it around. Give it some imagery."

"I've been sort of working on that," he said. "I've been trying to adapt it to the camera."

He told Mr. Gordon of his night sequence with the son going berserk in the amusement park on the pier.

"Good. Very good," was his comment. "A move in the right direction." Then, he added, "Of course, the first thing is to get rid of the idea of cancer. Get rid of it completely. People recoil at the very mention of the word. It'd kill the picture just as completely as it—" he waved toward the white square of empty screen—"killed the character in the play."

The indifferent way he said "the character in the play,"

as if it were any character and not a unique and powerful one, annoyed him. But he restrained his ego and said quietly, "That film we've just seen, Mr. Gordon, that's hardly my play. The theme is lost in the drabness of the reproduction. My play is not about cancer but about courage."

"Exactly." Mr. Gordon got to his feet. "That's why you can eliminate it." They walked back toward his office. "How about heart trouble or TB?"

"Hardly, Mr. Gordon." He spoke up now. "The greater the threat, the greater the courage. Cancer, as a killer, approaches the absolute and it takes a courage approaching the absolute to defy it. My play isn't my play without it."

Mr. Gordon stopped at the door. "We're not making plays, Mr. Martin," he said with the sort of smile a chief of staff might assume while reproving a buck private. "We're making pictures."

Mr. Gordon went into the outer office. The skinny, brazen, reddish stenographer was sitting at the secretary's desk.

"The barber is waiting for you inside, Mr. Gordon," she sing-songed.

"Thanks, baby," Mr. Gordon said and disappeared into the immensity of the inner office.

That was the last he had seen of Mr. Gordon in his remaining months at the studio. Nor did he hear from him again, for that matter. He decided he had been judged uncooperative, and had been written off as a mistake.

It was little less than a year ago from those days in the studio until now, he mused, from those days of silence that began the long descent until here this night with this woman when it was finally reaching its end. Less than a year ago, almost an infinity ago…

5.

He had first seen her as she came through the doors into the smoky, light-smeared din at Sicilia's, the tawdry café in the shadows not far from the garish incandescence of Main Street, where he had finally touched bottom.

How out of place, how unutterably out of place, she had seemed that first night when she came through the doors, her singular womanness sheathed in white; narrow black bands on both her wrists, a narrow black band around her neck, her hair tawny in the streaked dark. How he had been astonished. And how he had been immediately stirred with a strange excitement.

She is in my destiny, this woman, he had said to himself. How, I do not know. It is fantastic, it is mad, and it is true.

Sicilia's had been the end of the road for him. Night after night he ended his wanderings there, in the first booth by the doors where best he could watch the degraded come and go, seated usually with Tommy, the bouncer. Poor Tommy, sitting there glowering and drinking beer, his derby, the badge of his authority, unremoved from his head.

Poor Tommy. Yet, why poor Tommy? Sicilia's was his Romanoff's. Here was his world, here were his people. Where else could he, in his forties, a one-time fighter, punch-drunk, his little, black cruel eyes revealing through their only infrequent flashes of understanding the bruised mind behind them, where else could he, his derby still on his head, sit in the first booth with power and authority?

Tommy glowered at one and all. That was the role he played. But still these people, these sots, these derelicts, these were his people, this was his world. This had become, in a way, John's world too.

The descent had been casual at first.

He had continued to go to the studio for almost two months. He had not been too sensitive at the silence. He had declared himself and his conceit sustained him.

In those days, he was still living in what St. Lawrence called "The Great Expectancy." Each morning he would tell himself, "This is the day," confident that that day he would turn a corner or answer a telephone or open a letter and the silence would end and greatness would greet him again.

But the silence grew. It became palpable, ponderable. And little by little, as silence followed silence, his confidence in the inevitability of his good fortune began to wane. The idea of failure, black and total, began to move like a shadow in the corridors of his mind. He fought the idea, proclaiming even more boldly than before his faith in his destiny. He fought it, changing his way of living, seeking out strange places and strangers and, especially, strange bars and bartenders and the strange phantoms that are found in the bottom of a glass.

Soon, all that was left of his former life was his house in the hills and St. Lawrence. He had given up going to the studio long before the six months' term of his contract was up, and nobody sent for him or inquired about him or communicated with him. He had tried writing another play but his new way of living, particularly his drinking, got in the way. His late nights consumed the days, and it began to seem as if he were hardly out of bed before it was dark and drinking time again.

The evenings he spent with St. Lawrence were the only ones now that were without blur and distortion, and even some of these evenings, after St. Lawrence and he had parted, would find him off on his own to downtown Los Angeles, taxiing from one dive to another, desperately trying to reach bottom.

Then, St. Lawrence was sent to Italy to work on a picture and all that remained of the past was his house, and as the weeks went by he saw less and less of that.

Two nights before St. Lawrence left for Italy, they had had a long evening together. He had always remembered that evening, but of late, and tonight especially, sitting here watching the woman at the mirror, he remembered it.

What were those lines St. Lawrence used to quote? How often, especially how often of late, had they echoed in his sodden brain. How did they go?

"For low they fall whose fall is from the sky."

That was one of the lines, but how did the others go? They were about the drink of immortality, he remembered that. He had memorized them. How did they go? It was this whiskey that was killing his memory. He was getting drunk and his memory was going. That was good. Whiskey is a great invention. Greater than the wheel, greater than the electric light. Whiskey, the Memory Eradicator. A great invention. But he must not get too drunk, not this night. How did those lines go? Yes, he remembered them now.

> Lower than man, for I dreamed higher.
> Thrust down, by how much I aspire,
> And damned with drink of immortality.

Yes, that was it. Damned with drink of immortality. That was he. Lower than man, for he dreamed higher, thrust down by how much he did aspire, and damned with drink of immortality. That was he.

St. Lawrence had been in a good mood that night. Slightly tipsy and very voluble. Talked and quoted, quoted and talked. Very literate, very well read. Had a fine education,

St. Lawrence had. Had a strong faith in fundamentals. Loyola of Los Angeles. The Jesuit college, where skyward soars the tower and westward dreams the sea. That's the way St. Lawrence put it, in a sort of poetry, when he was drinking. He had been nurtured, not damned with drink of immortality.

St. Lawrence had been gay and gracious that night and it had not occurred to him that in his quips and quotations his friend was warning him, warning him against himself, warning him his fall would be profound, for his fall would be from the sky. St. Lawrence hadn't warned him directly. He was too sensitive for that. The warning had been subtle, casual, a gentleman's warning, and St. Lawrence had been weeks gone before he realized it had been a warning at all.

St. Lawrence was a kind, a good friend. But had he shouted the warning at him and branded it across his forehead, it would still have been futile. Nothing, he felt, nothing could have altered the descent that led to the bottom, to complete failure, to this woman and to this night.

The telephone and the mail, they had been the meters measuring the silence as it enveloped him. At first when he moved to the house in the hills, the telephone rang often. Invitations. Friends. Agents. Girls he had met at parties wanting a part in his picture. Insurance salesmen. Promoters. So, on and on. Then, little by little, the telephone ceased to ring except when St. Lawrence called. When St. Lawrence left for Europe, it ceased to ring at all.

Hours, days, weeks went by without its ringing, without even the false hope of a wrong number. Sometimes he would sit and stare at the telephone, saying to himself, it can't, with me here pleading before it, it can't stay silent. It has to speak. But it did not. It was like a thing that once had life but had life no more, like a corpse. Sometimes when he was drinking he, his ego surging, would stand over it and command it to speak. He would shout at it. But no sound came from it. Here, in this city of millions, hundreds of thousands of people were telephoning one another but his telephone did not ring. The silence, as time went on, became more and more significant, more and more dramatic.

It had been the same with the mail. The mail, with its promise and variety, had always excited him. He never knew what new hope a letter from Jonquist might bring or what enchantment might be promised by a fine, linen envelope addressed in a bold, feminine hand. When the personal mail ceased to come, he comforted himself by reading the advertisements.

Then came the days when there was no mail, except a few bills at the first of the month. He would mope out from the bedroom in his pajamas, his mind cloudy, his body depressed from the last night's drinking, and in a desperate hope would search the slit under the door. There would be nothing, no even small white indication of an envelope. He would fling open the door in a more desperate hope. But there would be none in the patio outside. Then, he would look out on the vast Hollywood plain, prosaic and practical in the daylight, and he would think of the thousands of people who lived and worked there, and his pit of loneliness would seem deeper and emptier than it had ever been before. Sometimes a surge of defiance would sweep over him. You can't destroy my identity, he would say, no matter how many millions of you there are!

One morning, his nerves quivering after a night's particularly heavy drinking, he had rushed out into the patio and, in the open, had wildly shaken his fist down at the vast plain, shouting, "You mediocrities! You won't destroy me! I shall survive, whatever you do, and one day I shall triumph, and I shall throw your silence back into your confounded faces!"

He had discovered the Japanese gardener with popping eyes listening to his shouted defiance over the whirring of his gas-motored lawn mower a short distance down the lawn and, abashed and suddenly limp, he had backed into the house and quietly closed the door. Inside, he had poured himself a stiff drink of whiskey. It was the first time he had drunk whiskey in the morning.

He looked down at the glass he held in his two hands. He could not blame whiskey. It had not caused the descent. It had only eased it.

He glanced at the watch on his wrist. Eleven minutes of twelve. Sicilia's would be blearily smoky now, convulsed with bodies dancing, brawling, noisy with coarse laughter, cursing, music, singing. He could see Tommy in the first booth, his derby black over his pasty face. He was sorry he would not see Sicilia's again.

He looked back at the woman at the mirror. How well he remembered that first night he had seen her at Sicilia's.

That night he found a reason for Sicilia's. Its place in his destiny, that was its reason, he had told himself. Now, as she entered into the streaked, smoky din, her hair tawny, her superbly drawn womanness wrapped in white, he had said to himself, this is ordained.

"Slummers," Tommy had growled as she and her escort moved down to an empty booth across the floor. Tommy did not like slummers, the dilettantes who toured the nether world with a patronizing air that in no way concealed their prurient curiosity.

The escort was in his early forties, well-groomed, urbane, with a Palm Springs tan and the jowls and paunch of a man of pleasure. As they moved toward the booth, the dive was hushed a moment and all eyes watched her, a hush broken only by the wail of the juke box and the breaking of a glass. After she was seated, the din rose again, sordid, hysterical as before, and she became another shadowy creature of the smoky haze. But not to him.

He did not take his eyes off her but she appeared to be unaware of his gaze. Still he knew she knew.

His feeling of excitement grew. It had been ordained, he told himself, that they should meet, and with her he would rise and walk the sky again. It was insane for him, a derelict sitting in the booth with the shabby Tommy, to think this way. He was mad, there was no question about it. Still, what he thought, what he believed, he was profoundly certain was true.

He so deeply concentrated his gaze on her that she would, he thought, be compelled to feel the physical pressure of it. Still she did not turn her eyes once his way. The escort had ordered Scotch highballs. After tasting his drink and finding it watered, he had put it aside, and gone to the bar to negotiate with the bartender for the purchase of an unopened bottle of whiskey. Now she was alone and this was his opportunity, he told himself.

He grabbed a pencil and pad from his waiter and wrote quickly, "You are my destiny and I love you!"

Underneath he had scribbled his name and telephone number. It was childish, this note, he knew now, but how inspired he had thought it that night.

The waiter delivered the note. She read it, calmly, easily. She glanced his way. It was the least of glances, casual but appraising. She did not look his way again.

She and her escort sat closely together, watching the sordid pageant, until they had finished two drinks. Then they rose to go, leaving the almost full bottle of whiskey on the table behind them. They passed the first booth closely enough for him to touch her. But she did not look at him.

Still he knew that she knew.

"You are my destiny and I love you!" Yes, that had been preposterous. It had been proved preposterous. Yet, now, this night, sitting here in this tawdry room with this same woman in all the final emptiness of his disillusionment, he could feel a surge of the excitement he had known that night in Sicilia's.

He had left Sicilia's soon after she was gone. He had the extraordinary thought she might call him that night. In his new confidence nothing was impossible. He had sat up till daybreak.

The next day he did not leave the house, moping through its emptiness hour after hour, waiting for the telephone to ring, for the corpse to come to life. As night came, there was a moment when he doubted. Why should she ever telephone him? How would she ever know he was not another creature crawling in the slime of Sicilia's? That was exactly what he had been doing, wasn't it? Why should he expect her to know in her brief appraising glance that those were not his people, that he was a stranger?

Then, as if in answer to his doubt, the telephone rang. It was the first time it had rung in months. With its ringing, his doubt vanished. He walked to the telephone very slowly. He knew it would not stop ringing. He knew when he picked it up it would be she.

6.

She lived in a small apartment on a tree-arched street near Santa Monica Boulevard on the fringe of Beverly Hills. She was dressed in a formal dark red evening gown as she opened the door to meet him. The gown did not strike him as being too elaborate, too much for the occasion. Nothing could be too elaborate or too much for this occasion, it seemed to him. He had dressed his best in his dinner jacket. He would have worn a white tie and tails if he had had them.

Their greeting had been quiet, easy. She, as he was to learn, was not given to words, and he was in awe of this moment which he felt so deeply was meant to be.

He asked her out to dinner. But she had had a little supper earlier and did not feel like dinner. He had had no dinner but he did not feel like dinner either. Neither mentioned Sicilia's or the note, or commented on the extraordinariness of their meeting. It was extraordinary enough but, for him, it had been so long ago plotted in his stars that he could not become vocal about it. For her, it was another experience, met in a way, as he learned, she met all experiences, great or small, with an almost wordless acceptance.

They sat, and he talked of inconsequential things, mostly of the apartment. It was very small, new, modern, clean and uncluttered, warm with wood, bright with chrome and glass. It was made for cloudless living, he said.

He could see into the bedroom through an open door. There were long draperies on the windows and he noted with curiosity that the color of the draperies was exactly the deep red of her gown. He was going to comment when he observed on the dresser in the shadows of the bedroom a cheap, vaguely luminous, blue-and-white ceramic madonna, the same cheap madonna that now stood on the shelf on the wall of this tawdry room here by the sea. It was a false note, false in the modern decor, and an archaism in the modern living the decor reflected.

His eyes came to rest on her, and there was silence. His heart beat strongly, rapidly. His hunger, his desperate, immature hunger for her was, he knew, burning in his eyes. She had to have seen it, had to have sensed it, but she spoke no word and sat in an indolent ease that was more challenging than any show of passion. It couldn't be indifference, he assured himself. Hadn't this hour been preordained?

In the silence, he got to his feet. Be quiet, he told his heart, be quiet. He walked deliberately toward her, determinedly slowing his pace. Be quiet, my heart, he said again, be quiet. All this was meant to be. He stopped before her, looked down on her bare, finely drawn firm shoulders. He put a hand on her shoulder and fitted it into the curve of her neck. Could she feel his hand trembling? She gave no sign.

He took her by her wrists, lifted her to her feet. Slowly, he took her into his arms. She was as he knew she would be, strong, substantial, with life latent. With her would he find fulfillment, with her would he become complete....

Those weeks, those first weeks after they met, how frantically happy life had been for him, how crazily, suddenly turned upside down!

He lived in an almost hysterically high excitement, up soon after daybreak every day and at work on a new play, drawing most of his sustenance from coffee, oblivious now to the diversions of daily life, unmindful even of the daily newspapers. His day began with his work and ended with her.

Every evening he would call her and race down out of the hills to her apartment. He lived only to be with her. Some evenings she would not be home and he would be desolate. But his desolation left him immediately he saw her again.

Little wonder in those days that St. Lawrence had, in his amused way, grown even more skeptical of his sanity. He was back from Italy and one day he had come up to invite him out for lunch. He had refused, indicating the coffeepot on the electric warmer on the low table beside him.

"I have no interest in the conventional," he had answered St. Lawrence. "I'm living life in all its essentials for the first time. I've grown young, and I'm seeing patterns and colors in life I have never seen before. I was born old, you must remember." Then he added jauntily, "'When half-gods go, the gods arrive.' Emerson certainly knew the workings of genius."

"Love or passion?"

"Both," he had answered. "Both intermingled magically, beautifully."

"Am I invited to the wedding?" St. Lawrence had asked. "I want to be sure to have my striped trousers pressed."

He had been unaware of St. Lawrence's subtle cynicism. "You are to be the best man!" he exclaimed. "Just as soon as I finish my new play." He had waved to the manuscript on the table. "I'm writing a truly great play. About a woman. About a woman and a man's soul, a man's artistic soul."

"Really?" St. Lawrence made no effort to hide his smile of skepticism.

"You can't understand! You can have no idea of the importance of my play until you meet the woman!"

"Aren't you overdoing everything a little bit?" St. Lawrence had asked.

"'Nothing succeeds like excess,'" he had quoted Wilde in reply.

St. Lawrence had gone away, shaking his head in mock despair.

St. Lawrence had been his only friend but the day came when he gave even St. Lawrence up.

She had come up to the cottage one evening and he had invited St. Lawrence over to meet her. He had made them cocktails and had himself stayed with his coffee. He was deeply disappointed that St. Lawrence had not made more ado over her. He was gracious, as he always was, but she was apparently just another woman to him. And the next day, when St. Lawrence's only comment on her was, "She's a few years older than you, isn't she?" he was angered. He made it a point not to see or talk to him again.

7.

He had never before felt so profoundly his dependence on her as he did the night he discovered her perfidy. He had worked out in the patio from early morning till dusk. With the coming of dusk, the million lights began to twinkle in the world below, and the evening became slowly vast and empty. He began to feel very small and alone before the spreading multiplicity of the lights and the dark arched immensity of sky. He felt a deep need for her.

He telephoned her and there was no answer. He waited and telephoned again. Still she was not there. He felt more and more alone. He could see the lamp-lit windows in St. Lawrence's bungalow on the terrace below. He knew how pleasant it would be there but his pride would not let him call. He drew the draperies of his windows, shutting out the lights and the evening. He felt more alone. All he had was she, in all the length and breadth of the world.

He turned on all of the lights inside. He made himself a new pot of coffee and drank from it. He telephoned again and still there was no answer. His loneliness grew. The loneliness of the house, the emptiness of the night began to unnerve him. He had to see her.

He got into his car and drove recklessly down the steep, winding road to Sunset Boulevard.

It was night now, and streaming automobile headlights mazed the boulevard, and the entrances to the night clubs and cafés were aglow with the coruscating costume jewelry of their lights. The spangled excitement of the boulevard made him even more lonely, and he continued to drive recklessly west and then south until he was before her apartment house.

He was certain he would find the windows in her apartment house lighted when he got there. But the windows were dark, dark, it seemed to him, with a hollow lifelessness. He was more depressed. He had a feeling that this was wrong, a betrayal of the new order of his existence.

He went into the vestibule of the apartment house and pushed the buzzer to her apartment. There was no response. He knew it was useless but in his desperation he continued to push the buzzer as if by his very insistence he might somehow summon her presence.

As he stood in the vestibule pushing the button, the manager of the apartment house, a tall, gray woman in a dark gray dress, came out from her first-floor apartment and approached him. Was he Mr. James? she asked.

He hesitated before answering, and in that black moment he had a sudden presentiment that the worst had happened and he had come to the end of all things.

Yes, he was Mr. James, he lied.

She smiled. Miss Garden wasn't sure he was in town, she said. She had left a message for him. She gave him a slip of paper. Miss Garden would be at that address, she indicated the writing on the slip of paper, and he could, if he wished, meet her there.

The manager returned to her apartment. He stood in the vestibule with the slip of paper in his hand. His presentiment was true. She had betrayed him.

He went to his car and drove slowly back north toward Sunset. Then, as he drove, he realized he could not return to the empty cottage in the hills. He could never endure there, with this cold dread in his heart, the lonely hours till the morning. He could never argue himself out of it. He would go mad.

He stopped the car, turned around and started south toward Wilshire Boulevard. There was only one thing for him to do. Go to the address on the slip of paper, see her somehow and demand the truth. Go now, dread or no dread. This minute.

The address was that of a house on a quiet, residential street off Olympic Boulevard. It was a white stucco house, Monterey style, with a red tile roof and a wooden balcony and a great dark oak front door. A misted yellow light shone from a heavy bronze fixture over the arched doorway and, through the drawn draperies of the tall, front window, he could see a faint glow of light inside.

He walked slowly up the curved, flagstoned walk toward the door, not wanting to face her, knowing his happiness and his future were tragically in the balance.

He stood for a long minute at the door. He braced himself and pushed the button.

After several minutes, a small window set at eye level in the door was opened. Through the ornamental black iron grill before the window, he could see the sallow brown splotched face of a mulatto woman.

He was Mr. James, he said, and could he speak to Miss Garden.

The face withdrew, the little window was closed. There was silence. Then, after what seemed like many minutes, he heard a bolt being slid back. The door was opened. The mulatto woman, in a fine black dress with narrow white cuffs and a narrow white collar, nodded him in with a small, routine smile. She bolted the door and led him into a large living room just off the entrance hall.

It was a dispiriting room, shadowy in a falsely dim light, artificial with a pseudo-oriental decor. It was a spurious room, especially so in contrast to the modestly shaded white stucco and the wholesome wood and tile of the Monterey exterior of the house. He wanted to turn and rush out into the California night. But he knew he could not. Now, after the bolted door and the ugly insinuation of this room, he knew he had to face her.

The recorded voice of a man singing sobbed into the room. It came from beyond the magenta-draped wide opening at the rear of the room. Lifelessly, he moved back toward the opening. Now he could hear the tinkle of glasses, then the sudden sound of a raucous masculine voice followed by a chorus of women's laughter.

He looked through a slit in the draperies. Beyond was a small playroom, dim and smoky. Against the walls were gambling machines and the cabinet of an automatic record-player from which the wailing voice came. On the cabinet lay a Stetson hat.

He opened the slit in the draperies and peered further into the room. Now he could see a small bar, chrome-bright in the dimness of the window side of the room. Before it were four girls in long formal dresses. With them was a tall, heavy man in a wide-brimmed Stetson. Behind the bar, a scrawny woman with a long face and one bad eye was pouring drinks. She wore a dark green housecoat with an artificial yellow flower on her shoulder.

So this is where his love had come. His emptiness, his lifelessness left him. He felt a great anger. He had a sudden desire to destroy all he saw. Then, he heard her voice behind him.

"I'm sorry," the voice said.

He wheeled and saw her standing in the dim light of the living room just inside the door. She wore the dark red formal evening gown she had worn that first night in her apartment. It was the gown that he had thought she, intuitively aware of the preordination of their meeting, had worn for the great occasion. All it had been was the routine costume of the profession. The decoy of elegance. Routine. So had been the matching of the bedroom draperies with the dark red of the gown. So had been her calling him the night after Sicilia's.

She stood on the edge of the cheap oriental rug, relaxed, patient, as if waiting for his pleasure. He looked at her but his anger would not let him speak. Here she was, his great love. The woman of his destiny!

Behind her, in the entrance hall, he saw the mulatto woman draw the bolt on the door and admit two tall young men in dinner jackets. They were airily drunk. This was a lark. They would be volatile, they would be gay.

They saw her just inside the door.

"Hi, Goldilocks," one of them called out.

"Rejoice Lorelei!" the other cried. "The great lover cometh!"

Then they discovered him in the deep of the shadowy room, noting, as they must have, the anger taut on his face.

"Oh, this dance taken?" the first youth grinned. "Beg pardon."

"Looks like a husband," the second said, making a face of mock terror.

Laughing, they continued down the hall toward the playroom. She gave only a casual glance after them. Routine. Just more routine.

His anger surged to his brain. He rushed at her. He slapped her face. Twice, three times, he slapped her face. He grabbed her upper arm, sank his fingers into its flesh and whirled her toward the door. He drew the bolt, flung open the door and pushed her headlong out, shutting the door behind him.

Outside, on the flagstoned walk, he seized her again, pushed her out toward his car. She did not resist. She met his violence with the resigned acceptance with which she met all things. He pushed her into the car.

He had driven wildly down Olympic Boulevard to the Coast Highway and continued on north. There were no policemen on the road but had there been it would have made no difference.

He would have raced any motorcycle or patrol car to his goal and he would have gotten there first. Any building would have served his purpose, any sturdy wall or embankment.

He was going to kill himself and her.

Blurredly in his mind was the idea of driving the two of them over the cliffs into the sea at Point Dume north of Malibu. The steep drop into the dark Pacific had a lure for him. It seemed a cleaner way to die, and more absolute and complete. But it was not important to him where the end came so long as it came.

He did not speak, nor did she. His silence was angry, fiercely concentrated, but hers was quiet, almost casual. They raced by the towering palisades where, he remembered in the blur of his mind, his mother and he used to sit and look over the bay and dream for hours on end. They roared along the dark highway that edged the sea. They passed the Malibu Colony set off by itself on an angle from the highway, a row of misted lights against the black water. They raced on through the beginning of the ranch country and when they turned left from the highway into the road that led to the cliffs of Point Dume, he spoke for the first time.

"I'm going to kill you! I'm going to kill both of us!" he shouted at her.

She, despite the wildness of the ride, had lit a cigarette and was smoking it. Now, after he had shouted, she made no stir or cry, revealed no panic, no, even, trace of fear. She continued smoking.

It stopped him, this quiet acceptance of his fury. He could not go on with his purpose. He had wanted to kill her and himself, not only to end once and for all his heartbreak and his inexorably futile existence but also to make her suffer as she had made him suffer. But she continued to smoke her cigarette. This was not the end as he had wanted it.

He slowed the car down, stopped it a few yards away from the edge of the cliff. He began to tremble. She put a hand on his arm. He shook it off and dropped his head to his arms on the wheel.

Now, his head still on his arms, he could hear her talking, she who had almost never talked. She spoke without emotion, in short sentences of mostly nouns and verbs, in simple, primitive speech. She had not told him about her life, she said, because he seemed happy and if she had told him it would have made him unhappy. She had not wanted him to be unhappy. She liked him, mostly because he was strange and talked as if he needed her. But she did not love him. She felt no need of him.

The life she lived, she said, she had been living since she was seventeen years old. She liked it. She had no wish to be any man's wife. Wives were different people to her. She did not like them or dislike them. She had no interest in them.

She liked her life in her apartment but sometimes she got lonesome for the life in a house such as the house tonight. Then, she would go to such a house. She didn't know why. She liked the women who lived her life. Perhaps that was it. She liked it that the men in such a house were almost always strangers, and came and went and were forgotten. Perhaps that had something to do with her going. She liked the music and the air of excitement and the feeling of being in a house that was not like other houses. Perhaps that was it. She did not know. Perhaps it was that through her life she had known so many of such houses and the women in them were her people and that was why she would get lonesome sometimes and go to them. She guessed that was mostly it.

After a while he was able to look at her without revulsion. Her natural candor had softened his anger if it had not softened his despair. His madness left him, and he felt only pity, pity for himself as well as for her....

8.

She finished at the mirror and got to her feet. She walked to the bed with one last glance over her shoulder at herself in the mirror.

A little while before at the mirror she had been careful

about her robe. Now, going to bed, she was careful again. Could it really be there was something going on in her mind that had not gone on in her mind before?

She sank deep under the covers. Still she had not looked at him. "I'm sleepy," she murmured. "Don't forget to put out the heater. Good night."

That was all she said, and in its intonation there was nothing to reveal even slightly what was in her mind. She had said very little through the evening, less even than usual. He had said nothing. Any talk would have been inane and superfluous. Any interest in what was going on in her mind now would be similarly inane and superfluous. In a few minutes she would be asleep, and what was in her mind, if anything was in her mind, would never be spoken.

It had been a short brief journey from that night on Point Dume to this tawdry bungalow and this final hour.

As they had driven along the Coast Highway that night, on the way back to the city, a full moon had risen pale and large over the massed blackness of the Santa Monica hills. On the level ground against the hills, they had come upon a bungalow court, set in a small grove of tall eucalyptus trees. He had stopped the car on the ocean side of the road, just above the gleaming spray and foam of the luminous surf.

The bungalows in the court had a facing of logs to suggest log cabins and these, with an imitation well and its wooden bucket in the middle of the court, gave the place an air of obviously false and cheap rusticity. Still, the tall, slender eucalyptus trees swayed above the bungalows, and the shining ocean was only across the road from them, and the moonlight with all its magic was over them, and behind them were the steep, high, proud dark hills.

In his desperation, in his deep need for her, an idea had come to him. It had come faintly at first, vaguely, but his desire had enlarged and distorted it till it had become strong and persuasive. If she could move to a place near the cleansing ocean and under the uncluttered sky, might she not leave her past behind her and learn to live a new life with him?

He had told her the idea. He had elaborated emotionally on it. His desperation had fed his hope as he talked, and his idea had become a conviction, and again, slowly, he had succumbed to his old delusion. Yes, truly all this was meant to be, he had persuaded himself....

There was a bungalow-for-rent sign on a stake in the ground at the entrance to the court. He had been sure this was a good omen, of pertinence to their lives.

She had reluctantly consented to the idea. It was only out of her sympathy for him at the moment, he knew now. But at the time he had convinced himself it was all part of a larger plan, their coming upon this place in the moonlight.

He had rented the bungalow that very night.

The next morning, he put his house in the hills up for sale.

Each day he had continued to go to the house in the hills, not merely so he could meet any prospective purchasers but because he was driving himself at his writing and his going had kept him, while working, away from the distraction of her presence.

Two weeks had gone pleasantly by. Afternoons or at night, he would drive down to be with her. She had seemed content.

Then, in the afternoon of the day before, he had telephoned her he would not be down until very late. He had had an uninspired day and was only then beginning to write.

She had spoken as always over the telephone, expressing no disappointment, saying little in her indolent, physical voice. Later, when dusk came to the hills and the million lights began to fret the immensity of the plain below, he had, as he often had at this hour, become painfully lonely for her. He had given up his work and, getting his car, had driven down to the shore.

It was dark when he reached the bungalow. She was not there.

He put on the lights and waited. He made coffee, sipped it and read a magazine and waited. An hour passed and she did not come.

He went outside. The night was clear with many stars high in the heavens. He stood in the starlit dark and watched the surf for a long time, only because he did not want to return to the bungalow. He knew the truth now. He watched the surf, monotoning his mind to its monotony.

He went back to the bungalow, got in his car and drove slowly into town. He turned from Wilshire Boulevard into the street that became a quiet, residential street as it neared Olympic Boulevard. He stopped near the shaded stucco house. He walked up the curved, flagstone path to the big, dark oak door.

He pressed the door button and waited. He waited without dread, waited emptily, wearily. In the time he had watched the monotony of the surf, almost all feeling had gone from him.

The little window behind the ornamental iron grill was opened and in the oblong opening appeared the sallow brown, splotched face of the mulatto woman.

"Miss Garden?" he asked. "I was here one night a couple of weeks ago."

The mulatto woman smiled her small routine smile. She closed the little window. She drew the bolt on the door.

She was in the house, he knew then. He had little feeling of any sort. He had known she would be there in that house back among her own when he had stood in the starlit dark on the beach and watched the waves breaking.

He turned and walked away from the door, walked down the curved, flagstone walk. He heard the door open but he did not turn around to look. He heard the door close and the bolt slide back into place.

The street was very quiet as he got into his car. He drove north to Santa Monica Boulevard and turned east....

That had been last night, a long, blurred night of cocktail bars. One of his last memories of it was his awakening St. Lawrence at five that morning to tell him he was a wise and good man.

9.

He watched her head on the pillow. He could not see her face beyond the raised covers, only her forehead and her blond hair. He could hear her breathing. It was deep, measured, but not yet deep enough.

She had fallen asleep as if nothing had ever happened between them. Could it ever be that the mulatto woman had not bothered to tell her of his visit to the door of the house the night before? That was difficult to believe. She would certainly have reported his coming to the door and his strange going away. Still she had said nothing.

He listened to her steady breathing. The answer to his curiosity became less and less important. In a little while it would have no importance at all.

Late that afternoon, after he had awakened in his cottage in the hills, he had observed with bleary and painful vision the rainstorm sweeping the world beyond his window. It was the storm that had given him the idea that got him out of bed and started him drinking again and drove him to drive down here to her.

It was good, this storm. It still grew in anger, as the gale driving it in from the ocean grew in strength, and the rain was now like a whip wildly lashing the house. The eucalyptus trees' cry had become a continuous moan, and their soaken leaves whirled and swirled on the roof in a melancholy ferment. He was grateful to this storm. Its music fitted the hour but more than that, it fitted his plan. It made easier his killing her, made it simple, beyond hurt to her and beyond detection.

His gaze shifted from her head on the pillow to the smoldering gas heater set in the wall. It was a sallow flame and it smelt meanly of scorched paint but it would serve his purpose well. The vent to the heater opened on the roof but the inverted top to the vent had, he knew, long since been blown away and now the vent opened flush on the roof. In a storm, leaves from the eucalyptus trees fell to the roof and choked the vent. The swirling leaves had choked it now, else the rain would be dripping down the vent and sputtering in the flame.

He listened to her breathing. It grew deeper, more measured. All he had to do was to sit and wait a little while longer. Then he would put out the light and go, closing the bedroom door after him—the door that now, leading into the little front room with its small fireplace, provided the only ventilation.

It would not be he, to make a fine point of it, who would kill her. It would be the heater that would kill her. It would consume the oxygen in the bedroom and consume her life too. Another death from a faulty gas heater. Another of many thousands of such deaths, week in week out, year in year out.

He would go to his house in the hills to keep his own rendezvous. An overdose of sleeping pills. Many a man while drinking had taken an overdose of sleeping pills. The two deaths would be simple, unconnected. No weeping, no disturbance, and afterwards, no associating the two of them in the newspapers, no cries of suicide pacts, no headlines of double killings. No scandal, no sensationalism, no public fuss and bother.

They would be well written, these final scenes, easy, natural, with no trace of the author. He looked into his glass. It was: almost full. He lifted it to his lips and drained it. She was sleeping deeply now. He got to his feet.

He made a step toward the bed and staggered. He grabbed the top of the chair and steadied himself. He must get control of himself. He must be calm, well ordered. He must not fail again as he had failed that night on the cliffs at Point Dume.

He moved again, this time a little more steadily. He moved to the edge of the bed and looked down on her. He touched her hair ever so slightly. Now, he said to himself, for the first time in all of my life, I dare meet reality face to face. Now there are no longer any wild ideas of destiny or patterns plotted in the stars. Now no longer am I victimized by fantasy or any other form of deceit. Now before me is the coldly rational reality of death. Yes, death is near for you and near for me.

You, Rena, incurable wanton, have completely destroyed me. I will destroy you. I will put you out of your wretchedness. I will put myself out of my wretchedness. Not life was ordained for us in our meeting, not life but death.

Goodbye, he whispered, goodbye to you. Goodbye to me....

10.

He was asleep, deeply, inertly asleep and he knew dimly he was asleep and he wanted to awaken but could not, and he had the feeling he was straining to lift an unendurably heavy weight from his body, a weight that had made him feeble and had smothered his breathing and stifled his brain.

He tried to close his hands but he could not bring his fingers up to meet the palms of his hands. If he could only close his hands, he felt, he would be able to get a grip on reality and stem his drift back into unconsciousness. But he could not close his hands.

He heard a voice at a great distance, then a second voice, but what they said he could not tell.

He felt a sting in his arm, a faint, dull, faraway sting. After a moment, he was able to close his hands, not firmly but limply, skin barely touching skin.

He opened his eyes. The lids were intolerably heavy and he closed his eyes again. In the moment they were open, he could see it was night and he was in bed in his own bedroom and there were two blurred figures of men in the room, one of which was familiar, though who it was he could not remember.

He heard a telephone bell ring. That was strange, the ring of a telephone in his house. Then his consciousness ebbed. His hands opened and he could not close them again. Sleep again came over his dim awakeness like the slow snuffing of a weak, small candle flame.

Now, he felt the sting in his arm again but this time not

so faint and faraway and, after a while, he heard voices, the same voices and they too were nearer. Now he could tell that one of the voices was familiar though whose it was he could not remember.

He opened his eyes. Now he saw it was daylight. The house and terrace were in deep shadow and he knew it was late afternoon. There were two figures of men in the room but this time they were not so blurred and one was a tall man with white hair and a young face and the other was St. Lawrence.

St. Lawrence saw his eyes were open and, smiling, he moved to the bed and took his hand. "How goes it, laddie?" he asked.

He tried to speak but could not. His head ached painfully. He could close his hands but his mind was heavy with a great weariness. He fell asleep again.

When he opened his eyes again he was alone in the room. It was morning. At first, he could feel the brightness rather than see the sunlight slanting down through the open window to the floor. Then, little by little, his vision cleared and his lethargy went from him. His head still ached dully.

He could now see through the window the great plain far below shining bright in the busy practical light of the morning. The plain was the last thing he remembered.

He had come back from the bungalow at the beach that night, Saturday night, and had come into the dark house and had not turned on the lights. He had seen the world below the window glowing with its myriad multicolored lights through the dark and the rain. The sight had inspired him to make a final gesture.

He had groped in the pantry and found a bottle of whiskey and poured himself half a tumblerful. He had stood there by the window in the dark and, looking down through the storm on the lights, had lifted up his glass in a toast. "Congratulations, you mediocrities," he had said. "Mine is the defeat and the failure, yours the victory."

His final gesture, his final, childish gesture. He had drained the drink. That was the last thing he remembered.

He had let himself get drunk. For all his resolution, he had bungled, he had failed. In his attempt at dying as in his living he had been a failure.

He was weary again. Had he failed at the beach too? Had he closed the bedroom door firmly after he left? He tried to remember. Why hadn't he made sure and jammed the vent with leaves? What a bungler, he cursed himself, what a blunderer.

Why had he got drunk? And why had he wanted to be so subtle, so flawless? He had a revolver, a loaded .32, right here in the drawer of the table by his bed. Why hadn't he taken it with him to the bungalow and killed her and himself like a man? It would have been vulgar and messy, and he would have been smeared across the newspapers from coast to coast. But what difference would it have made to him? He would have been dead. He and his idiotic conceit of himself as a dramatist! He had wanted the last scene to be without any trace of the author, the last curtain to fall on an empty stage. What imbecility!

Suppose she was alive. Would she suspect what he had tried to do? If she was dead, were the police called in? If she was dead, he, alive, was guilty of murder. He, dead, would be just as guilty of murder. But he, dead, would not know, would not be able to think about it, would not care.

Murder. It was an ugly word for one alive. It was an ugly idea for one alive. Murder, the unforgivable crime, the outrage for which no restitution could be made. Was he still drunk? Was it all a drunken dream?

He botched everything, living and dying. Everything except his play. Everywhere and always failure. Except for his play. How did the play ever happen? All this was worse than before. Sane or insane, drunk or sober, murder or no murder, he must end it. This time he would not bungle. This time it would be clean and final. Abruptly, angrily, he reached out to the table by his bed and pulled the drawer open. His violence sent the table lamp crashing to the floor.

The door to the bedroom was almost immediately opened and a plump, white-haired woman in a nurse's white uniform appeared in the doorway. "Well," she said pleasantly with a smiling glance at the fallen lamp, "you woke up with a bang, I'd say. How do you feel?" She moved over to the bed and picked up the lamp and set it back on top of the table, talking the while. "Bet you're hungry. People come out of those things very fast. How about some breakfast? How about some bacon and eggs?"

The telephone in the hall began to ring.

"That's probably that Mr. Gordon again," she said as she started out. "He called twice yesterday." She stopped in the doorway. "Do you think you're up to talking to him if I bring the telephone in?"

He shook his head. "What day is today?"

"Tuesday," she said and went on into the hall.

Tuesday. He had been asleep for more than two days. And the telephone had been ringing.

It had never rung in the days when he had pleaded with it to ring. And Mr. Gordon? Why should Mr. Gordon call? It had been almost a year since he talked to Mr. Gordon. Probably was chairman of some charities fund and was calling for a contribution. But why should he call twice yesterday? It was some other Mr. Gordon. It had to be.

The nurse returned. It was not Mr. Gordon, she said. It was a Mr. Nugent, a Mr. Daniel Nugent.

"I told him you were ill," she went on, "but he said he was down on Sunset at the foot of the hill and was coming on up anyway."

He sat up. "I can't see anybody. I don't want to see anybody."

"He was very crusty and talked like he was used to having his own way." She was troubled. "When I told him you weren't well, he said there was always something wrong with writers or else they wouldn't be writers and not to worry about it."

There was silence.

"I'd better get you some coffee," she said. "I've got some made. Maybe you'll have more of an idea what you want for breakfast after you get some coffee."

She turned to go.

"One minute." He stopped her. "When Mr. Nugent comes, don't admit him. Say I told you not to."

She nodded and went out.

Daniel Nugent? There was a Dan Nugent who was a motion picture director. What did he want? And why this presumption of his, this rudeness? He was one of the few film directors who might be said to be possessed of genuine talent, one of the best of the translators, as Jonquist would say. But what made him think he could come here when he was not wanted?

The nurse returned with the coffee service. On the tray were two letters.

Startled, he stared at the letters.

"The gardener stuffed them under the door just now," she explained. "Shall I pour your coffee?"

He shook his head, his eyes still on the letters.

"Oh, dear," she exclaimed. "I forgot. There's a letter came for you yesterday but the doctor said you were resting and he didn't want you disturbed."

She went back to the hall.

He continued to stare at the letters. Letters, after all these silent months. Mechanically, he opened the top letter of the two on the tray. It was from an agent who wrote he was quite sure he could get a writing job for him in one of the studios and would he please give him a call.

He opened the second letter. It was from Jonquist. He was negotiating, he wrote, for a London production of his play. He had reserved foreign dramatic rights when he sold the play to the studio and it looked very much as if the deal for the London production would be closed without a hitch.

He put the two letters on the table by the tray. It was strange, his getting two letters in one day, he who had not got a letter for so long. And the telephone ringing that had never rung? And this Mr. Gordon calling? And Dan Nugent on his way up to see him? And the letter that came yesterday? Was he awake? Was he still drugged?

The nurse came back with the letter. He studied her as she approached the bed. She was normal enough with her plump body and her round-faced smile. The sunlight slanting down through the open window, the shining bright plain far below, the strong smell of the coffee on the tray, all were normal enough. It was strange, this normality, this preposterous normality.

He looked at the letter the nurse gave him. The address was in a woman's handwriting but he did not recognize the handwriting. He opened the letter, glanced at the signature. It was her signature. He had never seen her handwriting before.

The letter was dated Saturday. Had she written him after he left that night? No, that couldn't be. The letter was mailed Saturday. She must have written it Saturday before she saw him.

"Dear Jack," the letter began. Dear Jack. The "dear" was a pure convention for she had never used the word dear, had never, for that matter, used any term of endearment while with him. Still the sight of the words, "Dear Jack," stirred him, revived the memory of his passionate love of her. His hands began to tremble. The letter in his trembling hands shook so he could read it only with difficulty.

"Bad news?" He became aware of the nurse's voice. "You're pale, Mr. Martin."

She stood by the bed with a cup of coffee in her two hands. He had forgotten about her.

"I'll have scrambled eggs," he said sharply to get rid of her, "Never mind the bacon."

She put the cup of coffee on the tray. Her round lips were in a pout as she went back out as if she sensed he was trying to get rid of her.

He steadied his hands against the bedclothes and began again to read the letter.

"Dear Jack," he read. "I just got back from town a few minutes ago and when I didn't find you here or any word from you I decided maybe you'd given me up for hopeless and I won't see you again. I'm sorry about last night. I got lonely here and went back to the house in town like I couldn't keep from doing it. It's hard to explain but I had the feeling I had to go. When I heard that you came to the door of the house to see if I was there, I felt very unhappy. It's the first time in almost as long as I can remember that I felt really unhappy. I guess maybe it's because I never made anybody unhappy like you before and I guess that's because I never knew anybody like you before. I think you're going to be a great man like you say and I think it'll be good for you if you don't see me anymore and that's why I'm writing you because on Sunday I'm going away from Los Angeles and you won't be able to see me any more even if you wanted to.

"To make a long story short, last night after you had gone away from the house in town I felt upset like I've never felt before and I left the house and went to Hollywood to see a girl who used to be in the house but who's married now and I got her alone and told her about you and about my being unhappy and how unhappy I'd made you. She said there was probably a reason for all that. She's something like you that way. She always sees reasons for things. She believes her car broke down one night when she was driving to the house just so she could meet the auto mechanic she's married to. That's the way she is. She saw a reason for my making you so unhappy and being so unhappy myself and she said it was so I would get wise to myself. She put me in her car and drove me down to a big church on Sunset Boulevard in Hollywood not far from where she lives. She knew I was born a Catholic and in the old days when we worked in the same house she always made me go to Mass with her on Christmas, Christmas being the only day on which she went to Mass. So she said to me outside the church, you go in there and go to confession and get wise to yourself. I'll go in with you and I'll go to confession too.

"I felt so unhappy I was willing to do anything. I hadn't been near a confession box for sixteen or seventeen years and the priest seemed kind of young and I was nervous, something I never am. Well, I told the whole story and the priest didn't seem to be surprised. Kind of young though he was, he seemed like he'd heard it all before. He told me I'd have to promise to give up the kind of life I was living and I promised. It wasn't bad at all.

"Well, I'm going to try to do as I promised. I'm going to try to be good and I thought the best way to give it a fair break was to get out of Los Angeles and go to San Francisco or Seattle and see if I can't get a job though I have no idea of what I can get a job at. The priest didn't suggest this. It's my own idea.

"I'm going to mail this now so even if you should come down here I won't have to tell you all this. I wouldn't tell it to you anyway. You might get mad again the way you were the first time. Monday morning when you get this I'll be gone.

"So long, Jack. You're going to be a lot better off without me around. I'm not your speed anyway. Bye. Rena."

He slowly folded up the letter and put it back in its envelope. Now he knew why she had delayed so long, why she had acted so unlike herself at the mirror Saturday night. She had wanted him to go.

This was the strangest of all the happenings, this letter, and her changing.

What was he doing, he suddenly asked himself, talking like this of her as if she were alive? She was dead. It was the effect of the letter. She was alive in the letter. But in life she was dead.

"When you get this I'll be gone," she had written. She had written more truthfully than she knew.

The doorbell rang. The sound of the bell ringing made him sit up from the pillows. That was Dan Nugent at the door, he was sure. This was also strange, Dan Nugent ringing his doorbell. The very ringing of the doorbell was strange. He could not remember when he had heard it ring before. Everything was strange. His being alive was strange. The telephone, the letters, her letter, the doorbell, all in this one morning out of all the mornings for a year, all were strange. The ordinance condemning him to silence had been lifted. He had the feeling he was losing his reason.

The doorbell continued to ring, boldly, insistently, as if it were not merely a doorbell ringing but a command.

One thought was flashing wildly across his bewildered brain. Could it be that his bungling Saturday night was meant to be? Could it ever be that she, she to whom the impossible had happened, she who had changed, also did not die?

He heard the nurse's voice and a man's voice over it at the door. An impulse, sprung from his new emotion, made him call out, "Nurse! It's all right, nurse! Let Mr. Nugent in!"

Almost immediately, he saw Dan Nugent appear at the door to the bedroom. He was a tall, bulky, awkward man in an old gray sweater, soiled blue denim trousers and worn tennis shoes. He came into the room in a sort of flat-footed shuffle, his graying-haired head and his shoulders thrust a little forward, his gray-blue eyes slightly squinted in apprais-al as he approached the bed.

"Hell, you look all right to me," he said gruffly as he approached the bed. "What'd they do? Get you tired? Don't let them get you tired, sonny. I'm Dan Nugent." He held out a large hairy hand. "I read your play. I think it's a hell of a play. I think it'll make a hell of a picture."

They shook hands. His grip was strong without forcing. His voice, his bulk, his vigor crowded the little room.

"I got one picture to do for Gordon," he went on, "and the play's it and you're the one to write it. Gordon's got an idea you don't want to write for pictures. How about it?"

Her letter was still in his hands. He looked down at it. Had the impossible happened, he asked himself again? Did she also not die?

Nugent was impatient. "Don't tell me Gordon's right and you're setting yourself up to be the world's greatest chump!" His voice was booming now. "Don't tell me you'd let one of those little echo boys at the studio write the script and feed his glory on your life's blood!" He leaned forward with his sharp, squinted look. "You're not scared, are you?"

He put her letter on the table. He had made his decision. The impossible had happened he was sure. He slipped carefully out of bed. "I feel as you do about my play, Mr. Nugent," he said, slowly standing up. "I think it'll make one of the greatest pictures ever made."

"Now you're talking like the man who wrote the play!" Nugent turned toward the hall. "Get a robe and let's get out in the sunshine. I got a couple of ideas I want to shoot at you."

He got a robe from the closet. He was weak, unsteady on his feet.

Nugent turned back from the hall. "I hope you're not married to that title *Defiance*. I got an idea I'd like to call the picture *Victory*. How does that hit you?"

"'Victory'? 'Victory' would be fine," he said.

Shaking, he put on his robe and looked through the window out on the shining day. Yes, he said to himself as a slight feeling of exhilaration came over him, yes, victory would be fine.

11.

He walked unsteadily out into the sunlight of the patio as if he were walking out into some unfamiliar, new world.

What a change in his life in a few hours, he said to himself, as he sat down in the young morning sunlight and listened to the compelling Nugent. Little by little, he began to forget the days and nights of silence and frustration and failure and the pathetic folly of his great love, began to forget Saturday night and his effort to destroy himself and her. She did not die, he began to be more sure now, just as he did not die. Had his drunken bungling also been plotted in his stars?

He must check about Rena, he warned himself, at the very first possible minute. He could telephone. No, that might not be wise. He might get himself involved, especially if his intuition were wrong and he had not bungled. The newspapers would tell him. He would check the newspapers at the first possible minute.

Nugent, strong, commanding, sitting in the patio, a sun-bright assurance of his new life, talked about the picture. Nugent had a fine understanding of his play. In his talk, he suggested a scene at the end to contrast the futility of the father's death with the strength of the mother's faith. "To me," he said, "the mother's faith has as much impact as the father's resignation. No one yet, as you know, has proved the end of life is death."

A few days before he might have found some objection to Nugent's suggestion. But not this morning. This morning he was not so sure of himself and his opinions as once he had been.

Noontime soon came and with it a proposal from Nugent they drive over to the studio for lunch. The idea did not appeal to him. In this new day he wanted no traffic with his past.

But Nugent was not a man easily resisted. Presently he was dressed and they were on their way to the studio in Nugent's car.

It was a triumphal return. Nugent was a Great Man in the studio. In the commissary Gordon welcomed him back as if he were his prodigal son. Even the skinny, reddish stenographer, passing him and the Great Man in the corridor, greeted him with a subdued and slightly awed expression. At last he had had his day. His grogginess went from him completely.

It was evening before he and Nugent separated and he went back up to his house in the hills.

The house was dark, chill, and at first he could not bring himself to go in. He knew inside he would have to find the answer to the dreaded question: was Rena alive or dead?

He stood out in the shadows of the patio. The exhilaration of the day ebbed from him, as if Nugent had been carrying him on his back since morning and had now let him slip down to his own feet on the ground. He was weak, shaky.

A sea fog crept in over the hills and made him cold. He began, in his weakness, to shiver. He turned and forced himself to go into the house.

He made a drink, a strong drink of Scotch and water. This was Tuesday night. He had not had a drink since Saturday night. He had bungled Saturday night, he and his drinking. Was it good that he had bungled Saturday night? The bans of silence and failure had been lifted. For today at least.

He turned to go back to the little porch outside the kitchen where, built into the porch, was a bin he used for old newspapers and magazines. In the newspapers he would find the answer. He dreaded going but he knew he had to go.

The doorbell rang. It was good to hear the doorbell ring. He welcomed the distraction. Any distraction was good that delayed the answer. He turned back from the kitchen and went to the front door. It was St. Lawrence. He was glad to see St. Lawrence. St. Lawrence was happy to see him.

He made St. Lawrence a drink. There was a fire laid in the fireplace and he lighted it. They sat by the fire. Outside the fog was now heavy on the hills and the night had become more cold. It was pleasant before the fire.

St. Lawrence told him it was he who had called the doctor for him. Sunday morning, he had read in the papers about Nugent and his play and he had gone over to the house to congratulate him. No one answered the doorbell. But when he was going away, he noticed the car was outside the garage and on looking into the house he saw him through his bedroom window, asleep in his clothes in a chair. He had gone in by the kitchen door and tried to awaken him. Then he saw the bottle emptied of sleeping pills and he telephoned immediately for his doctor.

"I knew you'd had too much to drink," St. Lawrence said, not taking his eyes from the fire, "and had taken too many sleeping pills. Lucidly you had dropped many of the pills. Otherwise the doctor would have had to report the incident as a suicide attempt. He decided—with some small hints from me—that if you had been mentally competent, if you had had a clear resolution to commit suicide at the time, you would not—at least, there was such a probability—you would not have dropped the pills."

St. Lawrence quickly—almost too quickly, it struck him—changed the subject. He spoke of Nugent whom he knew well. With a man of Nugent's talents directing, he said, his play would make a great picture, and win all the Academy

Awards and all the awards in New York and abroad as well. He was made, he declared. He had at last arrived.

They had a second drink. St. Lawrence's talk and gaiety raised his spirits. His depression, he told himself, was largely physical. After all, he had been in a sort of coma for more than two days. What did he expect himself to be a few hours later? Lighthearted and full of song?

Yes, St. Lawrence said, the world was his oyster now. How about his new play? Had he finished it?

Almost, he answered. He thought, he added carefully, it might have to have a new ending.

Then St. Lawrence said, "That girl, Miss Garden, you certainly were right about her, about her being your good fortune. How your luck has changed since she came into the picture!"

The words chilled him. His hands shook so he spilled his drink.

"Feel all right?" St. Lawrence was on his feet, looking down at him in concern. "You're still pretty shaky, aren't you?"

The telephone rang. He motioned for St. Lawrence to answer it. It was Jonquist telephoning from New York.

He made his way to the telephone. The deal for the London production of his play had just been closed, Jonquist said. He'd just received a cable and he thought he'd like to know. He'd have to plan to be in London for the rehearsals, Jonquist told him, and he'd fly over later and they'd both look into the possibility of a Paris production. It was a great day, Jonquist said.

He went back to the fireplace and, standing there holding to the mantel, he told St. Lawrence the news.

St. Lawrence was jubilant. This calls for another drink, he said. St. Lawrence made the new drinks and toasted him.

"Genius will out!" he said, laughing. "My neighboring cliff-dweller climbs the stars!"

St. Lawrence became tipsy, and as always when he was tipsy, he began to be very voluble. He was happy, very happy, he said. He was especially happy because, if he didn't mind him telling the truth, he was sure he had fallen into the deep pit and would never be heard of again.

"Saturday night, lost, forgotten, drunk and drugged and on the brink of extinction!" he exclaimed. "Tonight, greatness! Tonight, his play into a picture and a London production, tonight an artist on his way to wealth and glory!" A sudden thought entertained him. "Do you know, Martin," he went on, "in an olden time, after such an extraordinary metamorphosis, they'd say you had made a deal with Satan." Laughing, he held up his glass again. "That would be something, wouldn't it? Dr. Faustus of the Hollywood hills!"

The idea of Dr. Faustus in Hollywood, St. Lawrence found very amusing and exuberantly dilated on it. But he did not find it amusing. He felt more unnerved than before, and weaker and more depressed, and he let himself back down into his chair. He groped for his glass and drank from it. Whiskey would help. Whiskey always helped. Well, not always. There were times when whiskey couldn't help.

He could blurredly, distantly hear St. Lawrence talking on, gaily expanding his Dr. Faustus conceit. One mumbled an incantation, such as St. Lawrence was now mumbling in an elaborate mumbo-jumbo, and straightway to the music of the moans of the damned, Mephistopheles would appear in a gust of smoke. The world and the flesh, all that your desire demands, all in exchange for your soul. Mister! How about it? Want to make a deal?

Could St. Lawrence ever believe any of this stuff? Hardly. It had to be little more than a literary conceit with him. St. Lawrence should have been an actor. He liked to make speeches and act out parts, especially when he was drinking.

He could hear St. Lawrence talking. "Do you know what Satan said to Dr. Faustus? 'My best trick,' Satan said to Dr. Faustus, 'my best trick is to prove I don't exist.'"

St. Lawrence talked as if it were all real but a man of his sophistication couldn't believe that stuff. No man in his right mind could believe that stuff.

He could hear St. Lawrence going on, his voice becoming more blurred and more distant. "Satan said to Dr. Faustus, 'I'm a silly superstition, that's what I am. A silly superstition. *That's* my very best disguise.'"

Of course, Satan was a silly superstition. St. Lawrence's having Satan say he was a silly superstition was only a trick of rhetoric and didn't change that. Why was superstition always described as silly superstition? Superstition could be vicious, and fanatical, murderously fanatical, and there wouldn't be anything silly about that, would there?...

He could feel a hand gently shaking his arm. Then he heard St. Lawrence's voice. "You'd better get to bed, laddie. You'll sleep better in bed."

Slowly, dimly, he made out St. Lawrence leaning over him. "I guess I must have dozed off."

St. Lawrence raised him up a little in the chair. He could see St. Lawrence more clearly now.

"You're shot," St. Lawrence said. "Naturally. After what you've been through. I'm afraid my impassioned discourse on Satan and Dr. Faustus didn't help either." He smiled. "My friend Dr. Faustus seems to have upset you no end."

He sat up in his chair. He sat up carefully. He was fully awake now and on guard. "Dr. Faustus? What about Dr. Faustus?"

"You were talking about him in your sleep," St. Lawrence answered lightly.

Suddenly he was fearful. He had been talking in his sleep. "I'm still kind of drugged," he said. He tried to be casual. "It must have been the drug talking. What was I talking about?"

"Oh—" St. Lawrence hesitated. Then he said, "Let's skip it. You'd better get to bed now."

"No. I'd like to know now." He forced a smile and, anticipating the worst and beginning to set up a defense, said as easily as he could, "The picture—the picture we're going to make from my play—my mind's already whirling with ideas for it."

St. Lawrence turned away. "No, it wasn't the picture you were talking about," he said and it seemed as if he too was trying to be casual. "It was something about a woman—something mad about a woman and Dr. Faustus, about a woman and Dr. Faustus and Saturday night."

He tried hard to conceal his consternation. "I must be still drugged all right."

St. Lawrence nodded vaguely. "It could be," he said but his voice and manner were noncommittal.

He held to St. Lawrence's arm to steady himself, and got to his feet. He wanted to know the truth. "I guess I didn't make much sense," he ventured, seeking to draw St. Lawrence out further.

St. Lawrence put an arm around him. "Come," he said, "get to bed. We can go into all of this some other time, some time you're more yourself."

"Into all of what?"

St. Lawrence turned him toward the hall. "To bed," he commanded.

St. Lawrence helped him into his bedroom and sat him down in a chair. He then opened the windows and pulled back the bed covers.

He grabbed St. Lawrence's arm. "Tell me—tell me, please, what did I say in my sleep? I've had a few serious problems lately. I don't want to go gabbing away about them every time I doze off. I'd like to know."

St. Lawrence looked down at him a long moment. Then he said, "Forget about what you said in your sleep. Anyone can say almost anything in his sleep. I don't know clearly what you said in your sleep." He paused for the least moment and went on, "But I will tell you one thing, if you don't mind. I know your taking those sleeping pills was no accident. I know what you were trying to do and I have an idea you'll try it again. It would be a great tragedy, not only for yourself now with the world falling into your lap but also for your friends, for those of us who love you.

"I hope then you don't mind if I make a little suggestion. Why don't you tell someone what it is that is troubling you so deeply? It must be serious when you want to run away from it by killing yourself. Share it. Talk it out. You could go to a church, to the confessional if you believed in it. 'Whose sins you shall forgive, they are forgiven them. Whose sins you shall retain, they are retained.' Those are extraordinary words and they can be pretty helpful words. They've been spoken over the passions and crimes of man for almost two thousand years."

The mention of confession by St. Lawrence startled him. Not the idea of it in itself but its association with Rena. She had gone to confession. It seemed to him a part of the horrible fantasy of the night. Like Dr. Faustus.

"I understand," St. Lawrence went on, misinterpreting his agitation. "I can understand why you wouldn't like the idea of confession. It was just a thought I threw out. How about unburdening yourself to someone, to a doctor, to a friend? Have you thought of that? It's not like confession but it could very well do. You'll go mad if you don't. You'll go mad again, that's perhaps the best way to put it. How about it?"

He stared by St. Lawrence at the open window. The fog was very thick and gave a smoky gray tone to the dark. He could not see the lights below. He could see nothing but the smoky grayish dark.

"I have no friends," he said. "Except you."

"All right. Tell me. I'll never breathe a word. Maybe I can help you. I know a lot of people in this town."

Suddenly he grew hostile toward St. Lawrence. He was being unfair, he knew, but he also knew it was instinctive—it was his only protection. If he told St. Lawrence the truth, if he told him he had murdered a woman, St. Lawrence would be shocked, he was certain. He would tell him to get a lawyer and go to the police and make a clean breast of it. He would feel for him nothing but the greatest of pity, the sort of pity that in itself inspires pity.

"Thank you," he said coldly. "My rantings in my sleep must have misled you. There's nothing wrong, nothing wrong at all." St. Lawrence's face softened into a smile of sympathy.

"Martin," he said quietly, "for all your debauchery, for all your love of the gutter, you have an extraordinary naïveness about you—a childlike naïveness that seems untouched no matter what you say or do. Good night."

Straightway, St. Lawrence turned and left the room and the house.

He sat staring out at the smoky gray fog. What could St. Lawrence know? He himself did not know if the woman was dead, so what could he have said in his sleep? Nothing. Nothing of any import. He would go back to the paper bin. In the newspapers, he would find the truth.

Now, as he was in the hall on his way back to the newspapers, he became frightened again. He stopped, braced himself against the wall. He was trembling, from head to foot.

I'm shot all right, he said to himself, and I'm tired and I'm depressed. But most of all I'm frightened. I'm frightened at what I am going to find in the newspapers. But I have to know the truth. I've never been frightened like this before. I wish I could go back and throw myself on the bed right now and go to sleep. But I can't. I couldn't sleep. I have to go back to the paper bin and learn the truth.

He would have to find out even if he had to crawl on his hands and knees to the paper bin.

He continued on his way slowly, wearily, to the kitchen and the back porch.

The newspapers were in the bin the way the nurse had laid them. On top was yesterday's paper, Monday's, and under that was Sunday's paper. He took the papers into the kitchen and spread them out on the kitchen table.

Page after page, column after column, item after item, he went through the papers. Sunday's paper seemed interminable. In spite of his fear he found himself nodding over the last of its pages. There was nothing in Sunday's paper. Then, he remembered there could not be anything in Sunday's paper. Sunday's papers were already on the street before there was anything to be told.

Monday's paper, though not as large as Sunday's paper, also seemed interminable. His eyes became so weary he could hardly keep them open and only his fear kept him from dropping his head to his arms and going to sleep there and then.

Finally, he found the small headline. It was in one of the last columns on one of the last pages. The whole item was hardly an inch in depth. But it was all there, the truth he dreaded was all there.

Death from Asphyxiation, the headline read.…*A woman identified as Miss Rena Garden… Gas heater vent impaired by storm… Accidental asphyxiation…*

Hardly an inch of space but the dread truth was there.

12.

The whir of the gardener's gas-motored lawn mower awakened him. His eyes blinked before the brilliance of the morning shining on the hills and terraces wet from the fog of the night. He was still at the kitchen table where, in his clothes with his head on his arms, he had slept the night through.

Beneath his arms, the newspaper was still spread out to the page with the item announcing her death.

He mechanically read the item over again. It was unreal. Saturday night now seemed unreal. Last night seemed unreal. The sunlight, that was real. The glistening hills and terraces, they were real, and the whir of the gardener's lawn mower, that was real. There was a mockingbird vocalizing in a Chinese elm tree on the terrace below, he was real. But death…

Death of any sort was too dark an idea, too opaque and incomprehensible an idea to have reality in the splendor and vitality of the morning.

He stood up, stretched himself. He was a little stiff but he had slept well. He would start the coffee and take a cold shower. He turned to leave the kitchen. At the door he stopped. It was not as easy as he thought to leave the kitchen and the item in the newspaper on the kitchen table.

He went back to the table and, standing over it, reread the item. Her death had been inconsequential as her life had been inconsequential. Yet it was not easy to dismiss her death.

He sat down again at the kitchen table. He looked again at the item. Miss Rena Garden. It could be argued Miss Rena Garden was better off dead. She had reformed, yes, but who could say she would ever be able to hold to her resolution. She was what she was because of the chemistry of her inclinations not because of any persecution or dereliction. Miss Rena Garden could well be better off dead.

He got to his feet. Murder was a word, so was murderer. Thou shalt not kill, was an order issued by the chief to preserve the tribe. Thou shalt not steal, that was a similar order. Thou shalt not commit adultery, another. All tribal conventions, all of the same importance. Or unimportance.

The telephone rang.

The ringing of the telephone startled him. He stood looking down at the newspaper and the thought that had flashed across his weary brain the night before, the thought that her death Saturday night and the dramatic change in his life were somehow related, came to him again, this time heavily, forcefully, tuned to the insistence of the ringing of the bell.

The telephone stopped ringing.

He stood by the table in the brilliant clarity of the morning and he realized that no matter how coldly intelligent he might be, he could not explain away his experience.

The telephone rang again.

He listened a long moment to the telephone ringing. He looked out the window into , the splendor of the morning. The shining normality of the day put an end to his self-inquisition.

He went to answer the telephone.

It was Nugent on the telephone, gruff, impatient. Why the hell hadn't he answered the phone before? He was coming up in a studio car in a few minutes, he said, and they would take a ride around Santa Monica Bay to investigate possible settings for the house in the play.

He replaced the telephone. Beyond under the front door, he could see letters on the floor. He went to the door, picked them up. One was from the actor who had played the father's part in the play looking for the same part in the picture. One was from Mr. and Mrs. Gordon asking him to a cocktail party two weeks from Saturday afternoon. Another was from a girl he had met in New York She had read the great news and wanted to congratulate him and had he forgotten her and why didn't he write to her? There were other letters, one from an auctioneer, one from a maker of expensive lingerie.

The telephone rang again. It was the studio publicity department and when could he come to sit for pictures. He said he was busy but would see about dropping in tomorrow.

The doorbell rang. It was the Japanese gardener with a small cardboard box of oranges. They were from the two trees in the garden behind the cottage, the first fruit they had borne in several years.

While he was still talking to the gardener, a Negro man and woman came to the open door. Mr. St. Lawrence had sent them to clean the house. He said it was dirty and needed cleaning. They did work for Mr. St. Lawrence. Did he have a vacuum?

Yes, he had a vacuum.

They entered and took over the front of the house. He returned to the kitchen. He stood by the table as he had before and looked down on the newspaper. A shaft of strong sunlight now fell aslant the table and the newspaper. The muffled din of the vacuum was joined to the whir of the gardener's lawn mower. The mockingbird in his high jubilance could be heard above them both. Life was like a flame and a song all around him.

The telephone rang again. He did not answer it. He left the kitchen and went to the shower.

He was hardly dressed after his shower and had not yet had his coffee when Nugent arrived. The Negro woman answered the doorbell.

Five minutes later they were in the chauffeur-driven studio car headed for Santa Monica Bay.

13.

Nugent and he rode south along the bay as far as Portuguese Bend.

It cleared away the shadow of his fear, this ride along the shining bay. A man's best balanced and most rational life is lived in these sunlight hours, he assured himself. They rode close to the sea, and the sea had the stimulation for him it had always had since his boyhood. Nugent too was a stimulation. He was bright, inventive, and his belief in the play was even more of a tonic than sunlight and sea.

But that evening, when he was back alone in his home in the dark of the hills, the past returned and the remembrance of the woman he killed became strong again and insistent.

He began to worry if anyone had given her a funeral. He

had loved her deeply and he had held her in his arms and the thought that she might be in the city morgue troubled him. He would have to telephone the manager of the bungalow court.

It was doubtful if anyone at the court knew him. He had never given his name at the court. She had paid the rent. Still, it was dangerous, he was aware. If the police had any suspicion her death was not accidental, they would see to it a record was kept of all calls. Suppose they learned he called? That would not prove anything. Nobody could prove anything.

He would telephone. It was a chance he had to take.

The manager answered the telephone. He knew her as a small, dumpy weak-brained widow with dyed reddish-brown hair and great splotches of rouge on her cheeks, a spiritualist who spent most of her time at a ouija board trying to communicate with her late husband. She answered in an affectedly other-worldly voice and he was sure she had just come from the ouija board.

He told her he had just learned of the death of Miss Garden and wondered if the funeral arrangements had been made.

Yes, yes, indeed, she sighed, the poor dear had already been laid away. An aunt had come from Phoenix to claim the body and the aunt was very rich and she was sure the poor dear had the loveliest funeral imaginable.

Then, suddenly, with excitement, she asked, "Are you, by any chance, Mr. Martin, Mr. John Martin?"

Abruptly he replaced the telephone.

How did she know his name? Rena had probably mentioned it to her. But why should she ask if he who telephoned was John Martin? He grew more troubled and began to brood again. Did she connect him with the woman's death? He must be intelligent, he warned himself. After all, she had been dead only a few days and the memory of her and his killing her had not yet been permitted the balm of time. Would there ever be such a balm? Would the memory fade? Would there be, as time passed and his success grew, a gradual vanishing of his sense of guilt?

Why had that woman—the manager of the court— asked if he was John Martin?

Suppose she did know his name? What difference would that make? If the police had found out his name from her and had suspected him, they would have come to him long before.

If only, he said to himself, if only after he had killed her and failed to lull himself, life had gone on as before, empty, silent, frustrated, there would have been no problem. He would have killed himself at the first opportunity. But these strange, these unaccountable happenings, this incredible rush of good fortune that seemed so clearly related to her dying, they were what made him pause.

And this mad idea of St. Lawrence, the idea he was being somehow rewarded, that had made him pause too.

Thou shalt not kill was purely a tribal convention. Evil and Good, and their anthropomorphic personalizations, Satan and God, were the inventions of fear. The Dr. Faustus legend was the most fantastic of all legends. He must stay with facts, he must keep to the world in which two and two inevitably made four.

Rewarded? …

As well believe the woman he had killed had died a saint after her confession and gone to Heaven and was working miracles for him there. As sensible an explanation of the strange happenings of the last days as a pact with a nonexistent devil.

I'm a silly superstition, the devil said. My best trick is to persuade you I do not exist.

I'm losing my mind, he told himself.

The night was heavy in the house. He hurried about the hall and rooms turning on every light. He felt puny, helpless.

He went to the mirror in the hall and searched his face. His face was white.

Why do you go to the mirror? he asked himself.

Why do you always go to the mirror? You are always dramatizing yourself, as St. Lawrence says. St. Lawrence is right.

You dramatized your father's dying and death. You dramatized your first success. It was but the initial moment in your flight to greatness, you said. What greatness? You dramatized your frustration and degradation. You had fallen from the sky, you told yourself. What sky? You dramatized this common woman whom you killed. She, you said, was the woman of your destiny. What destiny?

You dramatized even your killing of her. It was to be the perfect final curtain to a confused and futile play. Now you are beginning to be obsessed with the idea there is a sinister power working to reward you. What sinister power?

Why not dismiss all this dramatization of yourself as a projection of a diseased and theatrical mind? Yes, diseased. You are not one of the nice, normal people. You are not one of those good, pleasant, how-are-you-this-morning people. You are crazed. You always have been. Yes, crazed.

He turned abruptly away from the mirror. Crazed. The house seemed dark in spite of the lights.

I am a murderer. There is no projection of a crazed mind about that. This woman was alive a few days ago as I am alive. Now she is dead. Now she is dead and buried. That is no delusion.

He was trembling.

He went back to the kitchen. The newspaper was still open on the kitchen table. He looked down at the item again. *Death from Asphyxiation....Miss Rena Garden.* There it was, the fact. That was no delusion.

He sat down by the kitchen table and stared at the newspaper.

The change in his life, the astonishing dramatic change in his life since her death, that is no delusion either. One day, one year of days, there were only emptiness and silence. Then suddenly after her death, there were only acclaim and good fortune.

I am in terror before the mystery, he said. I wish I could kill myself. It was easy Saturday night. But it is not easy now. I have not the courage now. I am in terror before the mystery and have not the courage.

His mind sagged before his fierce self-inquisition. Wearily he folded his arms on the table and dropped his head on them.

What is that quotation of St. Lawrence's? "Drunk with drink of immortality." No. That is not the way it went. "Damned with drink of immortality." That is the way it went.

Damned. Damned.

14.

Now, another night had come.

He drove south on Lincoln Boulevard on his way to Playa del Bey and as he drove, he said to himself, I am going to do what I am going to do because I am frightened and desperate. There is no lofty motive inspiring me. I am lost and in need of help and I know nowhere else to turn.

The night before, he had spent the dark hours begging for the quick coming of day. Morning would, as it had done before, restore him to courage, he was sure, and in the sane daylight, the abnormal, he hoped, would not be so abnormal, and the mystery would lose some of its terror.

But daylight this day brought him no courage. He greeted the dawn from the terrace before his house. The normality of the scene aroused only his resentment.

Laugh at me, he cried out wildly, you sane, good, complacent dwellers below! ...You, who have never known frenzy or dreamed of greatness...You, who are aghast at passion, at madness...at any excess or deviation....

Laugh at me, you complacent, good people, and go on into your ordinary routine day.... *Laugh at me, you who have never known gods...nor demons!*

His defiance faded. Words, no matter how bold, did not help. He backed away from the damning truth of the morning and returned to his house and slammed the door against it.

He drew all of the window shades and locked the doors, front and back. There, in the dusk of the house, he spent the day. The telephone rang and he did not answer. It rang again and again, and he did not answer.

The morning mail showed under the door but he did not go near it.

The doorbell and the telephone bell rang throughout the day and he ignored them. Once he heard an angry pounding on the front door and then an even angrier pounding on the back door. He knew it was Nugent. He quailed before the man's force and aggressiveness but he did not go near the doors. He did not dare to talk to anyone or see anyone for fear they would perceive the truth.

The day was interminable. He felt he was surely losing his mind. He would go to the mirror again and again and search his image for signs of madness.

"Murderer!" He would whisper the accusation at his image as if at a stranger.

Murderer!

As night approached, the accusation he whispered to the mirror began to echo through the empty dark of the house, softly at first, then more loudly and more loudly. But, as the night grew deeper it was not so much the word that agitated him, not so much his sense of guilt, but the fear of a sinister force walking the dark rooms with him like a companion.

Where will I go? he asked himself.

The first place his thought turned to was St. Lawrence's house. It was only a few steps away and there in it was his only friend. But St. Lawrence would see through him instantly if he did not already know the truth. St. Lawrence would break him down and he would confess. Then there would be the police....

Suppose he did do what St. Lawrence was certain to advise, go to the police? Would this even deeper, more tormenting, ever-growing sense of the sinister in life, would that vanish? Would he carry the burden of his fears to prison with him where, without the distractions of his new life, they would crush him completely?

To prison? And after that, the gas chamber? Why not? His giving himself up might inspire leniency. Might, but not of necessity.

By some emphasis of justice, he might well be sent to the gas chamber. He had been drinking when he shut the door on her asleep but nonetheless he had acted after reflection and with full consent of his will.

The gas chamber? When he shut the door on her asleep, he had turned her bedroom into a gas chamber. Why not the gas chamber for him too? It was fitting and fair. It was just. She died in a gas chamber. He would die in a gas chamber. The parallel was exact. The parallel was horrible and fantastic, as all things in life now were.

The gas chamber?

He began to shake violently. What has made such a coward of me, he asked himself. Saturday night I had no fear of death. Nor any night before Saturday night. But now I am terrified. Is there such a reality as conscience and has it made a coward of me?

No, it's more than a sense of evil and a sense of guilt. Those I could rationalize away.

It is this sinister thing that unnerves me, this sinister thing here side by side with me, my companion in the dark.

The doorbell rang.

He was startled. Who could be calling now in the night?

He waited tensely. The doorbell rang again. At this hour, he decided, it could only be St. Lawrence. He went to the door, opened it.

A dumpy, reddish-haired woman stood there in the dark with a package under her arm. He did not recognize her.

"Yes?" he asked, his voice shaking.

The woman's rouge-splotched face was fissured with an unseemly smile. "Why, Mr. Martin," she murmured, "don't you remember me?"

Immediately he remembered her voice, the weak, affectedly other-worldly voice that belonged to the manager of the bungalow court.

He stiffened in fear, searched the dark behind her for sign of the policemen he was sure were there.

"What's the matter, Mr. Martin?" the voice said. "You look like you've seen a ghost."

He snapped on the outside light. There were no policemen hanging back in the dark. "What is it you want?" he asked, trembling in spite of his effort to appear at ease.

"Now don't be angry, Mr. Martin," she went on. "I'll only be a minute. I have a package here for you."

She passed him the package. "It is eerie, my finding you at last, Mr. Martin. I saw your name in the movie news this morning and I read about the studio going to make your play and I said to myself, I said, 'That's him, that's the nice man who was so much in love with the poor dear before she died.' Do you mind if I come in?"

He stepped back and she waddled into the dark house. He did not close the door behind her. He was intense, fearful.

"Why are you in the dark here, Mr. Martin?" she asked.

"I happen to like the dark." He tried to be casual. "What is all this about, may I ask?"

"Our dear Rena sent me," she answered cryptically, smiling her unseemly smile. "When the dead give you a mission, Mr. Martin, you can never be at rest until you carry it out. It was the spirit of my dear husband on the other side who found you for me. I'm sure. I'm sure."

He was puzzled until he remembered her devotion to the ouija board.

"At the studio," she went on, little more than a voice in the dark, "they wouldn't give me your address till I told them I had an important package for you. Open the package, why don't you, Mr. Martin?"

He went on into the living room and turned on a light. She waddled in after him.

"This is from Rena?" he asked as calmly as he could. "Is that what I gather?"

"Yes, from Rena, Mr. Martin," she sighed, "the poor dear."

He began to open the package. She could see his hand shaking, he knew. He must keep control of himself, he warned himself.

Maybe she suspected him. Maybe this was a trick of some sort to get him to betray himself.

She watched his face intently, slyly. "It's eerie, isn't it?" she whispered. "Eerie."

He wanted to strike her down with all his strength. Instead, he said as easily as he could, "It is good of you to bring this to me."

"Yes, it's eerie," she said watching him. "Eerie. The night she died, the poor dear left a note under my door saying she was leaving early the next morning and if a Mr. John Martin ever came down to inquire about her, would I please be sure and see to it he got this from her room.

"So here you are, Mr. Martin, and glad I am to have found you. I can be at peace now."

He finished opening the package. It was the cheap blue-and-white ceramic madonna that he had first seen in the bedroom of her apartment. His hands shook so the wrapping paper rustled. He put the madonna down on the piano.

"Kind of shakes you, don't it, hearin' from the Beyond?" she whispered. "The poor dear, I hope her friends on this side haven't forgotten her."

He was sure, he managed to answer, her friends had not forgotten her, and he was very grateful for the statue.

"Good," she murmured. "It is a pity the way people forget the lonely spirits on the other side." She turned to go. "I must get back and report to the poor dear and tell her the mission is done. Goodbye, Mr. Martin,"

With that she waddled out. He followed her to the door. "Thank you. Good night," he said with effort.

She waved a stubby hand and went on across the terrace. He waited a moment and snapped off the outside light.

He returned to the living room. He picked up the madonna in his hands and studied it. It was even cheaper looking on close scrutiny, streaked now as it was with what was left of its original luminous paint. The last time he had seen it, it was on the little shelf on the wall of the tawdry bedroom in the bungalow court.

It had looked down on their last hours together. It had looked down on her death.

Why had she wanted him to have the statue? Did she want to leave him a remembrance of her? Could the statue have been an idea inspired by her religious fervor after her confession? It could have been. He did not know.

He put out the light so the house was dark again. Still the ceramic madonna glowed vaguely in the dark.

He collapsed into a chair.

I have lost my mind. I am destroying myself in spite of myself. The intangibles, the cold, enormous intangibles have crushed me completely. I need the personal, the concrete. I need compassion. I need compassion or my madness will destroy me completely.

St. Lawrence. No, not St. Lawrence. St. Lawrence leads only to the police. There is no compassion there.

He looked at the madonna glowing in the dark. Slowly an idea came to him, a mad, incredible idea....

15.

So, now, he drove south on Lincoln Boulevard on his way to the chapel at Loyola University at Playa del Rey.

It had been St. Lawrence's idea to begin with. It was St. Lawrence who had mentioned the confessional. He had finally accepted the idea as the only possible release from his terror, the only possible escape from his madness.

The statue and the remembrance it brought of Rena's going to confession had moved him strongly toward his decision. It was hard for him to define, this influence of hers.

In his hours of torment, he had become obsessed with the thought of her significance in his life, a significance that seemed more apparent with her dead than it had been with her living. She, for all her impassivity, had gone to confession. It was incredible. Now he was going to confession. That was incredible too.

It would have surprised St. Lawrence, he said to himself as he drove, that once he used to go to the confessional. Many years ago. So many, many years ago. Usually on Saturday afternoons, often with his mother. It was routine for Saturdays, as routine as the Saturday movies for children and the Saturday night bath.

"Bless me, Father, for I have sinned…I lied to my mother…I disobeyed my father…I put a caterpillar in Sister Veronica's desk…"

"Is that all, my child?"

"No, Father, I…I did something awful bad."

"Yes?"

"I…I didn't put the dime my mother gave me into the collection box."

"I see. Well, you won't do that again, will you? For your

penance say three Hail Mary's. Now make a good act of contrition…"

"Th-there's more than that, Father."

"More?"

"Yes, Father. I—I took the dime and a friend of mine, Tommy—I don't have to mention his name, do I, Father?"

"Oh, no. Just get on with your confession."

"I took the dime and a friend of mine and me, we bought a cigar and we smoked it."

"Well, well. You got sick, I suppose?"

"No, Father. Tommy—I mean, my friend, he got sick. I didn't get sick."

"I see. You will watch out about lying to your mother and disobeying your father, won't you, my child?"

"Yes, Father."

"Very well. For your penance say three Hail Marys. Now make a good act of contrition."

Confession. It was routine then, he said to himself as he drove along the Boulevard. It was not routine now.

Whose sins you shall forgive, they are forgiven them. Whose sins you shall retain, they are retained.

Those are not routine words, he told himself. Those are strange words, unimaginable words…. So strange and so unimaginable that for me they might well be sanely true.

He approached Playa del Rey. To the west lay the shadowy, quiet sea. Before him, to the south, dark against the pale, starry sky, rose the lofty tower of the Loyola University chapel. It was because of St. Lawrence he had decided to go to the Jesuits at the university. St. Lawrence was stamped with wisdom and charity, and wisdom and charity are what I direly need now, he said aloud, as he drove. The profoundest of wisdom, the deepest of charity....

He turned off the highway toward the university. A sudden thought chilled him. Suppose, he asked himself, the priest commanded him, as a condition of absolution, to give himself up to the police?

It was one thing to confess he had killed this woman and tell of his dread and ask for absolution and seek thus to free himself of the torments of guilt and fear. It was another thing to give up, as a price for this release, his extraordinary new life and its future happiness and achievements or, even, to give up life itself....

The gas chamber. Her gas chamber. His gas chamber. The terrifying parallel struck him again. His decision to go to the confessional had lulled him into a false sanity.

He drew up to the side of the road.

I must not go to pieces again, he told himself. I must go on. In the confessional, as St. Lawrence pointed out, men for centuries have left the burdens of their crimes. It is my only hope now. Should the priest command me, as a condition of absolution, to go to the police, I can refuse. I can leave the confessional no worse off than when I entered it. The priest is bound to silence and my secret will be safe. It is my only, my last desperate hope.

He turned the car back on to the road and drove on to the campus.

The campus was much quieter than he had expected it to be. The stubby palm trees lining the road were like sleepy sentries in the shadowy night. The massed red and yellow roses in the sunken garden before the main building appeared to glow in the starlight with a faint light of their own. His headlights picked up two young Jesuits, bareheaded and in their black cassocks, strolling on the lawn. It was very placid, almost pastoral. He, murderer, he who had deliberately taken a human life, felt like an evil intruder into the innocent peace and academic serenity of the campus.

But this was no time, he told himself, for more self-catechizing and self-chastisement. What he must do, he must do directly, boldly.

He saw the two young Jesuits he had seen strolling on the lawn enter a building just off the palm-lined road. He parked his car, followed them. He found a young man at a telephone switchboard just inside the entrance to the building. He asked him if it were possible to have a priest hear his confession. The young man nodded and, while working on the switchboard, told him to go to the faculty chapel in the same building and wait in the confessional there and a priest would come. It seemed very much routine to the young man.

He went back out and walked across the lawn to the small chapel that extended at right angles to the building. The chapel was dark except for a single overhead light in the rear of the church and the red sanctuary lamp by the altar. He found the confessional at the rear of the church. He went into the confessional and knelt down in the complete darkness and silence. There was no priest.

After a while, the darkness and silence began to suffocate him and he got up from his knees and went back out into the chapel. He knelt in a pew a little distance from the rear of the church. He looked at the tabernacle, hardly discernible in the dark.

He remembered some words from his boyhood. He had learned them by rote and they had never meant anything to him. Now they were tossed up from the clouded deeps of memory into his consciousness and they suited the desperate need of the moment.

Christ, he pleaded, I believe, help my unbelief. I believe, Christ, help my unbelief.

He heard the footsteps of the priest entering the chapel and going to the confessional.

Christ, I believe, he prayed again, help my unbelief.

He got up from the pew and went back to the confessional. He had not seen the priest. As he knelt in the confessional, the priest drew the slide that separated the confessor from the penitent.

There was a moment's silence. Then, he blurted out, "Father, I killed a woman."

He waited for the priest to speak. He was afraid the priest would be harsh, hostile. But the priest, when he spoke, spoke quietly. He asked if he knew what he was doing when he killed. Completely, he answered. It was premeditated and deliberate.

Then, without the priest asking, he told the whole story of the relationship of the woman and himself. The priest listened without a word.

When he was finished the priest said, "God has been very kind to you that you are still alive. When was your last confession?"

He tried to remember. It was twelve, possibly thirteen years ago, when he was a boy.

The priest suggested he make a complete confession, so far as he was able, to cover the years from then till now. The thought appalled him. But the priest was patient, and with the aid of his sensitive questioning the confession was made.

The first part of the ordeal is over, he said to himself. Christ help me, he prayed, Christ help me in what is to come.

"God has indeed been kind to you," the priest said. "For your penance, I want you to recite in full once every day for a month, a prayer I shall give you as you leave the confessional. Now, make your act of contrition."

He did not remember the words of the act of contrition. The priest told him to repeat the words after him.

"My God, I am heartily sorry for having offended You...."

He repeated the words.

"I detest all of my sins because I dread the loss of Heaven and the pains of Hell but most of all because I have offended You, my God, who are all good and worthy of all my love...."

The act of contrition was made. The priest pronounced the words of absolution in Latin.

He understood only the words, *Ego te absolvo*.

He listened tensely. The priest had said nothing about giving himself up to the police. Would he, when he was finished with the words of absolution, command him to give himself up?

The priest finished the words of absolution. "God keep you," he said.

He continued to kneel, tense still with uncertainty.

"Is there anything more?" the priest asked.

"I—I can't believe—I—I'm happy it's over with. Father," he mumbled lamely.

"I can understand," the priest said. "I might point out, however, that it is not all over with."

The priest paused as if to word his thought carefully. While the priest paused, his heart began to pound with fear. Now, he said to himself, he will tell me I must give myself up to the police.

Then the priest went on, "You are to say your penance without fail and with as much feeling of contrition as you can muster. You must reform your life and be determined to sin no more. You have usurped the power of Him who gives life and takes it away. If you had robbed one of money or possessions, you could strive to restore them. But you have robbed one of life. You cannot restore it. Your own life should be offered up daily in atonement. It is not all over with. I'm sure you understand."

His heart slowly stopped its pounding. The priest had not mentioned his giving himself up. Still he knew he would have to know the final truth if ever he was to have peace of mind. He hesitated. Then, trying hard to keep his voice from trembling, he asked, "Am I bound, Father, to give myself up to the police?"

There was silence a moment.

"Whether or not you are to give yourself up to the authorities," the priest said, "is not in my jurisdiction and the decision is not mine to make. Nor does the validity of this confession in any way depend on your doing so. Your sins are forgiven you. Go in peace."

His fear ebbed from him. He got up slowly from his knees. As he left the confessional, the priest passed him out a small leaflet. He saw only the priest's hand. He did not see his face.

He went dazedly down into the dark of the chapel and knelt in a pew. He heard the priest's footsteps as he left the chapel. Now he found himself shaking as his tension broke.

He began to sob.

Christ... You, revered as the healer of the possessed and the obsessed, the sick and the demented... You, loved as the Saviour of the lost and the damned... Christ, heal me... Christ, have mercy on me.

16.

He drove home slowly. He was still trembling. It had been only a little over a half hour since he had left the confessional. But the terror that had been his companion was no longer with him.

The boulevard was as usual alive with the lights of automobiles. His world seemed subtly to be righting itself. There was no shadow of the sinister in his thought. He had the curious feeling he had left the burden of his guilt back in the confessional, as if it were something substantial, like a package, and if he turned around and went back to the confessional he would come upon it.

He tried to analyze this feeling of having the dead weight of his guilt left behind him in the confessional. He had no surge of religious emotion. Could it be, he asked himself, psychological?

It had to be more than that. He had a complete conviction his great sin had been forgiven. He believed in spite of his unbelief. With his conviction of forgiveness came a growing feeling of peace.

My few minutes on my knees, he told himself, have changed me as all my hours of rationalization had not been able to change me.

When he reached the cottage, he felt himself weary with a completely physical weariness, an experience he had not recently known. He gave the sky and the plain a long look as if now they belonged to him and he were putting them away for the night. Gone was his dread of the cold impersonality of this world below him, gone was his antipathy to its people.

As he undressed for bed, he found in his pocket the little leaflet the priest had passed out to him from the confessional. It was the ancient psalm, the ancient cry for mercy, the *Miserere.*

He read from the psalm.

> Have mercy on me, O God,
> According to Thy great mercy.
> And according to the multitude of thy tender mercies.
> Blot out mine iniquity.
> Wash me yet more from mine iniquity,
> And cleanse me from my sin.
> For I acknowledge mine iniquity.
> And my sin is always before me.

On and on he read through the psalm. It grew on him, as he read the psalm, that many of the verses were strangely familiar. But he did not know why until he came to one of the last verses:

> A sacrifice to God is a troubled spirit;
> A contrite and humbled heart, O God,
> Thou wilt not despise.

Then he remembered it was a psalm his mother used to recite in a subdued and reverent whisper, not as a penance but as a prayer, after her confession.

17.

In the morning, the sunlight that awakened him seemed to have a special significance.

He made himself coffee and sat in the kitchen and drank it. Almost constantly, as he sat with his coffee, the telephone rang. He did not bother to answer it. The telephone, and the world of which it was the voice, had no particular relevance for him now.

How the pattern of his life had suddenly changed, he mused. Or had it so suddenly changed? Could it be that this was the pattern that had been forming from the beginning?

He had killed Rena and had he thereby saved her soul? He had killed Rena and had he thereby saved his own soul? Was that the pattern that had been forming all the while?

He finished his coffee. But the pattern was not yet complete. What was it the priest had said in confession? "You have robbed one of life. You cannot restore it. Your own life should be offered up daily in atonement. It is not all over with."

No. The pattern was not yet complete....

He drove slowly along the Coast Highway toward Malibu. He drove slowly by his beloved sea, taking deeply in every last detail of the day...the noisy gulls whirling about the fishing boat in the bay, the far tanker lumbering across the misty horizon, the regally self-possessed pelicans skimming along the crest of a breaking wave, the tumble and rumble of the surf, the white froth swirling endlessly on the sand... all the sights and sounds he had loved since a boy he took deeply in as if this were to be his last experience of them.

He drove by the rustic court with its log-faced bunga-lows. The tall graceful eucalyptus trees dozed in the sunlit calm. The bungalow where she had died had no clear, impel-ling identity for him now. In the sanity of the lucid day, it seemed like a place from some other life, from a drugged, hazy sort of life.

His clearest memory was of the cheap, blue-and-white

ceramic madonna she had always kept in her bedroom and had sent to him. There are three women in a man's life… mother, harlot, wife. There had been no wife in his life nor would there be. Could the three women in his life be… mother, harlot, madonna?

He drove on along the highway until he came to the Malibu sheriff station. He stopped his car at the curb before the station. He left the car and slowly climbed the flagstone steps to the entrance. At the entrance he turned and looked back out across the highway at the sea. The water was a shimmering greenish blue. The lumbering tanker was melting into the west.

He stood there looking out at the sea, reluctant to give up the final moment. St. Lawrence, he knew, would say he was dramatizing himself.

Suppose I am, he asked himself. Is it a deep fault in me to be aware of the drama of the moment? Only man can stand off and see himself as he is—and as he would like to be. Only man finds in himself, as I have suddenly found, intimations of infinite importance and only man can dramatize himself in a role of such importance.

So was I made. So have I lived, even when unaware of any importance, loving and dreaming in vast conceits and desiring greatness with my whole desire. So was I made, and so I believe I was meant to be to the end, the very last end.

He turned to the heavy wooden doors that led into the sheriff station.

This final moment, he said to himself, is this greatness at last? …

He walked slowly, erectly in quiet satisfaction. The doors closed behind him.

CLUNY MEDIA

Designed by Fiona Cecile Clarke, the CLUNY MEDIA *logo
depicts a monk at work in the scriptorium,
with a cat sitting at his feet.*

*The monk represents our mission to emulate
the invaluable contributions of the monks
of Cluny in preserving the libraries of the West,
our strivings to know and love the truth.*

*The cat at the monk's feet is Pangur Bán, from the
eponymous Irish poem of the 9th century.
The anonymous poet compares his scholarly
pursuit of truth with the cat's happy hunting of mice.
The depiction of Pangur Bán is an homage to the work
of the monks of Irish monasteries and a sign
of the joy we at Cluny take in our trade.*

"Messe ocus Pangur Bán,
cechtar nathar fria saindan:
bíth a menmasam fri seilgg,
mu memna céin im saincheirdd."

.

Made in the USA
Columbia, SC
13 June 2025